BOOKS OF A FEATHER

2/17	DATE DUE		
3/4/17	1558		

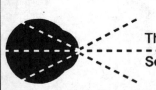

A BIBLIOPHILE MYSTERY

BOOKS OF A FEATHER

KATE CARLISLE

WHEELER PUBLISHING
A part of Gale, Cengage Learning

GALE
CENGAGE Learning·

Farmington Hills, Mich • San Francisco • New York • Waterville, Maine
Meriden, Conn • Mason, Ohio • Chicago

GALE
CENGAGE Learning·

LIBRARY OF CONGRESS CATALOGING-IN-PUBLICATION DATA

Names: Carlisle, Kate, 1951– author.
Title: Books of a feather : a bibliophile mystery / by Kate Carlisle.
Description: Large print edition. | Waterville, Maine : Wheeler Publishing, 2016. |
  Series: Wheeler Publishing large print cozy mystery
Identifiers: LCCN 2016023583 | ISBN 9781410492630 (softcover) | ISBN 141049263X
  (softcover)
Subjects: LCSH: Women bookbinders—Fiction. | Books—Conservation and
  restoration—Fiction. | Rare books—Fiction. | Murder—Investigation—Fiction. |
  Large type books. | GSAFD: Mystery fiction.
Classification: LCC PS3603.A7527 B67 2016b | DDC 813/.6—dc23
LC record available at https://lccn.loc.gov/2016023583

Published in 2016 by arrangement with New American Library, an imprint of Penguin Publishing Group, a division of Penguin Random House LLC

Printed in the United States of America
1 2 3 4 5 6 7 20 19 18 17 16

This book is dedicated to my friend,
the brilliant Susan Mallery,
with gratitude and affection.

CHAPTER ONE

The air inside the old bookshop was thick with the heady scents of aged vellum and rich old leathers. Heaven. I breathed in the lovely pulpy odors as I climbed the precarious rolling ladder up to the crowded top shelf to start cataloging books.

The aisles of the shop were narrow, barely three feet wide, which meant I could reach out and touch the volumes on both sides of the aisle — if I was willing to let go of the wobbly handrail, which I wasn't.

I had spent the last week helping my friend Genevieve Taylor conduct an inventory of the thousands of books that had been crammed onto these shelves over the last forty years. It was a dirty, back-straining, mind-numbing job, yet I didn't mind too much. It was fun to visit with Genevieve, a fellow book nerd; plus I was surrounded by old books. How could that be bad?

My name is Brooklyn Wainwright and I'm a bookbinder specializing in rare-book restoration. I hadn't been back to visit Taylor's Fine Books since Genevieve's father was murdered there almost a year ago. I hated to think of that moment when I found his body, tucked in a corner behind one of the brocade wingback chairs in the antiquarian book room. His throat had been slashed with a type of knife used in papermaking and bookbinding. Naturally, there was blood. A horrifying amount of blood. I'm a pathetic wimp when it comes to blood and tend to faint dead away at the slightest hint of a paper cut. For Genevieve's dad, though, I managed to keep it together, but it was a close call. Not something I was proud of.

Recalling that image, I had to clutch the ladder rail, feeling woozy all over again at the picture of all that blood seeping into the faded Oriental carpet beneath poor Joe Taylor's body. With all the dead bodies I'd come across since then, you would think I'd matured enough to at least maintain consciousness at the sight of blood oozing from an unfortunate victim. But it was still touch-and-go for me.

"I just found another first edition," Genevieve announced from the next aisle over.

I was grateful for the distraction. "What is it?"

"Bram Stoker's *Dracula*. Printed in 1897. Boards are slightly soiled, but the hinges are intact. Slight foxing. Spine's a little faded."

She said the words as though she were reading from a bookseller's brochure.

"A faded spine's to be expected," I said philosophically. "If it's in good condition otherwise, it's still probably worth ten thousand."

"Oh, wait," she said. "The pages are untrimmed."

"And the price just shot up to fifteen thousand."

She laughed. "That's what I like to hear."

I glanced down at the short stack of books on the floor. "So that makes what?" I wondered aloud. "At least a dozen first editions we've found just today."

"Fourteen by my count," she said, but seconds later I could hear her "tsk-tsking" in dismay. "I'm excited to find them all, but I'm also a little flipped out that they were just sitting here on the shelves. I love my dad, but he had a real humdinger of a filing system. I just wish I could figure out what it was."

I smiled. "At least he kept the books in alphabetical order. Sort of."

9

"Sort of," she muttered. "I found the *Dracula* crammed in with a bunch of paperback Charles Dickens novels."

"Well, they all start with *D.* Sort of."

She laughed, but I detected a bittersweet tone and I couldn't blame her. It had to be difficult going to work every day in the same shop where her father had died. But Genevieve was determined to carry on her dad's legacy as the premier antiquarian and rare-book seller in San Francisco. And given the dearth of good neighborhood bookstores out there, I wanted to support her in any way I could.

Besides the obvious disarray on the shelves, the shop had suffered at least three burglaries over the past few months. The thieves hadn't stolen money from the cash register; they had stolen books. Genevieve knew what had been taken, but she couldn't find a record of the books in her father's hopelessly antiquated filing system, which meant she couldn't file an insurance claim. That was when she decided it was time to do a major inventory.

All day long customers came and went while we kept working. They usually took their time, perusing the shelves and picking out a book or two. Some quietly minded their own business while others chatted away with Genevieve or her assistant, Billy. The store was busy, thanks to its location on Clement Street, a popular, ethnically diverse shopping and dining area in the heart of the Richmond District.

I continued to write down titles on the inventory form Genevieve had created for the task. Besides the book title, she wanted the author's name and the aisle and shelf numbers. The work was slow but steady, and when I finished with one shelf, I climbed a few steps up the ladder to work on the next one. I knew I'd reached the top shelf when my head skimmed the ceiling. I felt a little sorry for these books on the top shelves. A reader would have to be willing to risk an almost certain attack of acrophobia to explore all the way up here.

Hours later, I checked my watch and realized how late it was getting. "I'd better call it a day," I announced, and started to descend the ladder — but stopped when something caught my eye on the opposite shelf. With one arm looped around the ladder's edge for safety's sake, I leaned over and reached for the book, easing it out of its cramped spot. The title and splashy dust jacket were what had captured my attention.

One Flew Over the Cuckoo's Nest. It was

one of my mother's favorite books. After taking a minute to admire the almost pristine condition of the dust jacket — which proclaimed the price to be four dollars and ninety-five cents — I looked inside and found the author's flamboyant signature scribbled in blue marker on the front free endpaper. *Ken Kesey.* Was the autograph for real? I turned to the copyright page — 1962.

"I think I found another first edition," I murmured, tingling with excitement at the find. Call me a weirdo, but books could do that to me.

"Cool," Gen said from the next aisle over. "What is it?"

"*One Flew Over the Cuckoo's Nest.* And guess what. It's signed."

"Are you kidding?" she asked, her voice rising two octaves.

"Nope. The author's signature is right here on the flyleaf."

"Is the book a mess?"

"No, it's in beautiful condition except for a small rip in the dust jacket, but that can be fixed."

Gen didn't answer right away, probably pausing to calculate. "It's got to be worth ten or twelve thousand dollars."

"At least." I closed the book and turned it

around to study it from all angles. "I mean, it's in really good shape."

"Will you fix the rip?"

"Sure." Was she kidding? I would kill to work on this book! Even if it was something as simple as fixing a measly little tear in the jacket.

Instead of sliding the *Cuckoo's Nest* back onto the shelf, I scurried down the ladder and placed it on the short stack of books destined for the antiquarian room. That was where Genevieve, like her father before her, showcased the pricier volumes that would appeal to collectors and other booksellers.

Before I left for the day, Genevieve went to the computer and ran some comps on the seventeen first editions we'd found that day. I stood next to her and we both took guesses as to which book we thought was the most valuable — and we were both wrong. It turned out that a sweet little copy of *The Maltese Falcon* she'd discovered earlier that morning was similar to one that had sold recently for ninety-five thousand dollars.

Holy moly. I had to catch my breath. "I know someone who might be interested in *The Maltese Falcon.*"

"Please let them know about it," Genevieve said. "They can call or come by anytime to look at it."

"I'll call them tomorrow." I had to laugh at her expression. "You look gobsmacked."

"I'm beyond thrilled," she exclaimed, tossing her long, dark braid off her shoulder. "Can you believe all these beautiful books were buried in the stacks? I can't thank you enough for helping me out, Brooklyn."

"I'm having fun," I said, giving her a hug.

She snorted. "I wouldn't call it fun, exactly. But I appreciate everything you're doing."

"I'll be back Friday to help some more."

"I won't hold you to it."

"I'll be here," I said firmly, and started to leave, but then remembered something. "Hey, are you going to the Covington opening tomorrow night?"

The Covington Library was unveiling their new Audubon exhibit, the centerpiece of which was the massive Audubon masterpiece, *Birds of America*. The Covington was like Mecca for book lovers, so I was hoping Genevieve would be there.

Her eyes brightened. "I wouldn't miss it."

"I'm glad. So I'll see you there."

As I walked to my car, I had to admit I was pretty thrilled to be walking out with eight wonderful books to refurbish, including a battered copy of *The Grapes of Wrath*,

14

a charming hardcover edition of *The Merry Adventures of Robin Hood of Great Renown,* the signed *Cuckoo's Nest, Dracula,* and *The Maltese Falcon.* It was a win-win for both me and Gen and a nice reward for all my hard work.

It was a minor miracle that I was actually pulling into my apartment garage half an hour later. Driving from the Richmond District across town at this hour of the day when traffic was at its worst should've taken much longer, but I wasn't going to argue about my good luck. I parked the car and took the freight elevator up to the sixth floor. The noisy old wood-planked elevator was one of the wonderful holdovers from the 1900s, when this building had been a flourishing corset factory. It had sat empty for decades until recently, when it was refurbished and converted to trendy artists' loft-style apartments. The smart builders had kept the elevator intact, along with the original brick walls, the beautiful hardwood floors, and the large double-paned wire-reinforced windows.

Officially, we lived in the area of San Francisco known as SoMa, or South of Market, but since we were only a few blocks from AT&T Park, where the hometown Gi-

15

ants played baseball, some people considered the area more China Basin adjacent than SoMa. I wasn't too picky about these things, but San Franciscans took their neighborhood differentiations very seriously.

As soon as I closed and locked my front door, I sagged in relief. I usually worked at home, so being gone all day was unusual for me. But after a moment, I perked up, knowing Derek was already here; I'd seen his car parked in the space next to mine.

Derek Stone was my fiancé and . . .

Fiancé. I had to stop and breathe in the word. It was still so odd to say it aloud, let alone think it. But it was true. It was real. We were getting married, and how crazy was that? The two of us had almost nothing in common. I'd been raised in a peace-love-and-happiness artistic commune in the wine country and wore Birkenstocks to work. Derek had been a highly trained operative with England's military intelligence and he carried a gun. Think James Bond but more dangerous, more handsome, more everything. I was crazy in love with him. I figured that the old adage that opposites attract had to be true, because he loved me right back.

He had proposed two months ago, the night my friend Robin married my brother Austin. Of course I said yes. Duh! Since then, we'd barely had a chance to talk about a wedding or anything else related to getting married. We'd been living temporarily in Dharma in the Sonoma wine country, next door to my parents. commuting to the city while our apartment in town was being remodeled. The reason for the remodel was that Derek had purchased the smaller apartment next door to mine for the purpose of joining the two places together to make one very large residence.

Now the work was done and we had been back in town a week. Our place was still in a state of flux, to put it mildly. We'd been rearranging furniture and picking out new stuff and doing all those things you do when you suddenly have two extra bedrooms and a much bigger living room. It was fun and time-consuming and a little bit mind-boggling. I occasionally had to stop and pinch myself.

So no, there hadn't been much time to discuss wedding plans. We'd get around to it one of these days.

With a happy sigh, I slid the case that held my bookbinding tools under my worktable and set my satchel on the counter.

"Derek, I'm home," I called, even though he probably knew it already. He was preternaturally aware of everything that went on

17

around us. Besides, our freight elevator tended to shake the entire building when it rose from the basement parking garage, thus acting as an early-warning signal. I liked to think the noisy contraption made it more difficult for bad guys to sneak up on us, and yet they still tried it every so often.

"I've got books to show you," I shouted, excited to share my project with Derek.

"We are in here, darling," he called from somewhere in the vicinity of the kitchen.

We?

I heard a burst of male laughter, confirming that Derek was not alone. So much for showing him my stack of fabulous books from Genevieve's shop. I hung up my peacoat in the small closet by the door, trying to recall if we had made plans to see friends tonight. I was pretty sure we hadn't.

Not that I was paranoid, but I had to find a place to hide the books. Okay, maybe I was paranoid. I'd taken elaborate precautions before leaving Genevieve's shop, tucking the books away in a zippered compartment inside my satchel, which I wore strapped across my torso and clutched all the way to my car. I never took chances with books. Especially rare, valuable books. Our home had been broken into on more than one occasion by unscrupulous people who

18

were determined to steal a book from me.

Our friends and family were all completely trustworthy, of course, and I was sure that trust extended to whoever was visiting us tonight. Everyone knew I worked with rare and often priceless books, yet I rarely showed off the books I was working on. It was safer for everyone that way.

"I'll be right there," I called out, and turned in a circle, scanning my workshop for a long moment, looking for a good hiding place. There were lots of them. Besides my worktable in the center of the room, I had three walls of cupboards and counters and drawers that held all sorts of equipment and supplies. At the end of one counter was my built-in desk.

I grabbed my satchel and pulled out the eight books — the eight rare, extremely valuable books that I'd been entrusted with — and carefully slipped them into the deep bottom drawer of my desk and locked it. I would've preferred to stash them all inside the steel-lined safe in the hall closet near our bedroom, but this would have to do for now.

I felt almost silly for taking such precautions. It shouldn't have been necessary, since I was inside my own house. I wondered if I was being overly suspicious. But the answer was no, absolutely not. I was all too aware that there were people in the world who would lie, cheat, steal, or kill for a book. *So better to be safe than sorry,* I thought, and was about to rush out to greet Derek and whoever was visiting us when I spied a fluffy bundle of fur clawing at the old sandals I wore for work and kept under my desk.

"Hello, my little peanut," I said, and reached down to pick her up. "You're getting so big." I lifted her into my arms and rubbed my nose against her soft furry coat. It made me a little sad to realize that Charlie, our beautiful little kitten, was growing up.

"Who's visiting us?" I whispered. She simply purred, and I hoped that meant that our visitor was friendly. I held on to her as I walked through the archway that led from my office workshop into our living room.

Derek stood by the wide counter that separated the kitchen from the dining-and-living area, pouring red wine into three glasses. Another man, wearing a beautiful navy suit, had his back to me. I couldn't see his face, but I noticed he had straight black hair and was nearly as tall as Derek. He had just said something that caused Derek to laugh. I stopped and listened to that deep, sexy sound.

"And there she is," Derek said, spying me at last. "Darling, come meet Crane, one of my oldest friends."

"I'm not that old," the other man joked as he turned toward me. "Ah, how delightful."

If I'd been walking, I might've stumbled. The man was Asian and spoke with a British accent and he was simply . . . beautiful. Not as dashing or as blatantly masculine and tough as Derek, but then, who was? Still, Crane's smile was brilliant and his dark eyes twinkled with humor. He was clearly a confident man, and that made him even more attractive. *But no man should be that pretty,* I thought vaguely.

It was a bit overwhelming to have two such gorgeous males smiling at me, but I decided I could endure it. I set Charlie down and hurried over to the bar to give Derek a quick hug and kiss, then turned to our guest and extended my hand.

"Hello, Mr. Crane. I'm Brooklyn."

"It's just Crane," he explained, and his smile grew as he gripped my hand warmly. "Nobody calls me 'mister' unless they're soliciting for money."

I laughed. "Crane, then. It's nice to meet you."

"It's a pleasure to finally meet you, too,

21

Brooklyn. I've heard many wonderful things about you."

I glanced at Derek. He'd never said one word to me about his friend Crane before. And yet the man knew all about me? Hmm.

Derek bit back a grin, clearly reading my mind. "Darling, Crane and I were in school together. We haven't seen each other in at least five years."

"Closer to six," his friend admitted. "Although we chat on the phone occasionally."

Derek set the wine bottle down. "It's a good thing. I'm always wondering if you've ended up in a federal penitentiary somewhere."

I raised an eyebrow, but Crane just laughed. "And I always figured you'd be the one to wind up on the wrong side of the law." He shook his head in mock dismay. "Instead you joined forces with the good guys."

Derek shrugged. "Considering our misspent youth, it's surprising we both turned out this well."

Crane nodded at me. "It was always a competition to see which of us could cause the most havoc in school."

"You won in the end," Derek admitted, handing each of us a wineglass. "But only through a technicality."

I gazed at Crane. "How did you win?"

"I'm smarter?"

"He cheated," Derek said dryly. "His grandmother left him a sizable inheritance and nothing was the same after that."

"It's true — money changes everything," Crane confessed with a worldly sigh. "It's not as much fun getting into trouble when you know you can simply bribe your way out of a jam."

Derek chuckled. "I, for one, am grateful for a few of those bribes."

I looked from one man to the other. "I'd love to hear some stories of Derek causing havoc."

Crane leaned close. "I'll tell you everything, but first . . ." Straightening, he held up his glass. "I'd like to propose a toast, to old friends and new."

We clinked glasses and took our initial sips of the excellent Pinot Noir Derek had poured.

"And as long as we're toasting," Crane added, "I understand congratulations and best wishes are in order."

"Oh." I gazed up at Derek and touched my glass to his. I didn't know why, but I was truly moved that he'd told his friend about our engagement. Especially as the two of us had barely discussed it since we'd been home from Dharma. I looked over at his friend. "Thank you, Crane. That's so nice of you."

Crane raised an eyebrow and seemed to be gauging my sincerity. After a moment, he nodded briefly and turned to Derek. "You're a lucky man, Stone."

"I know," Derek said, and met my gaze as he leaned close and kissed my cheek.

Happily flustered, I moved into the kitchen and quickly put together a cheese platter along with a bowl of crackers and some olives. Derek ushered Crane over to the living room, where he offered our guest the big comfy red chair. I followed a moment later, setting the munchies down on the coffee table and joining Derek on the couch.

I glanced around and couldn't help admiring our newly remodeled space. Our living room was now almost twice as big as before and we had expanded the kitchen, too. We'd turned my second bedroom into a spacious office for Derek. The two bedrooms of the newly purchased loft had become a comfortable suite for guests that included their own kitchen. I was hoping this new addition would entice more of Derek's family to visit us from England. Especially now that we were getting married.

Married. There was that tingling feeling again. I couldn't help grinning as Crane regaled me with tales of wild adventures from their prep school days.

"But enough of that nonsense," he finally said. Changing topics, Crane leaned forward and rested his elbows on his knees. "Derek tells me you work with rare books. It would be fascinating to watch you do that."

A flash of guilt made me hesitate. I'd hidden all my pricey books earlier, unsure whether our guest was trustworthy or not. Now that we'd officially met and I knew he was one of Derek's oldest friends, I felt a bit silly for having hidden them from him. Still, the books were valuable, so I refused to feel bad for being cautious. "Yes, I'm a bookbinder. I take books apart and clean them up and put them back together again."

"She's being modest," Derek said. "Brooklyn has a unique gift for repairing the rarest of books and making them come alive again. Almost like a skilled surgeon."

"Without all the blood," I murmured.

"But she's also an artist," he continued. "She's designed some fantastic book art."

I felt my cheeks heating up. I knew Derek appreciated my work, but all this lavish praise was going straight to my heart.

He tapped my knee. "Darling, Crane has an impressive art collection. I think he would enjoy seeing your work."

"I would indeed," Crane said, helping himself to a cracker. "I collect all sorts of art, including books. As you might expect, my interests are mainly in Asian art, but I'd very much like to see your work sometime."

I gave Derek an assessing look, then said to Crane, "We'd love to have you join us tomorrow night at the Covington Library if you're free. They're having a big party to celebrate the opening of a new exhibit featuring Audubon's massive book of bird illustrations. It's a real masterpiece." I gave a self-conscious shrug. "And if there's time, I can show you some of my own work on display."

Crane blinked, clearly surprised by my invitation. But then he flashed me a spectacular smile. "I would like that very much. I was about to invite you both to dinner tomorrow night, but perhaps we could dine together this weekend instead. Are you available Saturday night?"

Derek and I exchanged upbeat glances and he said, "We are and we'd enjoy it very much."

"Sounds like fun," I chimed.

"Wonderful," Crane said, pulling out his

phone to send himself a reminder. "I'll make the arrangements and text you the details tomorrow morning."

"Perfect."

Crane settled back in his chair. "I must say, I find it remarkable that they're opening an Audubon exhibit while I'm in town. I don't believe I've ever told you this, but I happen to have a tenuous family connection to James Audubon."

"Is that true?" I asked.

Derek leaned forward. "I had no idea, Crane. Tell us."

Crane's laugh was self-deprecating. "When I say tenuous, I truly mean it." He considered for a moment and then held out his hand to count on his fingers. "It's to do with my great-great-great-great-great-grandfather. Five 'greats.' His name was Sheng Li, and he was born in 1795, the son of a prominent Mandarin scholar. His father arranged for him to be smuggled out of China to England because he wanted Sheng to attend Oxford and learn Western ways. Because he was an obedient son, my ancestor studied very hard. He spoke perfect English and was talented in math and science. But his true passion was art. He was a painter. And here's the big coincidence. It was his good fortune to meet the great

27

painter James Audubon while traveling the east coast of Scotland."

"That's amazing," I said, imagining what it must have been like. "What a co-incidence."

"Isn't it?" Crane said, giving me a smile that said he knew exactly what I was thinking. "Audubon saw one of my ancestor Sheng's paintings and invited him to work as a colorist in anticipation of the publication of his great work of bird illustrations."

I shook my head in wonder. "What a small world. And how excited Sheng must have been to get such a prestigious invitation. Although it couldn't have been easy for him, living as an artist in a foreign land."

Crane's lips tightened into a scowl. "No, it wasn't. He was living in Britain during the lead-up to the first Anglo-Opium War, and despite it being fought thousands of miles away in the ports of China, people in England looked with great suspicion on the Chinese living in their country, especially as opium's use grew in popularity."

"Was Audubon able to protect him at all?" I asked.

"Yes. At least, that is what Sheng wrote in his journal. Our family owes a debt of gratitude to him for that alone. And for allowing Sheng to work alongside him, as well."

Derek, who had been leaning forward, listening intently, sat back on the couch. "So it's possible we could see some of your great-great, et cetera, et cetera grandfather's work tomorrow night."

"I doubt it," Crane said with an easy chuckle. "But it is a fascinating story, isn't it?"

"You sure know your family history," I said.

"The study of one's ancestors is very important to Chinese parents." He nodded. "Mine made sure we knew who all those 'great-greats' were and exactly what they accomplished."

"Families are so interesting and complicated, aren't they?" I grabbed a cracker. "Do you have brothers and sisters?"

"A brother." He took a quick sip of wine. "And another odd story, if you care to indulge me."

"Yes, definitely."

He smiled. "Perhaps you have heard of the one-child policy of China?"

I pressed my hand to my mouth, chagrined. "That was so stupid of me. I forgot all about that law."

"No, no. I don't wish to make you feel

bad. It's a terrible policy that was finally changed just recently. My only point in mentioning it is that my parents were allowed to have two children."

"How did that happen?" I was really intrigued now.

"My mother's family is from Hong Kong and my parents were living there when my mother gave birth to me. She suggested that we stay there a few years longer in order to have more children. It was still a British protectorate at the time, so it didn't fall under China's one-child policy. The sad irony is that once we were there, my mother began having miscarriages, and the doctors decreed that she must stop trying to have children. The happy irony is that shortly after that we moved back to Beijing, and she found out she was pregnant. To avoid a forced abortion, she moved by herself to her sister's farm, where Bai was born. And that is how I wound up with one brother."

"Wow," I said. "So once you were reunited, I guess you must've felt pretty lucky. The only boy in town with a brother."

Derek cleared his throat and took a sip of wine.

Judging by that, there was something I didn't know. I glanced from Derek to Crane. "Did I just step in it again?"

Crane laughed. "No, no. Derek is reacting to the fact that he has met my unfortunate sibling."

"Oh dear." That didn't sound good. "I'm sorry."

"I appreciate your concern," he said. "But do most families not have what they call the black lamb?"

"Sheep," Derek corrected, smiling.

"Ah. Black sheep. Of course. I confess, my brother, Bai, is one of the reasons I'm here this week."

Crane pronounced his brother's name like the word *buy,* but I doubted it was spelled that way.

"He lives here?" I asked. "In San Francisco?"

Disappointment and sorrow shadowed his expression. "He is currently residing in the city."

I shot Derek a desperate look. Leave it to me to ruin this happy reunion with his old friend. "I shouldn't keep asking questions. I'm sorry."

Crane waved away my distress. "Don't feel badly. It's probably good for me to talk about it."

"Yes, it's therapeutic," Derek said with a grin, and Crane chuckled. This seemed to be a topic they'd discussed before.

31

I looked at Derek. "So you've met Bai?"

Derek took up the story. "When Crane was sent to Eton, his brother demanded that he be allowed to go, too."

"I'm afraid Derek was a convenient target for Bai's bad behavior. My brother was insistent on proving to Derek what a tough guy he could be."

"For some reason," Derek said with a shrug, "his brother didn't like the fact that Crane had so many friends at school. Bai blamed me for that."

"As a young man, my brother had what you'd call jealousy and rage issues."

"Give her some background, Crane," Derek suggested, and turned to me. "It really is an intriguing story, darling."

"I'm dying to hear it, as long as you don't mind talking about it."

"No. Not at all." Once again, Crane sat back in the red chair and told his story. "My mother is half English, the daughter of a prominent Hong Kong businessman. Like the father of my ancestor the painter, my mother wanted me to receive a Western education."

"Didn't she want the same thing for your brother?"

"No. Again, like my ancestor Sheng, my brother has a gift for painting. My parents wanted him to study at the Central Academy of Fine Arts in Beijing. It is quite possibly the finest and most selective art school in the world. My brother was quite proud to be accepted to the academy, but at the same time, he wanted to get out of China. He insisted he wanted to see the world. My being sent to Eton intensified his demands. He was very spoiled and reacted badly when he didn't get his way."

"So Crane's parents relented and sent him to Eton," Derek explained.

I frowned. "And something tells me it didn't go well."

Crane made a face. "You guessed correctly. Besides harassing Derek, Bai was in constant trouble and was finally kicked out. It was a source of great embarrassment for my family."

"I'm sorry."

"It upset all of us much more than it ever bothered Bai. And now he bounces around the world, enjoying himself. He still has a tendency to get into trouble, but he's a wealthy man and trouble never seems to cling to him for long. He's also a talented artist and has many connections in the art world, which makes my mother proud. Her family trust allows Bai a generous allowance every year, so he's free to do as he wishes. But now my mother is ill and wants me to bring him home."

"I'm so sorry," I murmured again.

"So that's the family business you were referring to," Derek said.

"Yes." Crane took a sip of wine. "It seems I am still my brother's keeper, as they say. But along with my mission to convince Bai to come home, I am also conducting company business while I'm here. I'll be meeting with the Chinese consul general this week to discuss opening up markets to bring new business to my country. And of course I wanted to see you, my friend, and meet the woman who captured your heart."

I couldn't help smiling. "Why does Derek call you Crane? Is that your real name?"

"In a manner of speaking."

I shot a quick glance at Derek, who was watching his friend expectantly. I had a feeling Crane had been asked this question before.

"My actual name is Sheng Li," he explained, "named after my honorable ancestor. But from the time I was born my mother called me Hè." He pronounced it *hua* with a raspy whisper, almost as if he were growling the name.

"Okay," I said slowly.

"Chinese mothers are very fond of nicknames," Crane said. "*Hè* is the Chinese word for a type of bird, which in English is called a crane."

"Your mother's nickname for you was a bird?"

"Oh, not just any bird," he insisted, grinning, "but the most revered of all birds. In Chinese mythology, the crane is thought to be immortal. There is often some magic connected to any story involving cranes. My mother can be fanciful at times."

Understanding dawned. "She sounds like my mother. I have a sister whose middle name is Dragonfly."

He held out his hands. "Ah, then you can relate. I believe my mother was a free spirit in her younger days."

"A hippie," I said with a laugh.

"Exactly."

"So, did you always call yourself Crane?"

"Not until I went to school in England. When I started at Eton, I was a sad, scrawny thing. And Chinese, of course. The other boys were relentless in their ridicule of me for so many reasons. My name, my ethnicity, my physique. Derek was already on his way to becoming the titan he is today, and as my roommate, he took it upon himself to threaten the others with fates worse than death if they continued to bully me. When he found out what my nickname meant in English, he started calling me Crane. It sounded so cool. The rest of the boys seemed to agree and the harassment was quelled."

"My hero," I said, patting Derek's knee. Turning to Crane, I said, "You seem to have, um, outgrown your scrawny phase."

One of his eyebrows shot up in a rakish glint. "Thank you for noticing, my dear."

Derek rolled his eyes and I couldn't help laughing.

Crane continued. "That, too, is due to Derek's influence. He insisted that we begin daily workouts in the school gym."

"So you could fight back if necessary," I said.

"Exactly."

In my mind Derek really was a hero, but I wasn't going to embarrass him by repeating it.

"But let's change the subject," Crane said. "I'm tired of talking about myself. Tell me more about the Covington collection. I've read about it for years, but I've never had the opportunity to see it."

"I think you'll be impressed," I said. "It's much more than just a library, although there are many exquisite books and so much history. But there's artwork, too, and beautiful gardens. And the building itself is impressive. I think you'll enjoy it."

"I'm sure I will."

Derek put his arm around my shoulder. "You should be aware that the place also has a sentimental meaning for Brooklyn and me. It's where we first met."

"Now I'm truly intrigued," Crane said.

I almost laughed at the way Derek made it sound so romantic. True, we'd met at the Covington Library, but it was only because my mentor was killed that night and I found the body. Derek, in his role of security expert for the priceless antiquarian book collection on display, had found me with blood on my hands and had immediately accused me of murder. Not the most starry-eyed way to start a relationship, but we'd managed to overcome those first few bumps in the road.

"And just think," I said, gazing up at Derek, "this time there won't be any dead bodies to worry about."

Crane seemed amused, but Derek was no longer smiling. In fact, he was staring at me as though he might've wanted to check me into the nearest loony bin. That was when I realized I had just tempted fate in the worst possible way. Right then and there, I began

to pray that my words wouldn't come back
to haunt me.

CHAPTER TWO

I woke up the next morning tempted by the alluring scents of bacon and syrup along with the seductive aroma of strong coffee brewing. The delicious smells could mean one of two things: either I was dreaming, or Derek Stone, international man of mystery and all-around awesome hunk, was making breakfast. Was it any wonder I was crazy about the man?

I breathed in more of the fragrance wafting through the house and knew I wasn't dreaming. Talk about seductive; I was the luckiest girl in the world.

I jumped out of bed and rushed to wash my face, then threw on jeans, a sweater, and socks. Minutes later, I ran out to the kitchen and wrapped my arms around Derek. "Thank you, thank you. I love you, love you," I murmured, ridiculously grateful that his mother had taught him the basics of cooking. Unlike mine.

"You only love me for my ability to cook bacon." But he hugged me back and planted a warm kiss on the top of my head. "Pour yourself a cup of coffee."

I did as he suggested and added a generous dollop of half-and-half to my cup. "Can I help with anything?"

He took a quick sip of his own coffee. "No, everything's ready." He piled bacon slices onto two plates that already held a thick waffle and chunks of apple, banana, and strawberries, and set them down on opposite sides of the kitchen bar.

I leaned in close and kissed him. "You are the best thing in the world."

"And so are you." He kissed me back, then circled around to the dining room side of the kitchen bar and sat.

I sat down on the one kitchen stool, facing him. After a long moment of silence during which we spread butter and poured syrup on our waffles, I said, "I had a dream about you and Crane tormenting your teachers at Eton."

He chuckled. "I still have those dreams myself. Nightmares, actually."

"You seemed really happy to see him." I studied him, watching as his gaze shifted. I could tell his thoughts were a thousand miles away and I really wanted to know

40

where those memories had taken him. And why they weren't making him smile.

We hadn't talked much last night, since I'd fallen asleep the minute my head hit the pillow. So now I asked, "Why have you never mentioned Crane to me before?"

He paused to chew a piece of bacon. "To tell the truth, Crane was a part of my past that I never thought I'd visit again."

"You make it sound sad. What happened?"

"We were chums, best pals for years. Then we parted ways and I didn't see him again for a long while."

"Did you have a fight?"

"No, no. We were in the final weeks of school when Crane received word that his father had died. The family expected him to come home at once and take over the family business. He was packed and gone almost before I could absorb the news."

I leaned an elbow on the table and gazed at him. "That's really sad."

"It was a bit of a shock, but he would've left a few weeks later anyway, when school ended." He sipped his coffee. "Don't feel badly, love. I've seen Crane off and on since then. But it's been a while since the last time we got together. Almost six years now. And that was under rather shady circumstances, I might add."

41

"Shady?" I stared at him. "What happened?"

His lips twisted into a rueful smile. "I can't go into too much detail, darling, but Crane was instrumental in helping us bring an elusive Middle Eastern prince to justice."

My mind reeled at the possibilities, but I knew Derek wouldn't spill any government secrets, so I moved on. "So you were just kidding when you said you thought Crane would end up in prison."

His lips curled in humor. "We always used to wager which one of us would end up on the wrong side of the law."

"It looks like you've both managed to avoid it."

"So far."

I had to laugh. Derek was practically the poster boy for honorable behavior.

After leaving school, Derek had joined the Royal Navy. From there he was recruited to work for MI6, the British equivalent of our CIA, and stayed for ten years before leaving to start his own security firm. Talk about avoiding the wrong side of the law. Derek was so lawful it was scary sometimes.

I broke off a piece of bacon and popped it into my mouth. "Well, I really like Crane. He seems . . . centered." I frowned and batted the word away. "Sorry. I sound like my mother. What I mean is, he seems to have a healthy attitude about the world. He didn't spend a lot of time complaining about anything or competing with you."

"No, he never did much of that." Derek paused to sip his coffee. "He's always been a stand-up sort of friend. Always there in a pinch if I needed him."

I gazed at him for a long moment. They hadn't seen each other in almost six years and suddenly Crane showed up? Was there something I should know? "Do you need him now, Derek? Is that why he's here? Is something wrong?"

Derek reached over and squeezed my hand. "Nothing's wrong, love. You heard Crane say he's in town on family business."

"Do you believe him?"

It was his turn to frown. "I'll have to wait and see. I admit I'm concerned about him confronting Bai."

"Me, too." I thought about my own family and was thankful we all got along. Derek's family was the same way. "Will he let us know if he needs our help?"

One eyebrow shot up. "*Our* help?"

"We're a team, right?"

He grinned and gave my hand another squeeze. "Yes, we are. But I doubt we'll be called upon to help Crane out of a jam. I just think it might be unpleasant for him to deal with his brother."

We talked and ate for another fifteen minutes. Derek told me about the new security agent he'd hired for his San Francisco office. We agreed that we'd order Thai food for an early dinner before heading over to the Covington Library tonight.

He was finishing his coffee when he suddenly remembered something. "I'm sorry, love. I forgot to ask you how your day went yesterday. Did you bring home any books?"

"I did. Eight beautiful books to be repaired. I'm so happy."

He grinned. "I trust the books are happy, too."

"I felt awkward when I came home last night, though. I heard you talking to someone, so I hid the books in my desk, just to be safe. And then later, after I'd spent some time with Crane, I was a little embarrassed for being so suspicious."

"You shouldn't feel guilty about taking precautions." He sighed. "We haven't had to concern ourselves with security issues since we've been away."

"True. I guess we're a little rusty."

"Not to worry," he said. "We'll be back to our usual paranoid selves soon enough."

Sad but true. No matter how much I loved

our building and how much I trusted our neighbors, being back in the city after spending so much time in Dharma was a culture shock. In my hometown, doors weren't just left unlocked; they were left wide-open. Of course, bad things happened everywhere, including Dharma. Usually, though, it was an idyllic spot to unwind and de-stress.

As we cleared our dishes, I gave him a brief rundown of the books I'd brought home from Genevieve's shop. "I'll show them to you tonight."

"I look forward to it."

A few minutes later, I walked with Derek to the door. As I kissed him good-bye, I ran my hand down the sleeve of his impeccable navy suit, just to feel his sinewy muscles through the richness of the fabric. "Have a good day at work, making the world more secure."

"You, too, love." He touched my cheek as he kissed me back. Then he left, and I sighed as I closed the door behind him. Like everyone, the man had his faults, but sometimes I just couldn't remember what they were.

I washed the dishes and cleaned up the kitchen, then grabbed a colorful chunky-weave scarf and headed back to my workshop. It was January, and even though we'd had very little rain this season, the air was chilly. My workshop was in the front of the house, closest to the street, so it was always a little colder than the rest of the rooms.

Unlocking my desk drawer, I removed the books I'd hidden there the night before and placed them side by side across my worktable. Then I sat down with my most powerful magnifying glass and a notepad and examined each book, making notes as I went. When I was finished, I lined them up again in order from least damaged to most.

I liked to work on the easiest fixes first because a quick, successful repair job always put me in a good mood. So first up was a loose front and back hinge on the extremely expensive copy of *The Maltese Falcon.* Carefully gripping the front and back covers, I splayed the book and held it up off the table. The text block drooped precariously, indicating that both the front and back boards had separated from the spine. Luckily, the endpapers were still intact with no ripping along the joints, so despite the sagging boards, this would be a wonderfully simple fix. I set the book down, pushed my chair away from the table, and smiled as I strolled around my studio, gathering various repair supplies and tools from the cupboards and drawers and counters built along three walls.

I had missed this room while we were living in Dharma. Oh, I'd had full use of my old mentor Abraham's workshop nearby and I'd done a small amount of book repair work while I was there, but it wasn't the same. It wasn't mine. I wondered now if some of my recent angst had been brought on by the need to get back to full-time bookbinding work. I did love my job.

After laying out my tools on the table, I walked over to the small sink in the corner and began to mix up my first batch of glue. Not that I was obsessive or anything, but it was vitally important to have the right glue for the right job. For this one, I preferred a mixture of sixty percent polyvinyl acetate to forty percent methyl cellulose. Others recommended a fifty/fifty ratio, but I liked the consistency of my sixty/forty blend better. I knew some book artists who favored PVA on its own, but I contended that adding methyl cellulose gave the glue more flexibility and allowed a bookbinder more time to alter and fine-tune her work. And once it dried completely, the combo was an even stronger adhesive than just the PVA on its own.

Clearly, I could be a real nerd on the

subject of glue. I'd watched students nod off in the middle of my impromptu glue seminars. But this stuff was important. I liked to say that my reputation as a bookbinder was only as strong as the glue I used to bind my books together.

I said clever things like that all the time but rarely found an appreciative audience.

These days anyone could purchase PVA already mixed in gallon containers. It was cheap and easy, so it just made sense. But when it came to methyl cellulose, I preferred to concoct my own. I could have bought it premixed as well, but where was the fun in that?

I found a clean pint container and poured in a few tablespoons of methyl cellulose powder. To this I added hot water and whisked it steadily for about five minutes. Once it was smooth and lump free, I added one cup of cold water and whisked again until the substance was clear and viscous. I wanted the consistency to be goopy but still pourable and easy to spread with a brush.

I left the concoction sitting on the sink counter to congeal further while I surveyed the books again. As I'd already determined, the most badly damaged was *The Grapes of Wrath*. Half of the text block had broken away from the spine, so the pages would have to be taken apart and resewn. The front cover was almost completely severed from the spine except for a few strands of linen cloth holding it together. All of the gilding on the spine had been rubbed off and the cloth here was tattered and split at every corner. One spot on the back cover had been worn down so badly that I could see the aged, heavy board beneath the cloth.

Genevieve had found comparable copies of this edition of *The Grapes of Wrath* selling online for forty-five thousand dollars. It would take a lot of work to bring this version up to that level, but I relished the challenge. For now I set the book aside and moved on to the next one.

Removing the dust jacket from the copy of *One Flew Over the Cuckoo's Nest,* I took a closer look at the rip along the fold. It was a little worse than I'd first thought when I found it on the shelf. Both sides of the tear had curled and darkened to a brownish yellow. I spread the dust jacket facedown on the table and studied it some more.

If I were a librarian simply trying to keep this book in circulation, I would follow the age-old bookbinder's maxim that a repair should simply keep the damage from spreading. If that was all I cared about, I would slap on a piece of acid-free document repair tape, slip the book into a clear plastic archival book cover, and call it a done deal.

But because this book was so valuable — a first edition signed by the author, after all — I approached it from a book conservationist's angle. I wanted to not only restore the book's health, but also make sure it would last another century or two. It would be a nice bonus if I could make it pretty, too.

Collectors were willing to pay a lot of money for Pretty.

I checked my decorative paper drawer to make sure I had enough Japanese rice paper to repair the tear and also plug up some of the small nicks along the edge of the jacket. For this job I would have to whip up a small batch of wheat paste, the type of glue that worked best with the fragile Japanese tissue paper. Wheat paste was persnickety and had to be mixed, then cooked, then diluted. And it only lasted a few days when stored in the refrigerator.

I told you I could be a real dork when it came to homing in on the finer points of glue.

I found several sheets of rice paper in three different thicknesses, so I pulled out one of each and tucked them under the *Cuckoo's Nest* to work on later. For now I wanted to concentrate on the easier jobs and take advantage of my fresh batch of PVA and methyl cellulose.

I picked up the copy of *Dracula* and inspected it closely. Genevieve's description was right on: it had been printed in 1897, the pages were roughly cut, or deckled; the boards were soiled, but the hinges were indeed still intact; the gilding and lettering on the spine were faded. She'd mentioned slight foxing, but she'd underestimated the problem. Those nasty little brown smudges thrived on a number of pages throughout the book.

I could try to clean the worst of the foxing with brushes and a dry bleaching technique I'd tried before, but I didn't feel comfortable taking the book apart and actually washing the pages in an aqueous solution unless Gen approved it. And frankly, I wasn't sure it would matter. With a book this old and wonderful, the foxing wouldn't detract all that much from its value.

This was another book that would have to wait until later in the week to be fixed. For now, I made notes and took photographs of all the books for my own reference. I always liked to take "before and after" photos to show my client and to post on my Web site.

I checked on my methyl cellulose and

found it had reached a perfect consistency. I poured some PVA into a small beaker and added enough of the methyl cellulose to reach my sixty/forty blend and whisked the two together. After a few minutes, I was satisfied that the final mix was smooth and lump free.

I assembled everything I would need to fix *The Maltese Falcon*'s drooping hinges on the table in front of me and began to work my tried-and-true bamboo-skewer fix. Basically, my glue, several sheets of wax paper, and two bamboo skewers. And the book, of course.

I stood *The Maltese Falcon* upright. Taking hold of the first skewer, I dipped the long, thin spike into the glue until it was completely coated. Careful to avoid the spine itself, I guided the glue-covered skewer into the small breach that was the inner hinge of the front cover. I twirled the skewer a few times to evenly distribute the glue, then removed the stick. I did the same thing to the back hinge.

I slid a piece of wax paper between each of the covers and their flyleaf pages, then closed the book. Grabbing my bone folder, I pressed the edge of it along the front hinge to emphasize the crease. I repeated the action along the back cover hinge, then placed a weight on top of the book. Ten minutes later, both covers were firmly affixed and *The Maltese Falcon*'s droopy text block was history.

That night, I walked through the doors of the magnificent Covington Library and felt almost giddy with joy. I couldn't help it. I loved this place. It was because of the books, of course, but also because the building itself was so striking, a glorious sanctuary and a loving monument to the written word. It was home to some of the most beautiful books ever created, and I'd fallen in love with every inch of the place the first time I visited when I was eight years old.

A grand Italianate mansion situated at the very top of Pacific Heights, the Covington overlooked the city and the bay. The views were breathtaking, both inside and out. And if books weren't your thing, the artwork throughout was spectacular and the gardens alone were worth visiting.

This was something else I'd missed while we were away. This place, the books, the wonderful reading nooks, the scents, the quiet. I'd missed my friend Ian McCullough, head curator and newly crowned president of the Covington Library and Museum. I'd heard about his promotion but hadn't had a chance to congratulate him. I couldn't wait to see him.

I waited for Derek inside the Covington's large, elegant foyer, next to the wide staircase that led to the upper levels. The foyer floor was a checkerboard pattern of polished black-and-white marble tiles and the centerpiece of the room was a gorgeous Tiffany chandelier hanging from the ceiling that sparkled dazzlingly above me. French doors on both ends of the foyer led to either the main hall or to another wide hallway that wound around to the West Gallery.

From the sounds emanating from the main hall, I could tell the party was already hopping and I hoped Derek found a parking spot soon. And by "hopping," I mean that guests were laughing and talking and enjoying the wonderful hors d'oeuvres and excellent wines while a string quartet played classical music from their perch on the second-floor balcony overlooking the main exhibit hall. So maybe "hopping" wasn't the right term, given the elegance of the crowd and the highbrow entertainment, but it sounded as though everyone was already having a good time. And with the exception of those few artistic types who perennially dressed in unrelieved black from head to toe, we were a colorful, sparkly group.

I checked my watch. We weren't expecting Crane to arrive for another hour. But that was fine; I would still have enough time to give him a quick tour of some of the exhibit rooms before the unveiling of the big Audubon book at nine o'clock.

"Brooklyn. Thank goodness."

I turned to see Genevieve Taylor rushing toward me from across the foyer. She wore a little black dress that fit her petite frame perfectly. Classic pearls and shiny black heels completed the outfit.

"Hi, Gen. Wow, you look beautiful." I reached out to hug her, but she was too anxious to notice. "Is everything okay?"

"I'm so glad I found you first thing." She fumbled with her purse and got the zipper open, then stopped abruptly. Glancing around, she asked, "Is Derek here?"

"He's parking the car, but he'll be here any minute. What's wrong?"

"Nothing. I'm just feeling a little paranoid, I guess."

"Why?"

She took my arm and pulled me a few feet farther back from the door, away from all the guests who were milling around the lobby area, greeting friends and checking out the crowd.

Pulling a small wrapped package from her

bag, she handed it to me. "I found this a few hours ago. Or rather, I found Billy walking away with it and took it from him."

"What is it?" I started to tear off the tape, but she grabbed my hand to stop me.

"Don't open it here," she whispered gruffly.

I frowned at all the intrigue but went ahead and slipped it into my purse. "I'll assume it's a book."

She smiled for the first time. "Yes. I'll let you have the fun of discovering for yourself what book it is, but I'll tell you this: it's worth as much or more than some of the books we found hidden in the stacks so far."

"Can you give me a clue of what's going on?"

She took a deep breath. "I thought things were starting to calm down. I mean, it's been a rough year, you know?"

I patted her arm. "I sure do."

The violent death of her father had been awful enough, but then to have the store involved in a string of burglaries? I couldn't blame her for being suspicious of every little thing.

"But now after today," she continued, "I'm afraid I can't trust Billy anymore."

"But he's your cousin."

"I know, but . . ." She shook her head in

dismay. "You didn't see his face when I caught him. He looked so guilty."

"You can't really believe he had anything to do with the book thefts."

"I don't. Not really. It's just that . . ." She shook her head and waved her hand dismissively. "Never mind. Can you just hold on to this for me? And, well, feel free to look it over and maybe clean it up a little and appraise it when you have a chance."

I almost laughed, since I would've done that anyway. "Sure."

"And don't tell anyone you have it, please."

"Of course not. How about if I call you tomorrow after I've taken a look at it? We can talk then."

"Thank you, Brooklyn. I know I can trust you." She glanced around again and then squeezed my arm. "I'll see you inside."

I watched her walk through the wide French doors into the exhibit hall and disappear.

I gripped my purse a little tighter. Apparently, Genevieve's paranoia was contagious.

Seconds later, Derek walked in and I waved him over.

"I'm surprised you haven't joined the party yet," he said, taking my arm and tucking it through his.

I smiled sweetly. "Just waiting for you, darling."

He gave me a sardonic look that made it clear he didn't believe me. I shrugged. "Something weird happened. I'll tell you about it later."

He held my arm a bit more securely. "I can't wait to hear all about it."

We walked into the main hall, and as always, I was struck by the beauty of the space with its three-story-high coffered ceiling and the fragile-looking wrought-iron balconies of the second and third floors with their rows and rows of books lining the narrow walkways. The room never failed to delight me.

We slowly made our way through the crush of people to the bar, pausing here and there to say hello to some familiar faces. It took us fifteen minutes to reach the far end of the room, and as expected, the line for drinks was long, despite three bartenders working behind the bar.

"Brooklyn! Derek!"

We both turned. "Ian!" I cried, and grabbed him in a hug. "I've missed you."

"Me, too, kiddo."

After a moment I let him go and he and Derek shook hands. "Great to see you both."

"Congratulations on your promotion,

Ian," Derek said.

"Yes, congratulations," I said. "That's such great news and well deserved."

"Thank you. It means a lot to hear that from both of you."

"Can we get you a drink to celebrate?" Derek pointed to the line.

"I wish I could say yes, but no, thanks." He grinned. "I'm on duty."

I started to ask Ian another question and Derek stopped me. "You stay here and talk to Ian, darling. I'll brave the line."

I squeezed his arm. "My hero." Watching him go, I realized I'd been saying that a lot lately. But then, he really was heroic sometimes.

Ian and I maneuvered away from the bar crowd over to an alcove that held a glass-fronted display of nineteenth-century American ephemera, including letters written by Walt Whitman, Henry David Thoreau, and Abraham Lincoln. We were laughing and catching up on all the latest gossip when Ian glanced around the room in an obvious attempt to locate someone.

"If you need to go and mingle, I'm fine," I said. "Maybe we can get together for lunch next week."

"I wanted to introduce you to someone, but I can't see where he disappeared to."

"Is it work-related?"

"Yes, he's got a book for you to repair." He craned his neck to search farther, then relaxed. "Guess he'll find us eventually. So, how's your mom?"

"Crazy as ever," I said, and launched into a funny story about my wonderful New Age Wiccan mother and her latest adventures. We were both laughing as a tall man wearing khakis, a denim shirt, and a sweater vest approached.

"Hey, Ian." He almost sagged with relief. "I thought I'd lost you."

"Not a chance," Ian said jovially. "Jared Mulrooney, I'd like you to meet Brooklyn Wainwright, the bookbinder I was telling you about."

We shook hands and I said, "Nice to meet you, Mr. Mulrooney."

"Believe me, Ms. Wainwright," he said, pumping my hand enthusiastically, "the pleasure is all mine."

"Please call me Brooklyn."

"Okay. Thanks, Brooklyn. I'm Jared." He glanced at Ian nervously as if waiting for permission to do something. To be honest, the man seemed like one big nerve ending. He was tall and very thin and a little gawky. He had big eyes, big teeth, and a large beak of a nose. I smiled, thinking how nice it was that book collectors came in every size and style.

"Jared is president of the National Bird-watchers Society, which has its headquarters in the Bay Area," Ian explained.

"Bird-watchers? Oh my goodness, how interesting," I said. Because truthfully, the man looked like a bird! A tall, skinny one, like a stork or a heron. Or a certain big yellow one on a popular kids' TV show. Except his eyes were more owl-like than anything else. I found him fascinating to observe. "You must be looking forward to seeing the Audubon exhibit."

"That's putting it mildly," he gushed. "I'm over-the-moon. Most of our members are here tonight, and Ian has promised all of us a private showing later this week."

"That should be exciting," I said.

"Go on, Jared," Ian said, hurrying the man along. "Show her the book."

"Oh. Right. The book." His mood shifted and he turned to face us head-on, as though he was shielding his actions from the crowd behind him. Flipping open the man purse he wore strapped across his chest, he handed me a book. "I sure hope you can fix it."

I took it from him and held it, weighing it in my hand for a moment. It was heavy for such a small volume, maybe four by seven

61

inches, an inch thick, and leather bound. Even at first glance, I could tell it was an exquisitely crafted work. On the cover was a lovely illustration of — what else? — a bird. I didn't know a lot about birds, but I would guess it was some sort of bluebird. Because, duh, it was blue.

"This is charming," I said, looking more closely at the artwork. The detail was extraordinary, with every feather visible. The color of the wings was almost iridescent and I had to marvel at the ability of the artist to capture the bird's bright-eyed curiosity. It was perched on a slim tree branch dotted with delicate purple and pink blossoms. "It's a glorious painting. Is this Audubon's work?"

"Yes, of course," Jared said, frowning.

I turned it on its side to examine the ribbed spine. *Songbirds in Trees.* "What a sweet title. And the gilding is still bright and unmarred. It's lovely."

"Open it," he said flatly.

I did as he instructed and felt my spirit deflate. "Oh my."

"It's my fault," he lamented. "I never should've taken it out of its display case. But I couldn't resist. It's just so spectacular, I wanted to get another look at it. I shouldn't have been drinking wine at the same time."

I didn't trust myself to speak. There were lovely illustrations of birds throughout the book, but more than half of the pages were badly wrinkled and stiff, as though they'd been dunked in a pool. Liquid was the natural enemy of paper — didn't everyone know that? I could imagine the hot blue fury flashing in my old bookbinding teacher's eyes if he'd been here to see the injury done to this book.

The wine Jared Mulrooney had doused the book with hadn't touched the leather cover, so he must have been holding the book open when the wine spilled. Frankly, I wished he'd spilled it on the cover rather than the pages, because that would be easier to repair or replace. I gave him a clenched smile. "I guess it's a good thing you were only drinking *white* wine."

He moaned softly. "Can you fix it?"

"I'll give it my best shot."

"She can fix it," Ian said proudly. "She can fix anything."

"I'll pay any amount," Jared assured me. "It's a treasure beyond price. I found it in a used bookshop in Scotland and it's become our society's most prized possession. We've always kept it inside a clear, locked Plexiglas display case at our headquarters. But I couldn't keep my hands off it. Why did I have to . . . Oh, what is wrong with me?"

"Now, settle down, Jared," Ian said, patting the man's shoulder. "It'll be all right. It's not like you killed anyone."

I blinked at Ian in shock, but he just grinned.

Jared's face grew even paler and I felt a wave of pity for him. He gave a furtive peek behind him and lowered his voice. "The others can't find out about this."

"You can trust me not to tell anyone," I promised, patting his other shoulder. Then I slipped the book into my purse alongside the other secret book I'd been given tonight.

This evening was getting more and more interesting by the minute.

CHAPTER THREE

I found Derek at the head of the bar line, and twenty minutes later, the two of us had managed to migrate through the crowd over to the dramatic octagon-shaped Shakespeare folio display, where we had a moment alone to enjoy our wine. I gave him a quick recap of my odd encounters with both Genevieve Taylor and Jared Mulrooney.

Shortly after I'd taken the book from Jared, he and Ian had slipped back into the crowd. I caught an occasional glimpse of Ian chatting and schmoozing with guests, but Jared had disappeared completely. Given the level of guilt and embarrassment he was suffering over the damaged book, I wouldn't blame him if he'd decided to skulk out before the Audubon was unveiled.

I realized I hadn't seen Genevieve, either, since our quick exchange in the foyer. But then, she was short enough to disappear from sight in a crowd this thick. I figured we'd run into each other again tonight at some point.

"Here he is," Derek said, glancing over my shoulder. I turned and smiled as Crane approached. I couldn't help noticing a number of women's eyes following his progression across the room. He wore another impeccably tailored suit tonight, as did Derek. Once again, I was struck by the overwhelming good looks of both men and knew I was the envy of plenty of the women in attendance.

"I'm glad you made it," I said, giving him a brief hug.

"Thank you, Brooklyn." He grinned as he shook hands with Derek. "I wasn't sure I would make it out of the consulate in time."

"Are you making enemies of the Chinese consulate staff so soon?" Derek bantered.

Crane gave a worldly shrug. "As always."

I must've looked concerned, because Crane laughed, then lowered his voice to add, "Actually, I'm about to increase the deputy consul's plenipotentiary powers to such an extent that, well, let us just say his mother back home will be very pleased."

I'd never heard anyone use the word *plenipotentiary* in real life, so I was impressed. "I'd love to hear all about it."

"I'm afraid it would put you to sleep," he

66

said, smiling so beautifully that I was momentarily captivated and willingly dropped the subject.

"Do we still have time for the tour you promised me?" he asked.

I checked my watch. "Sure. The Audubon unveiling doesn't happen until nine."

"That gives us a good half hour," Derek said. "Shall we start in the Children's Wing?"

Looking wistful, Crane scanned the room. "Is it too late to grab a cocktail?"

"Oh dear." I felt like a terrible hostess. "Absolutely not."

Derek pointed in the direction of the bar. "The lines have dwindled somewhat. Let's give it a shot."

"Lead the way," Crane said with a sweeping gesture.

Ten minutes later, after securing a gin and tonic for Crane, we stood in front of one of the most popular exhibits in the recently opened Children's Wing. It was a display of a dozen ingeniously designed pop-up books from different artists around the country.

I felt a little silly showing him my book arts work instead of the more somber restoration work I'd done that was on display in the main hall. For instance, there was an extraordinary copy of Goethe's

Faust, part of the Winslow collection that was still on exhibit in the main hall, and there were all the finely bound English women authors' books I'd restored last winter for the library's celebration of women in literature.

But this was one of Derek's favorites, so here we were.

"It's *Alice in Wonderland,*" Crane murmured, staring at the book in the middle. He glanced at me. "Are you telling me you created this?"

"Yes."

He stooped down and leaned in, getting as close to the glass as he could get in order to study my interpretation of the climactic scene in the book. An entire deck of cards swirled up and out of the book, flying two feet off the page and then plunging down as if to attack poor Alice, who valiantly fought them off.

A calligraphed banner lay at the base of the book that read YOU'RE NOTHING BUT A PACK OF CARDS!

"The cards look alive, don't they?" Derek said.

"And somewhat diabolical," Crane said. "I wouldn't want them coming after me."

I beamed. I couldn't have asked for a better review. "Thank you."

"That is spectacular," Crane said, straightening. "You are a remarkable artist."

"Thank you so much," I said, delighted by his compliments. "I love creating book art. Of course, I also love restoring old books, but that's an entirely different aspect of my work."

"Restoration, the way you do it, still requires an artistic temperament," Derek said. "It's much more exacting, though, with more rules to follow."

"I approve of that description," I said, then felt my shoulders droop. "I suppose that means I'm good at following rules. Not exactly what you'd call an artistic temperament."

"Do you think following rules makes you less of an artist?" Crane asked. "I certainly don't. I believe it makes you more considerate and wise."

I blinked. For some reason, his words made me choke up a little. "Thank you, Crane."

He continued. "When it's your free choice to follow the rules, it means you are being true to yourself. And that truth will naturally make you a better artist."

I thought about it for a moment. "I suppose you're right."

He gestured toward the display. "When I

look at this marvelous book, my first thought isn't, I wonder if she's following some rule. No, I'm thinking, How fun. How joyous. How fascinating. How did she do that? And yet it's clear that you were required to follow the most basic rules of mathematics, geometry, architecture, engineering, spatial order, harmony. An artist can try and pretend he is not following rules, but let's remember that nature itself provides rules. Gravity, for instance."

I laughed. "I'm grateful to hear you say that."

He bowed slightly. "And I am grateful to have been allowed to see this fine work of yours. It reminds me of *zhezhi,* the Chinese art of paper folding."

"I'm not familiar with *zhezhi,*" I said. "Is it similar to origami?"

"Yes." He smiled benevolently. "You could call it the Chinese version of origami, although I prefer to call origami the Japanese version of *zhezhi.*"

I smiled. "Good point."

He shrugged. "Ours is a much older art, naturally. The general way to tell the difference between a work of origami and one of *zhezhi* is that we Chinese tend to favor inanimate objects such as paper hats, boats, and the like, instead of the paper animals

70

that are so popular in origami."

"I didn't realize China had its own history of paper folding."

He sighed dramatically. "We Chinese come up with all the great ideas and generously hand them off to others to claim as their own."

I laughed again, as he clearly meant me to do.

"You'll find this is a common theme with Crane," Derek warned.

Crane waved his hand philosophically. "It's not easy being so superior."

"And with that," Derek said, chuckling as he pointedly checked his watch, "we should be heading back to the main hall. It's almost nine o'clock."

Crane grinned and tucked my arm through his. Derek took my other arm and the three of us chatted as we walked, making it back to the main hall with two minutes to spare.

Ian had wisely arranged tonight's reveal to take place on a raised platform so the assembled audience would be able to see the book when it was unveiled. Derek, Crane, and I stood at the back of the crowd as Ian began his short speech. I was so proud of him and could tell how much he'd matured with his new position.

He called this Audubon exhibit the Covington's most important exhibit since the Winslow collection opened here almost two years ago. That brought back a flurry of memories for me, of finding my mentor dying, of rescuing the *Faust* from his hands, of meeting Derek for the first time, of blood, of betrayal, of being accused of murder.

I had to force myself to shake away those memories and pay attention to Ian's words.

"Birds of America," he said. "This immense masterpiece, Audubon's legacy, is on long-term loan to the Covington Library from the Sheikh of Qatar, and we thank him and his country for their generosity." He was interrupted by polite applause and then Ian concluded, "Without further ado, I present to you James Audubon's magnum opus, the superbly illustrated *Birds of America,* for your enjoyment."

With that, he whipped the black velvet shroud away from the massive display case and the crowd erupted in loud applause and gasps of awe.

The book was enormous. From where I stood in line, it looked several feet wide and at least three feet tall. It was probably four or five inches thick as well.

The book was opened to a page that showed a large white bird with delicate white feathers cascading down his neck. On a wide screen above the display, the library had arranged slides of other illustrations from the book. One showed a tree branch with five songbirds perched in various poses. The colors of their wings vibrated bright blue, red, yellow, and green. Other slides showed snowy white owls quietly resting in their natural habitat; a family of ducks by a pond; a bright pink flamingo staring intently across the water; and a long-legged white bird standing at the edge of a pond, surrounded by tall grasses. The creature was bent over, his neck almost contorted, as he contemplated something on the muddy ground. A lizard or some kind of bug — I couldn't tell from here.

As I followed the crowd streaming closer, the colors on the page itself grew more dramatic and I could start to see the brush-stroke details in the white feathers and the bright eyes of the creature. It looked impossibly real and I began to understand, among other reasons, why this was such an important work of art.

When I finally stood directly in front of the display, it was daunting to see how large a book it really was. I knew enough about bookbinding history to know that the paper stock Audubon had used for his illustrations was called "double-elephant" paper and it was several inches wider and taller than the two-by-three-foot estimate I'd made while standing at the back of the room. In 1838, when Audubon published his illustrations, that was the largest-sized paper available.

The book was said to contain hundreds of stunning hand-colored illustrations of over seven hundred bird species. I stared at one of them now, a snowy heron or white egret. The delicate feathering detail was amazing. The bird seemed to be staring directly at the observer. In the background, a small placid lake appeared near a farmhouse surrounded by trees.

"Magnificent," Crane whispered behind me.

I nodded. Several minutes later, we moved away from the grand display and found a spot to carry on a conversation.

"I'm going to have to come back when it's not so crowded and take my time with it," I said. "Even the paper is beautiful. I'm hoping Ian will let me examine the bindings up close."

Crane glanced from Derek to me. "What a tremendous honor to be here. Thank you so much for inviting me."

"We're glad you could make it," Derek said.

"And we're still on for dinner Saturday night?" Crane said.

"Absolutely," I said with a smile. *Food? Yeah!*

He grinned. "Good. I'm going to take off now, but I'll see you both Saturday."

We watched him disappear through the double doors of the foyer and I turned to Derek. "I know you probably want to leave soon, but I'd like to try and find Genevieve before we go."

"Fine, love. I want to track down Ian and have a word with him. Shall I meet you back here in ten minutes?"

"Perfect."

Derek strolled away and I glanced around the room. The crowd had thinned out, but I still couldn't spot Genevieve anywhere. We'd talked about our favorite Covington displays in the past, so I wondered if maybe she had snuck off to see her father's beloved baseball cards display in the West Gallery.

Of course, she might've ducked outside to get some air and stroll through the gorgeous Covington Gardens. The thought of meandering around outside on such a cold winter night caused me to shiver, though, so I decided to try the Sports Gallery first.

I walked back to the hall we'd used earlier to get to the Children's Wing and turned in the opposite direction toward the West Gallery. There was plenty to see along the way, since the wide hall featured paintings from the modern era, including contemporary works by Richard Diebenkorn, Jasper Johns, Robert Rauschenberg, Ed Ruscha, and others.

One of the things I liked best about the Covington was the eclectic blend of items they chose to display. Besides all the historically significant ephemera and the many beautiful and rare volumes from great writers and historical figures across the ages, Ian also enjoyed juxtaposing the old with the new and the priceless with the prosaic.

For instance, along with the journals of William Faulkner and Ernest Hemingway, the Covington had included the diaries of John Lennon and Kurt Cobain. Ian and his subcurators had once filled a gallery with examples of advertising campaigns spanning the centuries from ancient Egypt, through the British Regency, and into the 1950s. They'd included a historical timeline of the quirky Sears catalogue, following it from its earliest pages in the 1880s up to modern times.

And there were the baseball cards. Joe Taylor, Genevieve's dad, had loved perusing all the players from the old days of the game to the present. I'd brought my own dad here to see them, too. They were displayed with other sports memorabilia in one of the smaller galleries off the West Gallery, so that was where I was headed.

The West Gallery was almost as large as the main exhibit hall. It had six doorways that led to other smaller galleries, and each of those usually contained a single-themed exhibit. Sports was one of them; the History of Cookbooks was another. Last year there'd been a gardening exhibit that featured gorgeous botanical prints. And the American West display was still going strong. Occasionally, a larger exhibit would be downsized and moved to a smaller space.

The West Gallery was still well lighted, but the lights in two of the connected display rooms had been turned off for the night. I checked my watch. It was almost closing time. Maybe Genevieve had already left for the evening.

I could see that the Sports Gallery still had its lights on, so I decided to check anyway. "Genevieve, are you here?"

The room was empty.

"Okay," I muttered, and turned to walk out. I felt bad that I'd missed seeing her, knowing how upset she'd been earlier. I would have to call her tomorrow morning to get the full story.

As I walked back through the West Gallery, I noticed the last room on the opposite side wasn't completely dark. Instead, its lights were set on dim, which I found interesting. Was there a new exhibit in there that demanded low lighting? I'd seen a museum employ this sort of lighting before, during a wonderful presentation of Leonardo da Vinci's drawings and letters. The paper and ink he'd used back in the fifteenth century had grown too delicate to withstand the glare of modern lighting.

I was curious to see what they were setting up, so I stuck my head inside the door to take a look around — and was immediately sorry I'd done so.

All I saw were legs sprawled across the floor, directly inside the doorway. I scrambled backward and then couldn't help myself. I screamed bloody murder.

I'm not sure how, but Derek was already halfway down the hall when I went bellowing around the corner. In seconds I was wrapped in his arms more tightly than I would've thought possible.

"What is it?" he demanded. "What happened?"

"B-body. In there. Dead."

Somehow he kept hold of me as he darted

to the doorway. He managed to shield me from the sight as he took a quick look.

"Genevieve," I moaned, burying my face in the warmth of his strong chest.

"Darling, it's not Genevieve. It's a man."

It took a few seconds for his words to penetrate through the buzzing in my head. I stared up at him. "A man? Who is it?"

"I have no idea." He continued to rub my back in soothing strokes. "I only took a brief look, but he's wearing trousers and his feet are quite large. I've met your friend Genevieve and she's rather petite."

"True. And she was wearing a dress. Duh." I finally managed to pull away from him because frankly, my curiosity was killing me. I mentally excused the pun.

Taking a deep breath, I tried to center myself and prepare my emotions for another shock. A small part of me was seething at the insult of my finding yet another dead body, but mostly I was sad and angry on behalf of the person who'd been left alone to die in a dimly lit gallery of the Covington Library.

Clutching Derek's hand, I moved forward slowly and leaned in to see inside the room again. Sure enough, the feet were large and the long legs were covered in khaki trousers. This time I looked above the man's waist to see the tan sweater he wore. No, it was a tan vest. So it was a man, all right. And not just any man, but Jared Mulrooney, the president of the National Bird-watchers Society.

My head was beginning to spin.

My first thought was that someone had killed him for ruining the bluebird book. But that was crazy. Or was it? How could I forget that people had killed for less, more often than I cared to remember?

My second thought was that the poor guy had committed suicide, unable to deal with the way he'd damaged the book. Either way, I felt heartsick over the death of the bumbling bird-watcher. I gazed up at Derek. "I know who it is."

Derek nodded. "We'd better find Ian and call the police."

Homicide Inspector Janice Lee walked into the main hall of the Covington Library and spied me and Derek sitting together on a padded bench along the wall. "Hey, looks like old home week around here."

"Hello, Inspector," Derek said, standing to greet her.

"Hi, Inspector Lee." I was so happy to see her I almost jumped up and gave her a hug. But that would've been a big mistake and I

80

felt foolish for considering it even for a moment. There had been times in the past, though, when I thought the two of us could be friends. I suppose it was still possible, but she didn't make it easy. Especially when the only times we ever saw each other were at the scenes of violent murders.

I confess, I'd developed a bit of a reputation for finding dead bodies. It wasn't my fault and it wasn't something I was proud of. It just *was.* I couldn't begin to explain it, but I appreciated the way my parents' spiritual leader, Robson Benedict, had put it, that somehow I'd been chosen to speak for the dead. To find justice and closure for their families. Was it mere coincidence that in every case, a *book* invariably played a central role in determining how or why the victim died? I didn't think so, but if I were to admit this out loud, I would have to give up my career. After all, who would hire a bookbinder if they knew her clients kept dying off?

On the upside, I had worked with hundreds of clients who hadn't died at all, so there was no reason to be paranoid. Was there? No, absolutely not. This wasn't about me. I was just here to help.

Each time I'd been involved in a murder in San Francisco, SFPD Homicide Inspector Lee and her partner, Nathan Jaglow, had been assigned to the case. I'd lost track of the number of times we'd all worked together. Ten times? Maybe more? So when she said it looked like old home week, it was obvious why.

Inspector Jaglow walked in directly behind Lee and grinned at us. He was older, somewhere in his fifties, slightly balding with unruly gray hair. A sleepy smile belied his sharp powers of observation, and his infinite patience was the perfect counterpoint to his partner's shoot-from-the-hip style. "Hello there, Commander, Ms. Wainwright. Haven't seen you two in a few months."

"We've been out of town," Derek explained, and shook the man's hand. The cops had referred to Derek as "Commander" from day one, mainly because that had been his rank in the British Royal Navy and it said so on his business card. But beyond those points, the title just suited him. He was tall, dark, handsome, and a bit dangerous-looking. And he easily commanded the attention of everyone in the room.

I was grateful that Derek's connection to law enforcement automatically exempted me from the police suspect list. It hadn't always been the case. On the contrary, the first few times I'd found a dead body, I'd been lucky they hadn't thrown me directly into jail. Thank goodness those days were long gone. At least, I hoped so.

"You cut your hair," I said to Inspector Lee. "It looks beautiful."

"Don't try sweet-talking me, Wainwright," she said.

I laughed, despite the unfortunate circumstances. "I'm not. You look great."

"Thanks," she muttered. Self-conscious now, she ran a hand through her jet-black straight hair. She'd cut several inches off the length and she was wearing bangs. It was adorable, but I wasn't about to mention that out loud.

Janice Lee was first-generation Chinese-American. She was very pretty and thin, although she'd thankfully put on a few pounds over the last year, owing to her quitting smoking. I was horribly envious of her wardrobe. The woman knew how to dress for success — or for intimidation, maybe, which probably spelled success in her book.

"Nobody ever comments on my hair," Inspector Jaglow said mournfully.

I grinned. "Your hair is lovely, Inspector."

He flicked an errant curl coquettishly. "Why, Ms. Wainwright, I'll bet you say that to all the fellows."

"You're a sick puppy, Jaglow," Inspector Lee said, rolling her eyes.

Jaglow gave me a quick wink, then glanced around the room at the twenty or so people left from the party. "Were these the only people here tonight?"

"No," Derek said. "Your officers took names and information from a number of others and let them go. These people here are acquainted with the deceased."

"Ian will have the full invitation list if you want to contact the ones who already left," I said.

"Will do," Jaglow said. He conferred with one of the officers for about five minutes and then announced aloud that the remaining guests could go home. There were sighs of relief and even a few tears as the group filed out of the hall. I figured many of them had been friends with their bird-watcher president and felt sorry for their loss.

Derek led the two inspectors around to the West Gallery and showed them where we'd found the body of Jared Mulrooney. I tagged along, naturally.

Ian had assigned two of his security guards to protect the scene and they stepped away from the door to allow the two inspectors and Derek to enter. I tried to follow, but one of them stepped in front of me. "Officials only."

"I'm official," I lied.

"Let her in," Inspector Lee grumbled. "She's already got her footprints all over the place anyway."

"I only took one step inside," I argued.

"I know, but it's always fun to give you grief."

I smiled. "So you've missed me."

She snorted. "Yeah, I have. I really have."

Despite the snort, I believed her.

Jaglow skirted the body and walked to the far corner of the room. He stared toward the open door as if trying to get some perspective on what might've taken place here.

"Who was this guy?" Lee asked, staring down at the body. "Looks like a professor type."

"He was president of the National Bird-watchers Society."

She frowned. "Are you serious? And somebody killed him? Why?"

I hated like heck to tell her about the damaged book, mainly because she would probably take it from me. Unfortunately, though, I felt it was my duty to tell her the whole truth. Not telling her would've been withholding evidence and would get me in more trouble later. So I pulled the small book from my bag.

"Earlier tonight, he gave me this book to repair." I handed it to her.

She stared at it, frowning as she turned it over a few times. Then she opened it. "Oh man. What a mess."

"I know. I just hope I can fix it."

"Good luck with that," she said, and handed the book back to me.

"You don't think it might be important?"

"Do you?"

The fact that she was asking my opinion was a first. "It might be, in terms of motive. But the book itself won't do much good stuck away in an evidence box."

"Yeah, I agree. So as long as I know you have it, I figure it'll be safe."

"It will be." I gave her a limp smile and said nothing else. I was pitifully relieved to get the book back and stunned that she was at least willing to admit that someone might actually be willing to kill over a book. Another first.

On the other hand, I couldn't imagine that Jared Mulrooney had been killed over this particular book, no matter how much damage he'd done to it. I planned to look it up online when I got home, but it didn't seem all that rare or valuable.

Jaglow, kneeling by the body, looked up at

his partner. "Stabbed."

Lee just shook her head in disgust. The two of them began a cursory examination of the area around Jared's body, so I had started to walk out of the room when Inspector Lee stopped me. "Oh, hey, Brooklyn, that reminds me."

I stopped and looked back. "What is it?"

"I've got a book I'd like you to look at, maybe see if you can spruce it up a little. Mind if I swing by your place tomorrow sometime?"

I had to force myself to stay calm and try to keep the absolute shock from showing on my face. "Um, sure. I'll be glad to take a look at it."

"Great, thanks." She shrugged, obviously uncomfortable about asking for my help. "It was my mom's and I kind of destroyed it when I was a kid. She went ballistic and I'm surprised I survived. Anyway, I found it in one of her drawers the other day and took it, hoping you would fix it up for me. It's her birthday next week."

"I'll be glad to give it a try."

"Thanks, pal."

On the drive home, Derek and I discussed the murder of Jared Mulrooney and the fact that Inspector Lee had actually been willing to admit that the book might be related to his death.

"I was pleased that she considered it," Derek said.

"Me, too. Although I can't really see the connection between the book and his death."

"We often don't get the connection until later when we have more facts. But there's always a connection, especially where you're concerned."

"Oh yeah." I gulped. "Thanks for that."

He reached over and took my hand in his. "Sorry, love, but facts don't lie."

"I know." We drove in comfortable silence for another thirty seconds before I gasped out loud. "I forgot all about Genevieve's book!"

I immediately pulled the wrapped package from my purse and stared at it. "I guess I can wait until we get home."

"Of course you can."

"Who are we kidding?" I ran my finger under the taped end and eagerly pried open the small bundle. And stared some more.

"It looks like some sort of old magazine," Derek said after a quick glance down at what I was holding.

"It's actually an almanac," I murmured.

"Interesting."

"I'd say so. It's a first edition of *Poor Richard's Almanack,* and it's over two hundred and seventy-five years old."

CHAPTER FOUR

After breakfast the next morning, Derek left for work and I went into my workshop and called Genevieve. "Are you kidding me?"

"No." She obviously knew who was calling and exactly what I was talking about. "Look, I'm sorry about all the cloak-and-dagger stuff last night, but I didn't know who else to talk to."

"So tell me what happened."

"All I know is what Billy told me. He says he found the *Almanack* shoved behind another book and he was just going to put it in the office for me to look at. Except that he had his hand on the back-door knob and it looked like he was leaving, so I'm not sure what he was really planning to do with it."

"Maybe he was just going out for . . . I don't know, lunch. Or a jog around the block. Maybe he didn't realize how valuable it was. I mean, it doesn't look like much."

"I highly doubt that was his plan, but I

appreciate your sunny optimism. Lately, I'm more the overly suspicious type, I guess."

"I can be suspicious, too," I insisted. "But I just can't see your own cousin doing something to hurt your business. Or doing something unlawful, either." I was referring to the past burglaries because I had a feeling that was where Gen's suspicions lay.

"Maybe I've lost perspective," she lamented, "but can you blame me? After all that's happened this last year, my spirit is a little weakened."

"Oh, honey, I hear you. But look, there could be a perfectly innocent explanation for all this. It's Billy, after all. He doesn't have a larcenous bone in his body."

"He never used to, but maybe someone else is luring him over to the dark side."

I paused to consider that possibility. Billy was a sweet guy, but not the brightest bulb in the lamp. If some nefarious book collector had swayed him with money or promises, he might buckle.

"I suppose it's possible," I said. "But I'm holding out for a happier explanation."

She laughed. "I hope you're right."

"So you missed the excitement last night," I said, changing the subject.

"I know. I left before Ian unveiled the book. I was just too bummed out to have a good time."

"The Audubon is spectacular. You'll have to get over there to see it. But no, I'm talking about a murder. Someone was killed in one of the small rooms off the West Gallery."

She didn't say anything and I thought we might've been disconnected. But finally she said, "O-oh my God. Are you kidding? I spent at least half an hour in the West Gallery last night."

"I actually went looking for you over there, hoping I'd catch you before you went home. That's when I found the body." I didn't mention that at first I'd thought the body might be hers.

"Oh no, Brooklyn. You found the . . . ugh."

"I did." She was well aware that I'd found her father's body, too. I hated reminding her all over again of that sad time. Heck, I hated reminding *myself* of that.

"I'm so sorry," she said. "Tell me what happened. Do the police have a motive? I can't believe someone would kill anyone at the Covington. It seems so wrong. What is this world coming to?"

I didn't want to mention that this wasn't the first time a murder had occurred at the Covington Library. It seemed like a good time to change the subject again.

"So let's talk about this *Almanack*," I said cheerfully, staring down at the rare papers on my worktable.

"Isn't it amazing?" she said.

"I was dumbstruck when I saw it last night and I still can't quite believe it." As much as I loved old rare books, there was a part of me that was almost terrified to touch this thin tome. Its age. Its history. At the same time, though, those were exactly the reasons why I was excited to have it.

"I was fairly dumbstruck myself," she said. "In a good way, I mean. Aside from the fact that my own cousin might've been trying to filch it from the store."

"Filch is a good word."

"I like it, too."

She sounded a little perkier than she had a minute ago, but since we were in danger of venturing into cousin Billy territory, I steered us back to the *Almanack*. "The first thing I'd like to do is clean it as much as possible with a brush and maybe a dry sponge. Then I'll sew the pages back together. I've already done some research on the proper thread, the kind they used in the seventeen hundreds. I think it'll really improve its value."

"Even filthy dirty with loose pages, it could be worth somewhere between twenty

93

and forty thousand dollars, I found out."

I smiled. "It'll be worth more than that when I'm finished with it."

"I love you so much."

We both laughed and I was glad to hear the natural lightness in her voice returning. We talked more about the work I planned to do on the *Almanack,* including constructing a protective storage box to keep it from deteriorating any further than it already had done.

"Thanks, Brooklyn. I don't know what I'd do without you."

"Well, don't forget I'll be back to help you finish up the inventory tomorrow," I said.

"Are you sure? You've done so much already."

"I'm sure." Besides, it would give me a chance to corner Billy and get the real scoop on what he was thinking when he'd tried to filch the *Almanack.*

I spent the rest of the day doing preliminary work on both the *Almanack* and two of the books I'd brought home from Gen's shop earlier that week. This included sweeping each page with my softest long-handled sheep-hair brush to get rid of any minute bits of dirt and dust or carcasses of tiny bugs that might have crawled between the pages.

If you'd ever had a nice book collection or simply a bookshelf filled with books, you'd undoubtedly found remnants of silverfish or other bugs once in a while. Hopefully, they were dead and dried up on the shelf, not alive and eating their way through the insides of a favorite book.

In my own experience, silverfish were the worst. They were slimy and slithery and liked to munch along the edges of books until the pages more resembled fine lace than a solid book. I would be perfectly happy if I never saw another one of those little buggers again.

Beetles are disastrous, too, but rather than chewing along the edges, they prefer to bore straight through a book cover and into the pages, devouring everything in their path. One telltale sign that a beetle has been at your favorite book is a tiny pile of fine sand-like particles nearby. This is known as "frass" and it's the, uh, natural output of an insect's food intake.

Some conservationists suggest freezing books to get rid of a bug infestation, but there are too many problems associated with this solution for me to sign off on it.

One natural remedy I'd found only semi-useful was tea tree oil — rubbed on the wooden shelf itself, not directly onto the book.

Book preservationists frown on applying insecticides to books, but other options along this line include pheromone lures and sticky traps on nearby shelves. In my opinion, though, the best way to prevent bugs from snacking on your books is to individually wrap each volume in clear archival plastic and keep them in a cool, dry place that's dusted regularly.

The front door buzzer sounded and I was startled out of my reverie. Jumping down from my work chair, I grabbed the phone. After hearing Inspector Lee announce herself, I pressed the button to let her in, then waited several minutes while she took the freight elevator up to my floor. I finally took notice of the clock above my desk and realized it was almost time to start cleaning up and getting ready for Derek to come home. I also realized I was starving. I'd been so wrapped up in my work I'd forgotten to fortify myself with chocolate. That just never happened.

I quickly grabbed a handful of chocolate-covered almonds and munched them as I waited at the door for the inspector.

"Hey, Brooklyn," she said as she walked into my studio. "Thanks for doing this."

"I'm happy to do it. Would you like something to drink? Or some chocolate?" I indicated the half-empty bag of chocolate almonds on my desk.

"No, thanks."

"Okay, let's sit down and take a look at the book." I led her over to the worktable and we both sat.

She glanced around the room. "Convenient having your workshop at the front of the house."

"I think so. I figure if someone's here on business, they can come right into my office without going through the rest of the house."

"Cool." She pulled a heavy square book from her bag. "Here it is. You can see what a putzy kid I was."

On the cover was a column of Chinese characters next to an intriguing painting of a Chinese woman in workers' garb. In small letters along the side, it read in English, THE FINE WORKS OF CHINA FAMOUS OIL PAINTER ZHANG SONG. I turned the book over and opened it to the title page. It was written completely in Chinese. No English anywhere. On the facing page someone had taken a box of crayons and scribbled incoherently in ten different colors.

I nodded. "Oh yeah. Very nice crayon work."

"Yeah, thanks. And you'll notice I tore some pages out. But they're still in there in case you think you can tape them back together."

"I can do that easily. But the crayon marks are a little trickier."

"That's what I was afraid of."

I paged slowly through the book. There were only about sixty pages, but the paper was thick, as in many coffee table art books. It gave the book more heft. "These are beautiful paintings."

"I thought so, too. Which is why I tore them out and taped them to my wall when I was five years old. Idiot child."

"I'm sure your mother understood."

She shrugged. "Not exactly. I can still see it vividly. My mother's face crumbling as she burst into tears and ran from the room. I wanted to throw the book away after that, but I just couldn't. She must have tucked it inside her drawer that day because I don't remember seeing it around the house again. Not until the other day."

"I'm so sorry."

"Yeah, me, too. But if you can fix it, it'll be the greatest gift I've ever given her."

I continued turning pages. The paintings

were portraits of different Chinese women wearing richly woven traditional robes and clothing. Each woman was as beautiful as the next. Some were partially nude. Others were dressed in rigorously formal dresses. The brushwork was exquisite. The colors were soft and sensual and so tangible, I felt I could almost reach out and feel the satiny textures of the clothing.

As I paged through, admiring the artwork and the subject matter, it began to dawn on me that the paintings were all of the same woman. She changed her looks, her attitude, and her hairstyle for each picture, but it was clear to me now that it was the same model. This book was all about her. I wondered who she was and I was willing to bet that the artist had been in love with her.

"This woman is so striking," I said. "And these paintings really are fabulous. Have you seen any of the originals?"

"You could say that," she said, twisting her lips into an irreverent smile. "That's my mother."

I might've opened my mouth, but no sound emerged. I was speechless. I grabbed my bottle of water and gulped down a few ounces.

Inspector Lee began to laugh. "Now you

know why I wanted to tape the pages to my wall."

"Wow," I said, finally able to speak. "She is a gorgeous woman. I see where you get your looks."

"There you go again, trying to butter me up, but it won't work. I'm not going to divulge anything about the murder case, so don't bother asking."

"That's not fair." I let my shoulders slump for dramatic effect. "Okay, fine. You look nothing like your mother. Is that better?"

"Much more believable."

"You're impossible," I muttered, shaking my head. The woman just couldn't take a compliment. Although I was willing to bet that if Derek had said it, she would've blushed and giggled and thanked him. To be fair, though, I'd never heard her giggle in my life.

"So, what do you think?" she asked. "Can you get rid of the crayon marks or not?"

"Probably not," I confessed, quickly adding, "I'm going to try, but it's tricky. They've been stuck on there for years, so it's likely that even if I could lift the crayon wax off the page, the color will have seeped into the glossy paper."

I flipped to the back of the book, where little Inspector Lee had scribbled on the shiny flyleaf. "This page, I could simply remove without too much hassle." I held the book up and stared at the variegated doodles of a five-year-old. "It almost looks like modern art."

"Yeah, I was a real Picasso," she muttered.

I turned back to the title page with the multicolored crayon scribbles on the opposite page. "This frontispiece page presents two possibilities. Since it's a blank page — or was, once upon a time — I can either try to replace it with a brand-new page or, well, I was thinking you could simply leave it as it is."

"As it is? No." She shook her head mulishly. "No, no, no. The whole point is to fix it."

"But hear me out. Imagine you are your mother, and your grown-up daughter gives you this book you thought was ruined all these years. You open it up and the pages are all put back in their proper places and you see these earnest drawings done by your darling little girl when she was five years old. Be honest. Wouldn't you love it?"

"Love it? Seriously?"

I ignored the note of incredulity in her voice. "Come on, you were only five! You didn't know you were doing anything wrong. So give yourself a break. I'm thinking if you simply give it to her as it is, it'll be a delightful surprise."

"You are insane."

I ignored that, too. "I can reattach all the torn pages and they'll look like new. Trust me, she won't be able to tell the difference. And I can design a beautiful box for it. Derek brought me some gorgeous art paper from Hong Kong last year, so I'll use that. It'll go perfectly with the book's cover art. And listen, on the top of the box I can fashion a plaque with the book title and author's name. And under that, we could write something whimsical like 'original artwork by Janice Lee.' "

"No way."

"It'll be adorable. Your mom will love it."

She snorted. "You don't know her."

"Is she as tough as you?"

"Tougher. The original Tiger Mom."

"She sounds formidable. But if she's anything like you, I'll bet she's got a gooey marshmallow center — just like yours."

It was her turn to be speechless, but not for long. "Excuse me?"

I brushed off her intimidating tone. "Look, don't you think she'll be pleased and excited that you remembered the book after all these years? And now it'll be as good as new — well, except for the darling scribbles by her baby girl." I put my hands over my heart. "It's so sweet."

"You are so off base here." She pushed away from the table and paced around the studio, grumbling and shaking her head, as though she was carrying on her own private conversation. Finally, she stopped and waved her hands in the air. "Okay. Fine. Go ahead and fix whatever you can and leave the rest. You're really wrong about how my mother will take it, but what the heck? Just . . . let's do it."

"The box, too? And the plaque?"

She rolled her eyes dramatically. "All right. Sure. Whatever."

Just then I heard a "meow" and glanced down. Charlie was looking up at Inspector Lee while one of her little paws batted the toe of Lee's stylish black pump.

"Well, hello there," Lee said, and stooped down to pick her up. "Aren't you a cutie pie? Yes, you are." She nuzzled the cat for a long moment and then seemed to realize she had an audience. She glared at me. "What are you looking at?"

I had to fight to keep a straight face and not utter a word about gooey marshmallow centers. Instead I said, "I really can't wait to meet your mom."

■ ■ ■ ■

The next morning, I showed up at the bookstore, greeted Genevieve, and went right to work on the last row of bookshelves. "Where's Billy?" I asked after a few minutes.

"He called in sick."

That wasn't a good sign.

She seemed to know what I was thinking. "I'm afraid I'm going to have to fire him."

Something occurred to me. "If he's involved in something illegal, it's possible he could be hiding from someone."

"Oh God. Now you're scaring me."

I wanted to kick my own butt for saying it out loud. "Look, I'm just letting my imagination run away with itself. He's probably got a stomachache and you'll see him tomorrow, no problem."

"Yeah, maybe." She thought about it for precisely two seconds. "I'm going to call him back."

"Good idea."

Five minutes later, she came out of the office. "He's coming to work right now."

"Interesting."

"Yeah. He said he had something to tell me."

Twenty minutes later, Billy walked into

the store. His straight brown hair was still wet from his morning shower and he wore a grungy thin flannel shirt over a black T-shirt and skinny jeans. He was a sweet kid but always looked a little undernourished. I figured he could gain from a regimen of weight-bearing exercises and healthy eating.

I waved to him and he nodded but kept walking toward the office at the back of the shop, where Gen was working. It was still early enough that no customers had shown up yet, but if anyone came in, the cheerful bells over the front door would announce them loudly enough to be heard in the office, even if Gen shut the door.

I couldn't help myself; I skipped down the ladder and sidled toward the back office, hoping to hear some of their conversation. It was a bad habit of mine, but how else was I supposed to find out what was really going on with the *Almanack*?

"What's his name?" Genevieve asked.

There was a mumbled response from Billy.

"I've never heard of him," she said. "Is he a customer? Is he paying you?"

"Well, yeah, he pays me a little. I mean, it's not against the law. I'm sort of a —"

"A what?" Gen demanded. "A liar? A cheater?"

"No!" Billy huffed and puffed for a moment, then said, "I'm a helper. I'm helping the store make money."

She laughed. "Oh, really? A helper?"

"Yeah. I mean, sure, he gives me a finder's fee, but he still pays the store the money for the book."

"Is that what you were doing with the *Poor Richard's Almanack*? Being helpful?"

"Yes. I mean, it was dated like a zillion years ago, so I knew he might be interested. He likes old stuff."

"It looked to me like you were taking it out of the store."

"I wasn't," Billy insisted, sounding a little desperate. "I was just taking it with me into the office. I was going to call him and describe it over the phone."

"So why did it look like you were getting ready to walk out the back door?"

I knew the back entrance to the store was located inside the office.

"I was closing the door," he insisted. "Not opening it. You have to believe me. I wouldn't cheat you."

"How much does he pay you?"

"Usually about fifty bucks."

"Where did you meet him?"

"He came in one day when you weren't here."

Oh boy. I was willing to bet the guy had

specifically waited for a moment when Genevieve wasn't around.

"How many times have you called to tell him about a book?" she asked.

"I don't know. Maybe six or seven times."

"And each time you've called, he's come into the store?"

He paused. "Well, I've never actually seen him come in, but I'm not here every day. I just figured you waited on him."

"So how do you get your finder's fee?"

"We meet down the street at the brew-pub."

Oh, Billy, I thought, shaking my head.

"When was the last time you called him?" Genevieve's tone had softened. She had to be realizing the same thing I had, that Billy was being taken for a ride. Young and gullible, he was an easy target for a con man.

"Yesterday. I called to tell him about the *Almanack.*"

"Even after I took it from you?"

"He still might be interested in buying it."

"Do you remember the other books you recommended to him?"

"Yeah. He likes mysteries and thrillers, so I told him about the collection of James Bond books we got from that estate sale. That was about two months ago."

"And that was around the last time we

107

were robbed. Do you know what was taken?"

"You never told me."

"It was a collection of five first-edition James Bond books. Worth about sixty thousand dollars."

There was a pause and then Billy said, "I — I don't believe it."

"You're willing to believe a stranger, but not your family? Billy, honey, I know you had nothing to do with the burglaries, but this guy is using you to steal from the store."

I could hear him start to cry and felt like weeping myself. I was also really worried about the *Almanack* now, since Billy had already alerted the thief. I had to remind myself that it was no longer in jeopardy at the bookshop but securely locked in my safe at home.

"I'm so sorry, Gen," Billy said. "I didn't think he —"

"It's okay, honey. It's okay. But we're going to call the police, okay? And you're going to describe the man to them."

Late Friday afternoon, Derek was just pouring us each a glass of wine when the doorbell rang. He raised an eyebrow. "Are you ready for this?"

"Are you?" I asked.

"As ready as I'll ever be," he said, and held up his glass. "Here's to welcoming our first official overnight guests to our new home."

We clinked our glasses, took a quick sip of wine, and then hurried to the door to greet our visitors.

"Sweetie!"

"Hi, Mom," I said, and was instantly wrapped up in a happy hug.

Yes, my mom and dad were our first visitors in our new space. Even though we had spent the past three months living next door to them in Dharma while the house was being remodeled, I felt as if I hadn't seen them in a long time. Maybe because so much had happened since we had come home.

Mom hugged Derek next and said, "This is so nice of you to let us stay for the weekend."

"We're happy to have you both, Rebecca."

Mom blushed and I couldn't blame her. Derek was one of the few people who called her Rebecca, and she seemed to glow whenever she heard him utter her formal name in his charming British accent.

"Hey, punkin'," my father said, sweeping me into his arms for a robust hug. "You look great."

"Thanks, Dad. So do you."

They were both dressed casually and

109

Mom had her pretty blond hair brushed back in a ponytail.

"Hey, Derek." Dad shook Derek's hand, then pulled him in for a manly hug, too.

"Jim, great to have you here," Derek said. "How about a glass of wine?"

"Music to my ears," Dad said.

"Good. I've got a Medoc that is spectacular. I held off opening it until you got here."

"You rock, man."

I closed the front door and followed them into the spacious living room.

"Say, this is snazzy," Dad said, gazing around.

"Your new space is lovely," Mom said. "I know you'll be very happy here."

"We are very happy indeed," Derek said. "Now how about that wine?"

"I'll take your bags into your room while Derek pours the wine." I grabbed Mom's rolling suitcase.

"I'll go with you, sweetie. I want to see everything. Oh, I just love the energy in here."

My mother was always big into energy, vibes, the hum of electricity in a place. But this time, I had to agree completely. Our shiny new apartment was filled with happiness, and that was just how I wanted to keep it. "Thanks, Mom."

"And after we've had a few glasses of wine, I'll be ready to perform a transformation ceremony to initiate your new space. It's a new one I've been practicing and it's guaranteed to snap your garter belt."

I grinned at her. I couldn't help it. "That's quite a claim."

"You know I mean it. I brought my white sage and crystals."

"Super-duper, Mom," I muttered, and glanced back at Derek, who was laughing too hard to make a comment.

Once Mom and Dad were unpacked and we'd all had a glass of wine and a bite of cheese and crackers, we walked a few blocks over to the best sushi bar south of Market Street. Mom and Dad were in town to attend a Grateful Dead reunion party Saturday night and a wedding for the daughter of some old friends on Sunday afternoon. Now that we had extra space, we had invited them to stay with us for the weekend.

My parents had first met at a Grateful Dead show over forty years ago. To be specific, they met at the tie-dyed T-shirt booth in the makeshift parking lot bazaar before the show. It was family legend by now and we could all recite their ages (Mom was nineteen and Dad was twenty-two), what they'd been wearing (Mom was dressed in button-fly cutoff jeans and a skimpy T-shirt that advertised "Bed & Becky," and Dad wore . . . well, that detail never much mattered to the story), and Dad's opening line ("I sure hope your name is Becky"). It was pretty much love at first sight for the two of them and it was plain to see they were still in love to this day.

When I was eight years old, my parents moved my five siblings and me up to Sonoma County, where their beloved guru, Avatar Robson Benedict, had established the Fellowship for Spiritual Enlightenment and Higher Artistic Consciousness. We complained for a while, but it turned out to be the best move ever. I met my best friend, Robin, and my bookbinding mentor, Abraham, that year. And much of the initial sixteen hundred acres of farmland that Robson — or Guru Bob, as we kids called him — shared with his new commune members was lush vineyards.

My parents were simply the two sweetest people in the world and I loved them with all my heart. My dad was still laid-back and friendly despite running a billion-dollar winery operation and the Dharma Town Council. Mom was the original free spirit who'd been at the forefront of every New

Age trend I'd ever heard of — and a few I doubt really existed. Her current position as Grand Raven Mistress of her local druidic coven kept her busy and happy.

Our dinner was a laugh-filled, chatty food fest. We tried all sorts of intriguing combinations of raw fish and seafood oddities and taste-tested three different sakes. Walking home was an adventure, to say the least.

As we reached the door to our apartment, our neighbor Alex sauntered into the hall to greet us. She looked gorgeous as usual in her high-powered black business suit and stilettos. I started to smile but noticed she did not appear pleased.

Derek took one look at her grim demeanor and instantly snapped into protective mode, gripping my shoulder to keep me from advancing toward her.

"What is it?" he demanded.

I tried to soften the question. "Is something wrong, Alex?"

"Wrong?" She scowled. "I'll say there's something wrong. Someone tried to break into your place."

CHAPTER FIVE

"But you stopped him." It wasn't a question. I knew Alex would do anything it took to stop a thief in his tracks. She'd done it for us once before, and if this latest incident was any clue, she would have to keep on doing it for as long as we were all living here. We had wonderful neighbors, but Alex was the best, thanks to her covert training and awesome defensive skills. And the fact that she made absolutely fabulous cupcakes.

"Her," she corrected me. "I stopped *her.*"

"A woman tried to break in?" Derek and I exchanged looks of concern. Who in the world could it be?

Dad glanced around the hallway. "Did you already call the police? Are they on their way?"

"I didn't bother," Alex said, disgusted. "She ran away before I could grab her. I didn't even get close. To be honest, I barely noticed her as I was getting off the elevator.

When I got closer and saw her fiddling with your doorknob, I shouted and she tore out of here faster than I've ever seen anyone run. I swear she must've flown down six flights of stairs, because I chased after her, but she was long gone by the time I got to the street."

I squeezed her arm softly. "Thank you so much. We owe you."

"No, you don't." Disgust colored her tone, and her expression left no doubt that she was kicking herself. "I should've stopped her and I didn't."

Derek glared at her. "You're not to blame yourself."

"Derek's right," I said. "We're just grateful you happened to arrive home when you did."

She sighed. "That was lucky, I guess." She took a wobbly step toward her apartment, then stopped. "I think I broke my heel."

"We'll buy you a new pair of shoes," Derek insisted.

"We'll buy you *two* new pairs," I said. The momentary adrenaline rush was wearing off and I wanted to cry. We hadn't been in our brand-new apartment for more than a few weeks and already we'd been targeted again. It wasn't fair.

Alex must've noticed, because she held

out her arms. "Come here," she said, and gave me a hug.

"Let's all go inside," Mom said gently, rubbing my back.

Derek nodded. "Good idea." He unlocked the door and pushed it open to allow Mom and Dad to go inside. Then he turned to Alex. "You'll come in for a few minutes."

"Of course."

Derek put his arm around my shoulder as we walked into the house. After a few minutes, Mom and Dad said good night. Then the three of us sat around the kitchen counter.

"Can I pour you a glass of wine?" I asked.

"No, thanks," Alex said, slipping off her shoes. "It's getting late. I just wanted to tell you what I saw. And I'll be glad to talk to the police if you'd like to go ahead and call them."

"Do you recall what time it happened?" Derek asked.

"Yes. It was about twenty minutes before you got home."

"What did she look like?" I wondered.

"Tall, thin," Alex said. "She moved like a cat. I couldn't see her face. Couldn't even see her hair color. She wore a mask."

"Great," I muttered. "Catwoman."

Alex gave me a wry smile.

"Sights, sounds, smells?" Derek's words had the effect of snapping Alex to attention. The two of them occasionally spoke in a shorthand that I couldn't always decipher. Months ago, they had bonded over their shared history in covert operations — and their mutual desire to improve my pitiable self-defense moves.

"I got nothing," Alex said, frustrated. "She wasn't wearing perfume. She didn't make a sound. And she wore gloves."

"You're sure it was a woman," Derek said.

The question made her smile. "There's no doubt in my mind."

He shrugged. "You never know."

Something had been bothering me and I finally figured out what it was. "If you rode up on the elevator, she must've heard it coming. It shakes the whole building. Why didn't she leave before it arrived on our floor?"

"I wondered about that, too," Alex said. "She could've been gambling that it would stop on one of the lower floors. I think that's what I might've done."

Derek pondered the possibilities. "And even if it made it all the way up to our floor, she was close enough to the stairs to believe she'd have time to escape."

I grinned. "She wasn't expecting a former

covert operative to come strolling down the hall."

"They never do," Alex said wryly.

"We're very grateful," Derek said.

"Hey, you'd do the same for me."

"Absolutely," Derek and I said at the same time. I quickly added, "But I hope we never have to."

She leaned across the counter and patted my hand. "You and me both, pal."

First thing the next morning, after pouring myself a cup of coffee, I called Inspector Lee. I didn't want to examine too carefully the fact that I had her phone number on speed dial.

"Hey, Brooklyn," she said. "Don't tell me you're finished with the book already."

"No, not yet. The reason I'm calling is to let you know that someone tried to break into our apartment last night."

There was silence for a moment, and I could practically see her sigh, then brace herself. "Tried?"

"Yeah. Our neighbor Alex was just coming home and saw the burglar, but she got away. That's why we didn't call the police."

"She?"

"Yes. According to Alex, the intruder was a woman."

"That's different," she murmured.

"Yeah, I'll say. I can't imagine who it is."

Another pause, and then Lee said, "But everyone's okay?"

"We're fine. We were out to dinner with my mom and dad."

"So, you want me to get someone to come by and take statements?"

"I don't think it's necessary," I admitted. "I can ask Alex to give you a call, but she didn't see much. She did say that the woman was wearing a mask and gloves, so Alex couldn't get much of a description and there aren't any prints. Oh, she was tall and thin. That's about all Alex could discern."

"Okay, I'll make a note. You might want to think about hiring some private security, Brooklyn."

I was beginning to think the same thing — although when I thought about it, I *lived* with private security. Who could I hire who would be better than Derek? There was no one better. "I'll talk to Derek about it."

"Something tells me he's already considered it."

"I'm sure you're right," I said, wondering if he might've already put someone in place. "Anyway, I just wanted to let you know what happened. Not that there's any connection, but it's just weird that it happened

one night after the murder at the Covington."

"You're right. It's weird, but I can't see a
connection, either."

"Except for the fact that both incidents
are really disturbing."

"I hear you." She seemed to hesitate, then
said, "Listen, this might sound lame, but
could you keep an eye on my mom's book?
It's not as valuable as some of those classics
you usually work on, but it's sort of rare.
You know, one of a kind."

I thought it was sweet that she was so
concerned about her mom's book, but I
wasn't about to say so out loud. "I understand completely. Please don't worry,
though. I've gotten used to keeping all the
books I'm working on in my safe. It's very
secure."

"Cool," she said. "Give me a call if you
happen to hear from any other neighbors
about the break-in, or if you decide you
want us to come by and check things out
after all."

"I will. I really appreciate it."

I hung up the phone, amazed. It felt as
though I'd just had a conversation with a
friend. Well, besides all the murder-burglary
talk. But hey, my friends were used to that
kind of talk around me, so what the heck?

My point was, Janice Lee and I were becoming friends. Hallelujah.

I laughed at myself, then wondered if I should've mentioned the *Poor Richard's Almanack* that was currently tucked safely away in my hall safe along with her art book and all the books I'd brought home from Genevieve's to repair. If I had to place a wager, it was an easy bet that the *Almanack* was the reason for the attempted break-in. That was especially true after overhearing Billy tell Genevieve that his friendly neighborhood book thief knew about the *Almanack.*

What if the thief couldn't find the rare booklet in the bookshop? What if he'd followed Genevieve to the Covington Library? What if the guy had watched her hand the *Almanack* to me?

What if I was being followed?

I wondered, not for the first time, if the *Almanack* had something to do with Jared Mulrooney's murder. But how could it? What was the connection? Unless Genevieve knew Jared somehow. It didn't make sense, but still. What if . . .

I should've asked Inspector Lee if the police had made any progress in finding Jared's killer. Not that she would tell me anything, but it would help to know that they were doing their best to solve his murder. I couldn't help feeling a connection to the odd-looking bird-watcher, if only because I had his book in my house.

Could Jared be the connection? It made sense. He had been murdered, and one day later, someone tried to break into my house. The part that didn't make sense was the book itself. How could a simple, pretty little book about birds be important enough to kill over? I didn't have a clue.

I rubbed my arms as a chill skittered across my shoulders.

Shaking off my nerves, I walked into the kitchen to refill my coffee cup. My parents had decided to sleep in, a luxury they rarely indulged in at home. This afternoon, they would meet up with friends for an early-afternoon concert in Golden Gate Park before the main event tonight at the Fillmore.

Thinking about my parents, I replayed last night's events. We'd been having such a good time until we got home and found Alex waiting for us. I wondered again what the intruder could possibly be looking for. I made a mental list of all the books in my safe, and when I got to the *Almanack,* I gasped out loud. What with the arrival of my parents and all the trauma over the attempted break-in, I'd completely forgotten to tell Derek about Billy's con man entanglement.

"I'm a knucklehead," I muttered, and went to track down Derek. I found him working in his nice new home office — formerly my second bedroom. He was talking on the phone but held up one finger to indicate he'd only be a minute, so I leaned against the doorjamb and waited until he finished.

"Hello, love," he said. "Come in and talk to me."

"I can't believe I forgot to tell you something," I said, taking a seat in the chair next to his desk. "It might be important."

He angled his chair to face me head-on. "Go ahead."

I told him about eavesdropping on Billy and Gen's conversation the day before. "Naturally, I jumped directly to the conclusion that I was being followed and whoever tried to break in last night was trying to steal the *Almanack*."

"Unfortunately, that's not an unreasonable deduction to make." He frowned and considered the situation. "After our intruder's run-in with Alex last night, I doubt she'll try to break in tonight. But I've decided not to take any chances. With all of

123

us leaving the house tonight, I've asked George to watch the place until we get home."

"You already called him?"

"Yes."

My mood brightened at the news. So Derek *had* been thinking about private security. George Thompson was one of his best agents and I'd worked with him twice before. The first time was while I was working on the traveling antiques show *This Old Attic,* and then once again more recently while we were staying in Dharma and a friend required security.

"So George can do it?"

"He'll be here at six."

"That's great."

"Yes. He'll park across the street and watch for anyone who comes near the front door of the building."

"Is it necessary for him to stay outside?" I wondered. "He's welcome to come inside the house and stay warm."

"I'd rather have him catch the woman outside the building than inside our home."

"I see your point. But I hate to think of poor George sitting out in the cold all night."

He broke into a smile, leaned over, and squeezed my hand. "You have a good heart.

But to be perfectly honest, I offered him the choice and he elected to remain outside."

"That's because you're his boss. You intimidate him."

"Every chance I get."

I smacked his knee, but managed to laugh as I stood up. "I love you," I said, bending over to give him a kiss.

"And I love you." He grabbed me around the waist and pulled me close. We stayed huddled together for a long moment; then he gazed up at me. "We'll have to find some time to discuss our plans."

I knew he meant our wedding plans and it made me smile. "Yes, we do. But let's wait until after my parents leave."

"Excellent idea. I'd rather not make any decisions by committee. Especially as they might include a drum circle ceremony where I'm clothed in nothing but daisies."

"Hmm." I laughed at the image but knew just what he was talking about. "We're in perfect agreement."

I left him to his work and walked down the hall to the closet that concealed my safe. I kept a few jackets hanging in there to distract a would-be thief. Pushing them aside, I slid open a small panel in the back wall, revealing a combination lock. I dialed in the six numbers, opened the door, and pulled out *Dracula, Cuckoo's Nest,* and the *Almanack.*

This closet had once functioned as a dumbwaiter back in the days when the building was a corset factory. Now it served as a fireproof safe lined with a one-inch-thick layer of solid steel. I trusted it to keep my books secure — as long as I remembered to put them in here every night. After a few scary break-ins over the last few years, I'd developed the habit.

After locking the safe and rearranging the jackets on the rod, I took the books to my workshop.

Since it was Saturday, I only planned to work until Derek was free. We'd talked about walking up to Union Square that afternoon to do some after-holiday shopping. And this evening we were going out to dinner with Crane. I was looking forward to it, especially now that George would be keeping watch over our place. If Derek hadn't thought of it, I would've worried about it all evening and spoiled my appetite. And that would've been tragic.

I should've been able to zone out on my mundane work of cleaning the *Almanack,* but my mind was buzzing too much about the murder of Jared Mulrooney at the Covington and the attempted break-in last night. There had to be a connection. I finally gave up working, pushed my chair away from the worktable, and went to talk to Derek again.

"Are you busy?"

He glanced up and sat back in his chair. "Just making notes for a meeting with a new client on Monday. But I'm glad you're here because I want to run something by you."

"What is it?"

"I was thinking of having a small party next Saturday."

"Here?"

He grinned. "No. Although it would be a good idea to schedule an open house one of these days so our friends can see the new space."

"I'll start looking at the calendar."

"Great. But next Saturday's party will be at my office. A meet-and-greet reception for Crane. I'd like my partners to get to know him and see if we can't drum up more business with him in China."

"What can I do to help?"

"I'll have Corinne send out the invitations and contact the caterers." He grabbed my hand. "You just need to assure me you'll be my date for the party."

"Of course I will." I gave him a toothy smile. "It sounds like fun."

He pursed his lips, studying me, and I wondered how he could look so cynical and sexy at the same time. "I don't believe you for one moment, darling," he said. "But I appreciate your willingness to take one for the team."

I laughed. "I'll admit that first office party was a little rough." That was putting it mildly. The women in Derek's office had decided I was public enemy number one because I was dating the boss. It wasn't pretty. But Derek's secretary, Corinne, was a doll and most of his agents and partners were great fun.

"But this year's Christmas party was lovely," I continued. "And you'll be there, so my life is complete."

"As is mine." He tugged my hand and I ended up sitting on his lap.

"That was clever," I said, wrapping my arms around his neck.

He took full advantage of my position and planted his mouth on mine. I could feel his heart pounding against my own as he moved across my cheek, kissing and nibbling his way over to my earlobe. Then he traveled down to my neck, leaving more kisses along my collarbone.

After a long moment, he rested his forehead against mine. "I thought you were working."

I smiled. "I was. But I was thinking about something and actually came in here to ask your advice."

"So you're not here to have your way with me?"

"Oh, always." I laughed but then sobered. "Seriously, I was trying to figure out how the intruder got inside. Everyone in the building knows better than to open the door for someone they don't know."

"The woman is clearly a professional if she managed to elude Alex." He shrugged. "She could've been watching, lying in wait, and followed someone else's guest inside."

I heaved a sigh. "I'm inclined to call Inspector Lee and tell her I've changed my mind. I'd like the cops to come and conduct interviews with everyone. One of our neighbors could've seen something."

"I'll call her," Derek offered.

Instantly, I had second thoughts. "But wait. Am I making too much of this? I mean, she didn't get into the house."

His eyes narrowed. "But next time she might."

Two uniformed officers showed up an hour later. After a brief discussion with Derek and me, they went off to the other units to ask questions.

With nothing better to do than worry, I started back to work on the *Almanack*. I'd already swept away all the loose dirt from the pages, so now I was ready to use my dry sponge and see if I could get rid of some of the ground-in dirt and dust that had blackened the corners and edges.

I had one drawer devoted to cleaning products, and that was where I found the vulcanized rubber sponge I'd used a few years ago for a set of books that had been damaged in a fire. The books hadn't burned, thank goodness, but they'd sustained a lot of smoke damage and were covered in soot and dirt. A set of cookbooks from the same fire had been coated in a layer of grease.

The rubber sponge acted like an eraser, removing more than ninety percent of the grime and particles off the surface of the smoke-covered pages and the book covers, too. I was hoping it would work as well on the *Almanack*. If not, I would pull out my trusty tub of Absorene, a goopy, pliable substance that I could mold into a lump of soft putty and use like an eraser. The stuff reminded me of Silly Putty, and when massaged onto the surface of the paper, it absorbed dirt and grime. What remained were little crumbs that could be vacuumed up or swept away.

But I started with the sponge. It was always a good idea to test things first to make sure something wouldn't actually damage the paper. So I turned the booklet over and carefully rubbed the sponge along one small corner of the back page. The result was positive. I was thrilled to see that a tiny amount of dingy brown surface dirt was gone. Obviously, I took my victories where I could.

I turned the book over and began to work on the title page. This time it went much slower because this opening page had taken the brunt of hundreds of years of mistreatment and was much more fragile than the other pages. It didn't help that the book had no actual cover. That was because *Poor Richard's Almanack* had first been published as a booklet — by Benjamin Franklin himself. The publication comprised twelve or more stitched-together pages called "self-wrappers."

The copy I was working on featured the phases of the moon for each month of the year, along with a number of essays, most of which seemed to be written tongue-in-cheek. There were woodcut illustrations throughout as well, including a diagram of Leonardo da Vinci's famous anatomical man, which was used to signify the different astrological signs.

It contained invaluable instructions and advice, such as the best time to plant a peach tree. And Mr. Franklin had also scattered a number of clever aphorisms throughout the publication, such as "Guests, like fish, begin to smell after three days."

"We're ready to go!" my mother bellowed from the far end of the living room. "Come see how we look."

I set my chunk of rubber down and jogged out to see them. Mom and Dad were decked out head to toe in vintage Grateful Dead wear. Mom was wearing worn, holey jeans and a suede leather vest, complete with fringe, over a long-sleeved rainbow tie-dyed T-shirt. Dad's outfit was similar except for the fringe. He also wore a beaded leather band around his forehead to keep his hair out of his eyes.

I felt like a proud parent at Halloween. "You guys look so cute."

"Your costumes are ingenious," Derek said.

Mom laughed. "These aren't costumes. This is what we used to wear on a regular basis."

Dad fiddled with his hair. "I haven't worn

this headband in dog's years."

"It still turns me on," Mom said, and started to dance in front of him, causing her fringe to go wild.

"Oh boy." I glanced at Derek. "I've got to go back to work."

"As do I," he said, his eyes wide with alarm. Lord only knew what they would do next.

Mom and Dad's laughter followed us out of the room.

I spent another hour working on the *Almanack* pages. I had pulled the thin frayed cords loose and now a row of individual pages lay across my worktable. It was hard to believe that Benjamin Franklin himself might've touched these pages, might even have stitched them together with his own thread. It was an incredible discovery and I thought again how lucky it was that Genevieve had caught Billy before his contact was able to steal the book.

I had gone online to find comparable versions of *Poor Richard's Almanack* and calculated that this copy was probably worth twenty to thirty thousand dollars. That was nice to know. But in fact, the historical value of this booklet rendered it virtually priceless.

A ruthless collector might be willing to risk going to jail for the chance to steal it.

That night we met Crane at the Slanted Door, one of the trendiest restaurants in San Francisco, if not the world. It was a large, colorful, noisy room, and great fun for people-watching. Both the Vietnamese food and the service were phenomenal. The view was incomparable as well, since the restaurant was situated in the Ferry Building along the Embarcadero overlooking the bay, the bridge, and the hills of Berkeley beyond the wide stretch of water.

It was wonderful to see Crane again. He and Derek regaled me with stories all through the meal, which consisted of at least six courses of incredibly delicious food. There was wine to accompany each dish and I was able to relax and enjoy the company, the food, the ambience, and the view.

Halfway through the third course, a really good-looking Asian man approached our table. He wore a gorgeous dark gray suit and I thought he might be the maître d' — until the guy slapped Crane's shoulder and said, "Fancy meeting you here, bro."

Crane looked up and did a double take. "Bai." He jumped out of his chair and gave

his brother a hug. Bai made a face but toler-
ated Crane's affectionate gesture, although
he barely lifted his arms to return the
embrace. It was a bratty-younger-brother
thing to do and Crane didn't appear to take
it personally.

Crane turned to Derek and me. "Derek,
you remember Bai."

"Of course." He stood and shook the
younger man's hand. "How are you, Bai?"

"I'm great," he said. "Why wouldn't I be?
My life couldn't be better."

I was taken aback by the underlying
defensiveness in his tone, but Crane didn't
seem to notice. "Brooklyn, allow me to
introduce you to my brother, Bai. May I
suggest that the two of you have something
in common, since he is also a wonderful artist?"

"It's nice to meet you, Bai."

"Hey, you, too," he said, shaking my hand.
His gaze moved up and down my torso so
subtly that Derek and Crane didn't notice.
"So you're an artist?"

"I'm a book artist and I also restore old
books."

"Good for you." He made a show of
glancing around the restaurant, looking for
someone, anyone. Then he turned to his
brother. "I saw you from across the room

135

and wanted to say hello, but I've got to get going."

"All right," Crane said. "Let's talk later."

"Yeah, whatever. Nice meeting you, Brooklyn. Good to see you, Derek." Then he took off across the room and disappeared out the door.

I felt my cheeks heat up at the thought that I'd mistaken Crane's brother for the maître d'. But in my defense, we were sitting in an Asian restaurant and everyone who worked here was Asian and beautiful and dressed impeccably.

Crane and Derek sat back down. Crane appeared slightly rattled. Derek was trying to mask his annoyance with a bland smile. I knew the look and I couldn't blame him. Bai had barely uttered five sentences, yet he had come across as arrogant and condescending. But maybe I was being overly sensitive on Crane's behalf.

"That was interesting," I said lightly.

"He does that," Crane said. "Like a mini tornado, he swirls in and shakes everything up and then disappears into the wind."

"He looks good, though," Derek said. "Seems calmer."

"Yes," Crane murmured. "I hope it lasts."

We continued with dinner, but for some reason, I wasn't as relaxed as I'd been before we were interrupted by Bai. I didn't like the way he had treated Crane, I was perplexed by the tone he'd taken with Derek, and I definitely didn't care for his appraisal of me. Bai had only been in our presence for a minute or so, but Crane's mini-tornado description of his brother was apt. I found myself shaken by his slapdash arrival and cavalier attitude.

After a sip of wine and another sliver of Derek's lemongrass-grilled rib eye, I did my best to forget about Bai and enjoy dinner. Now and then, though, my mind kept slipping back to a picture of poor George sitting cold and alone in his car while he kept watch on our place from across the street. But what if the thief didn't come to the front door? What if she snuck into the garage and took the elevator or the back stairs up to our apartment? Every entry was locked securely, but that didn't seem to provide enough of a barrier to this particular intruder.

"Darling," Derek said, "are you feeling ill?"

"No, I'm fine. Just a little preoccupied."

He reached for my hand and squeezed it. "Would you feel better if I called George and asked him to go upstairs to make sure everything is copacetic?"

"Would you mind?"

"Not at all." He pulled his phone from his pocket and walked outside to make the call.

I glanced at Crane. "I'm sorry to be such a drag. It's been a wonderful evening."

"You're not a drag at all," Crane said. "I did notice you've seemed a bit thoughtful this evening."

I smiled. "That's a nice way to put it. Unfortunately, we had an incident at home last night, so I'm just a little —"

Derek walked back to the table. "George didn't answer his phone. I've called the police. I'm sorry, Crane, but given everything that's happened lately, I think we'd better go home."

Crane insisted on following us home, and by the time we arrived, a police car was pulling up to the curb. Derek didn't bother to wait for the garage security gate; he parked on the street. A minute after that, Inspector Lee drove up and parked.

I was hoping and praying it would be a false alarm, but George was too good an agent to let his phone go dead or simply not answer it. Something had to be wrong.

Derek ran across the street to George's car, but returned a minute later. "He's not in his car."

Two police officers walked up as Inspector Lee joined us. "I'd like to get upstairs as soon as you can get the door opened, Commander."

Derek keyed in our security code and six of us entered the unattended lobby. Inspector Lee turned to the two uniformed cops and pointed to the wide stairway directly ahead of us. "The stairs are faster if you're inclined to run. I'm taking the elevator. It's slower, but I won't need a lung transplant by the time I reach the sixth floor."

"Understood, ma'am," the taller male said. He looked so young and cute, like a dark-haired teen-idol type. "I'll take the stairs."

"You go for it, Vogel," Lee said.

"Right behind you," his partner said. She was a petite redhead with a name tag that read LOVE. I assumed that was her last name and not some sort of philosophical statement. She and Vogel both took off running.

"These kids today," Lee muttered, and led the way to the freight elevator. "Let's get going."

When the doors finally opened on the sixth floor, it was clear that we'd made it up there before the two cops. *Good to know,* I thought, as Derek raced off the elevator and down the hall, only to stop abruptly when

he saw George Thompson lying crumpled
on the floor in front of our door.

CHAPTER SIX

"I don't need to go to the hospital," George grumbled. He sounded cranky and defensive and I didn't blame him. Especially when it was his boss insisting that he go after being bested by some devious intruder.

"You may have suffered a concussion," Derek explained.

"I'm fine, boss."

"Of course you are," Derek said calmly. "But I won't let you back in the office without having a doctor sign off on your condition."

"All right," George mumbled. "But I'm not going in an ambulance. I feel dumb enough already."

"I can take him, sir," Officer Vogel said.

"Vogel here was an army medic," Inspector Lee added.

Derek nodded in approval. "I would be grateful for your help, Officer."

Inspector Lee glanced at Vogel. "Think

he's in any condition to answer a few questions first?"

"Let me see." Vogel sat down in front of George. "How do you feel?"

"Stupid."

Vogel smiled. "Any nausea? Headache?"

"A little headache. No big deal."

"What's your name?"

"George Thompson."

"And what day is it?"

"Saturday." He glanced at Derek. "Although I'm not sure how long I was out. It might be Sunday morning by now."

"Not quite," Derek said.

Vogel unclipped a small flashlight from his belt. "I'm just going to check your vision. This will be uncomfortable for a minute."

He flipped the flashlight on and shone it directly into George's eyes. He blinked rapidly in response. "Can you focus directly on the light?"

"I'll try."

Vogel watched for another moment, then turned the light off. "Okay, all done." He stood and nodded at Inspector Lee. "Go ahead, ma'am."

Inspector Lee sat down in front of George, who gazed from the inspector to the cop. "Wait. How'd I do?"

"You did good," Vogel assured him. "Your pupils were focused on the light and they constricted as they should. If you were seriously injured or in danger of having a stroke, you might have little or no response to the flashlight."

George heaved out a breath. "Good to know."

Inspector Lee introduced herself to George. "I'd like to ask you a few questions."

"Please go right ahead."

"Thanks. So what made you leave your car? What did you see?"

He glanced back and forth from Derek to the inspector as he spoke. "A group of partiers came to the door of the building. I tried to count them all and estimated there were ten of them. I couldn't tell if they were all together in one party, because it seemed like there were a couple of stragglers. So I got out and followed them into the lobby."

"Smart thinking," Derek said.

He scowled. "Yeah, well, I'm not so sure. Anyway, by the time I got into the lobby, they were all filing into the elevator. I counted heads again and it didn't look like there were ten people in there, so in an abundance of caution, I took the stairs up to your floor."

"Go on," Lee prompted.

"I didn't see anyone up there, so I was going to return to my car, but I decided to check your doors first, just to cover the bases."

"And what happened next?"

"I got bashed in the head," he said, disgusted. "Never saw it coming."

"You didn't hear anything?" Lee asked. "Smell anything? Feel anything? Besides the bash, I mean."

"Not really."

"You don't sound absolutely positive."

He grimaced. "I can't explain it, but I guess if I had to try, I'd say I caught a vibe."

That sounded perfectly reasonable to me. Inspector Lee leaned forward. "Tell me about this vibe."

"It's like . . . the energy changed." He shot a quick look at Derek to see if his boss was making a face, but Derek's expression remained composed.

"I felt the floor shift," George continued. "It's hard to describe, but this is an old building and underneath all that sisal carpeting in the hallway is old hardwood flooring. There should've been a sound, but there was nothing. The floor didn't creak or squeak or anything. But I'm telling you, I got a feeling of movement under my feet. I

144

started to turn around and . . . bam."

"I'm so sorry," I said, lightly squeezing his arm.

"I'm the one who's sorry," he said, clearly in the throes of self-loathing. He frowned at Derek. "He must've been closer than I thought."

"Or *she,*" I murmured.

"A woman?" George rolled his eyes and then winced in pain from the slight movement. "That would be just perfect. So, did they get inside?" he wondered. "Was anything stolen?"

"No, and no," I said.

"At least as far as we know," Derek added, the voice of caution.

"None of my books are missing." I met Inspector Lee's gaze and she gave a brief nod of appreciation. The first thing I'd done after we brought George inside the house was check my closet safe. It hadn't been disturbed, thank goodness.

"Electronics and computers are all safe," Derek said.

"What about artwork?" Crane asked.

Inspector Lee studied Crane for a long moment and frowned. "I'm afraid I didn't get your name."

"I'm sorry, Inspector. This is Crane," I hastened to explain. "One of Derek's oldest friends. The three of us were out to dinner when Derek realized George might be in trouble."

I turned to Crane. "Crane, this is Homicide Inspector Janice Lee. She's the best there is."

"I don't doubt it at all," Crane said, his gaze on Lee as he reached out to shake her hand.

Lee's eyes were narrowed and focused on Crane. She didn't look one bit happy to be meeting him. "Hello, Mr. Crane."

"It's just Crane," he said, holding back a grin. "And it's a pleasure."

There was a long pause before anyone spoke again. And that was when it hit me. Inspector Lee and Crane! Oh my goodness, I thought. The energy vibrating off the two of them was electric. Didn't they make an attractive twosome? My mind took off in a whole new direction and I wondered if there was something I could do or say to push the two of them toward each other. Wouldn't that be fun? I realized it would be best if I kept my thoughts to myself, but my head was filled with sparkly romantic possibilities.

As Officers Vogel and Love prepared to leave and take George to Urgent Care, Derek promised to come by his stalwart employee's house the next day to check on him.

"Please, boss, that's not necessary," George said, his tone bordering on whiny. Again, I couldn't fault him. Who wanted your boss checking up on you? Especially when you'd goofed up the job so badly? Not that I blamed him for being attacked. But that was what George was probably thinking.

"I'll be there," Derek repeated.

"Resistance is futile," I said lightly, patting George's shoulder. "In case you've forgotten, Derek takes his role as 'the boss of you' very seriously."

"How could I forget?" George wondered, and I hid my smile because he looked so miserable.

After the officers and George left, Crane looked at me. "Your instincts were correct."

"Unfortunately, yes. I'm not very happy to be right."

"No, I imagine not. But it was good that we got here when we did."

"Yes, and thank you for coming along. You didn't have to."

"I wanted to make sure you were both safe." He glanced around, looked from me to Derek. "What else can I do?"

"It appears everything's in order," Derek

said. "Once again, the intruder didn't make it into the house."

"I'm glad to hear it. I'll take off, then."

"We'd like to return the invitation to dinner," Derek said. "Maybe sometime this week?"

"I would enjoy that. Let's talk in the morning."

"And there's a party next weekend," I reminded him.

He beamed. "For which I'm truly grateful and looking forward to it." He turned and bowed slightly. "Inspector Lee. An honor to meet you." Without waiting for a response, he walked out of the house.

She looked flustered and unsure of herself for the first time since I'd met her. Again, I didn't dare say what I was thinking, which was *He likes you, he likes you!*

I could be so juvenile sometimes.

"I know it's too late now," Inspector Lee said, "but first thing tomorrow I'll have Vogel and Love knock on doors to see if anyone got a look at George's attacker."

"Thank you for being here, Inspector," Derek said. "I'm sorry this was a somewhat wasted trip."

"Oh, it wasn't wasted," she murmured cryptically.

She had to be referring to us introducing

her to Crane. I started to smile and instantly she jabbed her finger in my direction. "Wipe that smile off your face."

"I can't."

"Don't make me hurt you, Wainwright." Her composure regained, she nodded toward Derek. "Have a good evening, Commander." And with that, she took off.

"What was that all about?" Derek asked.

I grinned. "Didn't you see the looks that were passing between Inspector Lee and Crane? I think they might be interested in each other."

He smiled tolerantly. "Ah. No wonder she told you to mind your own business."

"She didn't exactly say that," I demurred.

"But I am saying it, darling." He slid his arm around my shoulder and we walked to the bedroom. "Crane will only be in town for another week or so and Inspector Lee doesn't seem the type to be interested in a one- or two-night stand."

"I don't see why not," I said, grinning. "But you know your friend Crane better than I know Inspector Lee."

"I'm not saying Crane wouldn't be interested," he said, chuckling. "I'm just saying it might not be fair to Inspector Lee."

"All right," I said with a sigh. "I won't try to be a matchmaker. But I'll make a deal with you. If one of them asks one of us about the other, we can revisit this conversation. And if that doesn't happen, I'll consider the subject dropped."

At that moment, someone began yelling outside the front door, startling me. Someone else laughed and I relaxed. It sounded like some of our neighbors were having a party in the hall.

Given all the excitement we'd been through tonight, Derek wasn't taking any chances. He walked to the front door and swung it open.

"It's just us," Mom said jovially as she strolled into the house. Then she noticed our expressions. "What's wrong? Did we wake you? It's still pretty early, isn't it?"

"You didn't wake us," Derek assured her. "We just got home a little while ago ourselves and were just about to go to bed."

Dad walked in a few seconds later with his arm tucked around a complete stranger.

I watched Derek's eyes widen and I was pretty sure mine did the same.

The guy hanging on to Dad looked downright homeless, with a full gray beard that was stringy in places and badly matted in others. He wore an old black trench coat over filthy, baggy clothing that had long ago passed its expiration date for washing.

Maybe this was his Grateful Dead costume? But no, I didn't think so.

"This is Goose," Mom explained. "He's one of our dearest old Deadhead friends and he's fallen on some hard times. He's going to spend the night in our room and we'll take him to a shelter in the morning. I hope you don't mind."

Goose blinked and stared at us, then lifted his hand and flashed us the peace sign. "Hey, man. Cool digs."

"Thank you," I murmured.

He gazed around the room. "Whoa. You guys must be rich, right?"

Mom's smile was tentative as she looked from me to Derek and back to me. "It'll be okay."

I suddenly felt like the parent in this picture.

"I'll watch out for Goose," Dad murmured to Derek.

Derek's smile was tight. "Thanks, Jim." He glanced down at me and I telepathically reminded him that I'd warned him my parents were crazy. Good-hearted but crazy.

"Sleep well, everybody," Mom said.

"You, too," I said, and we watched as she and Dad led Goose toward their rooms down the hall.

Derek and I must have been in a state of

shock, because we said very little as we got ready for bed, then went out to the kitchen for two glasses of water.

A minute later, Mom joined us. "I've got Goose all settled. He didn't want to sleep in the second bedroom, so he's sleeping on the floor in our room."

"Maybe that's more comfortable for him."

"I hope we didn't upset you," she said. "We just didn't feel right leaving him there on the cold sidewalk when what he needs is a safe place to sleep and maybe a shower."

"You're a good person, Mom." While I, on the other hand, was fighting off this feeling of being appalled. I would never admit that to my kindhearted mother, but I had been completely stunned when they walked into our house with their scruffy friend.

"Oh, honey," she said, "we've been given so much. Once in a while, we need to give back."

It was so like my parents to embody that philosophy, and it made me feel downright mean and uncharitable for reacting with shock earlier. "You're right, Mom, and I appreciate you reminding me of that." I reached into the freezer for a few ice cubes. "I don't remember you ever talking about anyone named Goose."

"You don't? But he was one of our closest

buddies from the good old days."

"What's his last name?" I asked, thinking maybe I'd remember him that way.

She pursed her lips in thought. "You know, I can't quite recall. The good old days are a little foggy sometimes."

Derek smiled and gave her a peck on the cheek. "I hope you sleep well, Rebecca."

"We'll see you in the morning," I said.

"Good night," she said. "Thanks for understanding."

I squeezed her hand. "I love you, Mom."

"I love you more."

I chuckled and we headed for the bedroom. I'd always known my parents were good-hearted, but they'd proven it in spades tonight. For that reason, I hated myself for even once thinking that Benjamin Franklin's old saying about guests and fish might be true after all.

The next morning we were all up bright and early — except for Goose.

"He's still asleep," Mom said as she poured coffee for herself and Dad. "I've never seen anyone sleep so soundly. I guess he was able to relax for once."

"It's got to be so stressful sleeping on the streets," I said.

"It's no kind of life," Dad agreed as he

doused his coffee with a teaspoon of raw sugar. "Sadly, we know an alarming number of people who've ended up there."

"Some of our generation seemed to slip through a wormhole years ago," Mom said. "I don't know how else to explain it."

"I'm sorry about your friend Goose," I said, feeling helpless.

"We'll do what we can for him," Mom said, patting my hand. "So, what're you kids doing for breakfast?"

"Derek and I were going to walk down to the South Park Bistro. I've been craving their Belgian waffles."

"I'd love to take a walk this morning," she said, and glanced at Dad. "Do we dare leave Goose alone for a few minutes?"

"He'll be asleep for another hour or two," Dad predicted. "Maybe longer, poor guy."

Mom could tell we were reluctant, so she said, "You two go ahead and we'll get something later."

Derek gritted his teeth for a quick moment, then said, "If you don't think it'll be a problem to leave him alone for a little while, we can all go together."

I was so proud of him for having faith in my parents' judgment, although I could tell it cost him. It was costing me, too, but I was trying to hold my tongue.

"I completely understand if you'd rather not leave him alone," Mom said. "Jim and I will stay home."

"Maybe if we ordered everything to go and brought it home," I said.

"That's it," Dad said. "We'll walk there with you and get our breakfast to go. That way we won't be gone more than half an hour. Goose can't get into much trouble in that amount of time."

"Would that be okay?" Mom asked. "I really just wanted to take a walk anyway."

Derek nodded. "Then it's settled. I just have to make a quick phone call and we can go."

I assumed Derek was calling to check on George and I used the time to brush my hair and dab on some lip gloss. We all donned heavy jackets because the morning air was so cold lately.

We walked three blocks to Third Street and turned left. Two short blocks later, we reached the tiny enclave of South Park, a block-long green park and playground surrounded by small offices, apartments, a few shops, a coffeehouse, and several restaurants, one of which was the Bistro, an adorable haven for wonderful café au lait and fabulous Belgian waffles.

Unfortunately, the line outside the Bistro

was longer than we'd anticipated.

"Darn," I said, turning to Derek. "I'm glad we're getting it to go."

After twenty minutes we received our piping-hot orders of waffles to go along with separate containers of fluffy butter and golden syrup, plus sides of bacon. Mom had thoughtfully ordered breakfast for Goose, too, so we each grabbed a bag to carry and headed for home.

"This will be more fun anyway," Mom said, glancing at a charming shop window filled with kitchenware and linens.

I linked my arm with hers. "I think so, too."

"Gosh, I miss the city sometimes," she said, tightening her grip on my arm.

I chuckled. "Is that why you're shivering?"

"The chill is part of the ambience."

"Good point." In San Francisco, the weather was like a key character in a movie. The famous fog that rolled in almost every afternoon, blanketing the city, actually had a name. San Franciscans called it Karl. I'd heard a rumor that Karl the Fog had its own Twitter account.

I could hear the murmurs of Dad and Derek chatting a few yards ahead of us.

"Oh, I just remembered," Mom said. "You have that wonderful machine that makes café lattes, don't you?"

"Yes. I'll make one for you."

"I would love that."

"What time do you leave for the wedding?" I asked.

"Two o'clock. We'll have breakfast and then get dressed and ready to go. I'll wake up Goose as soon as we get back and encourage him to take a shower. It might boost his spirits a little."

"A shower always makes me feel better."

Chuckling, she patted my arm. "Me, too."

"I would offer to wash his clothes, but I think they might fall apart."

"True. And he might not be willing to trust you with them anyway."

"I understand." I rested my head against my mom's. "Poor Goose. Did you talk to him last night? Does he remember much of the old days with the Grateful Dead?"

She sighed. "He remembers the music, of course, and dancing. He says he remembers me and Dad, but he couldn't remember any of our other friends."

"That's too bad."

"It's okay," she said grimly. "We'll do what we can for him. And on the way to the wedding, we'll stop at one of the shelters in the Tenderloin and see if we can get him a bed for the night."

157

"I hope you can do it. I read in the paper a while ago that they've started requiring some kind of medical certificate proving he doesn't have tuberculosis before they'll let him stay the night."

"Oh dear. I wonder if he has one. Maybe we should bring him home to Dharma with us. Gary Jenkins has taken in a few homeless folks over the years, ones who were willing to stay sober and help around the farm. It's a much healthier environment."

"You'll have to ask Goose how he feels about that. Some people have a hard time stepping out of their comfort zone, even when that zone is as gruesome as living on the streets."

"I'm afraid you're right, sweetie. It's sad, isn't it?"

The four of us traipsed through the lobby and piled into the freight elevator.

"It smells so good in here," I said, gladly changing the subject.

Mom sniffed the air. "I think it's the bacon."

"And the syrup," I added.

Derek agreed. "My mouth is watering."

Dad was regaling us with the latest winery gossip as the elevator shuddered to a stop and we walked down the hall to our door.

"Stop," Derek ordered suddenly. "Jim,

step back. Brooklyn, please go see if Alex is home."

"What's wrong? What happened?" But then I saw that the door was opened an inch and I felt sick to my stomach. I ran down the hall and knocked loudly on Alex's door. When she answered I said, "Can you come over, quick?"

"I'll be right there."

I raced back to our apartment in time to see Derek pushing the door open. Mom and Dad remained in the hall, but I followed cautiously inside, wondering if Goose had left the door open. Was he still here? Did he steal everything in sight and run away? If so, he was a lot more devious and agile than any of us had given him credit for.

But everything seemed to be in perfect order. So what had happened here? Who had left our front door open?

Derek's voice was deadly calm. "Brooklyn, please go out to the hall and call Inspector Lee, will you?"

"Why? What happened?" I glanced around him and got a look at the hall where Goose lay spread-eagled on the hardwood floor. At least it *looked* like the man named Goose who'd come home with Mom and Dad last night. Except . . . he was clean. His hair was shiny and his beard was gone. Shaved off. He looked almost handsome and that would've been wonderful but for the fact that he was sprawled across our hallway floor, his back pressed up against the door to my closet safe. He wore a plush burgundy bathrobe that I recognized as Derek's. It had fallen open to reveal blood seeping from a gaping wound in his gut.

Now I had a whole new reason to feel queasy. There was blood. And Goose was dead.

CHAPTER SEVEN

Derek knelt down and checked Goose's neck for a pulse. Glancing up at Mom, he shook his head and confirmed my worst fears. "I'm sorry, Rebecca. He's dead."

"But he shaved," I muttered, then regretted it immediately, because the fact that Goose had shaved was possibly the least important aspect of the dreadful scene before us. No one seemed to notice my absurd comment, though, as they all stared at the body. Derek had taken it upon himself to get his phone out of his pocket and call the police. Dad had his arms wrapped around Mom. Her face was buried in his sweater, and her shoulders were shaking in grief.

I felt my own eyes burning with tears at the sight of Mom's pain. Once again, death had come into our home. It was going to sound completely self-centered of me, but I actually considered it good news that I hadn't been the one who found Goose's body.

Officially, that would be Derek, who didn't seem at all flustered by the discovery. But since I was still close enough to witness the crimson blood streaming from Goose's gut, did it matter? I might as well have been the one who had stumbled over the poor guy.

Blood. To this day, I just couldn't handle it.

It dawned on me that the reason Derek had asked me to go out to the hall and make the phone call was that there was so much blood. I just never seemed to handle it well, and this time was no exception.

Feeling like an idiot once more, I had to turn and walk away before I passed out from the image of all that dark red liquid oozing from Goose's stomach onto our floor.

I took the opportunity to pace the perimeter of the living room, taking deep breaths and trying to calm myself as I made a cursory search of the space. I checked my workshop, too, but didn't find anything out of place. I saw my sandals on the floor under the desk — and gasped. "Charlie! Where are you —"

I started to dash out of my workshop when I heard a plaintive mewing from right under the desk. I crouched down and peered into the small dark space. "Are you in there, sweetie?"

"Mew."

"Aw, come here. I won't let anything hurt you."

She crept closer and I pulled her into my arms. "Poor thing."

I wasn't about to let her go while Goose's body lay on the floor. I wanted more than anything to check my closet safe and make sure my books were still inside and secure, but I knew we couldn't move Goose's body until the police arrived.

I circled back around to where Mom and Dad were consoling each other. I had to avoid looking down at the poor man, knowing I was still light-headed from seeing our hapless murder victim's blood oozing from his wounds.

Ugh. There went my roiling stomach again. I silently argued that maybe it was a good thing I still reacted this way at the sight of blood. After all, I hadn't turned completely cynical about murder. And I also hadn't fainted this time. So three cheers for me.

Derek finished his phone call and slipped the phone into his pocket. "Inspector Lee and Inspector Jaglow will be here shortly."

163

"Good," Dad murmured.

Alex knocked briefly and walked in. "Everyone okay over here?"

"Not everyone," Mom said. "Our friend Goose was attacked while we were out taking a walk."

Alex's eyes widened. She walked over to take a look at the body, then scowled as her hands curled into fists.

"Stop," I said, before she could speak. "Don't you dare blame yourself."

"But —" She let out a breath. "I'm sorry, guys. I didn't hear a thing."

"It's not your fault," Derek said sternly.

She stared down at Goose. "Who is it?"

"An old friend of ours," Dad said.

She reached for Dad's arm and then Mom's and gave them each a gentle squeeze. "I'm so sorry for your loss."

"Thank you, Alex," Mom said. And the tears started to fall again.

It was alarming to see my mom so devastated and I was in danger of tearing up myself. I slipped my arm around her shoulder. "Let's go sit down, Mom."

"All right."

"That's okay, honey," Dad said, lightly squeezing my shoulder. "I'll sit with her." He led Mom over to the living room couch.

"I can stick around if you'd like," Alex said.

"You don't have to," I said, rubbing my hands up and down my arms. I wasn't sure if it was a nervous reaction or a way to get my own blood moving. "We're just waiting for the police to show up."

Derek agreed, adding, "We might give you a call later if something comes up."

"Okay."

But she still looked distraught, so Derek added, "You're not to feel bad. This is our fault for leaving him here alone."

"Where were you?" she asked.

"We walked down to South Park and got breakfast to go," I said. "We were barely gone half an hour."

Alex shook her head in disgust. "If it's the same woman who tried to break in the other night, she works fast."

"Yes, she does," Derek said through clenched teeth. "I have a feeling she's been watching the house."

"Probably. How else would she know the right time to break in?"

I didn't like the look of fury and frustration on Derek's face. It was a dangerous combination for a man with his skills and background. He would be even more determined than before to get to the bottom of

165

this. Not just for poor Goose and what his death had done to my parents, but because our *home* had been violated.

I knew just how he felt.

Alex left a few minutes later after promising to come back that afternoon.

Derek and I joined my parents in the living room.

"I'm fine," Mom insisted, lifting her chin and blinking like a sun-blind woman in a futile attempt to stem the tide. "I never cry."

"She cries at pet food commercials," Dad said.

We all had a good laugh and Mom smacked Dad's knee.

"Oh my God," I said suddenly.

"What is it?" Mom asked in alarm.

"I just remembered, we never ate our waffles."

"You're trying to make me cry again," Mom wailed.

It might've seemed wrong to an outsider, but it lightened our hearts to hustle off to the kitchen to heat up the waffles and bacon.

As we ate in silence I had time to ponder what had happened here today. I was raised to believe that life was a circle. Death and birth and everything in between were simply what happened during our cycle on earth. But did that mean we should be comfortable with sudden death? It saddened me to think it might be true. We weren't being blasé about it, I insisted to myself, but I wondered if we were becoming inured to the reality of it. It bothered me to think that maybe we were, and I was determined to fight the feeling.

I left the table to make another pot of coffee and came back to finish my meal. "These are the best waffles in the world."

"Goose would've enjoyed them," Mom said, then glanced around at our looks of alarm. "Don't worry. I won't start crying."

"Good," I muttered. "Because in case you haven't noticed, nobody cries alone when I'm in the room."

Dad glanced toward the back hall, where Goose's body remained. Looking at the rest of us, he asked, "Where did Goose get that bathrobe?"

Derek gritted his teeth. "I believe it's mine."

I gave him an apologetic look. "I believe you're right. Never mind. We'll get you a new one. Something Turkish and elegant."

"Oh no," Mom moaned. "I'm so sorry, Derek."

"Please, Rebecca." Derek reached for her hand. "Don't worry about it for a single moment. It was insensitive of me to blurt that out."

Dad leaned closer to Mom and threw his arm around her shoulders. "Come on, honey. It'll be all right."

"But Goose is dead and Derek's bathrobe is ruined and we never should've —"

"Rebecca, please," Derek quickly intervened. "If wearing my bathrobe gave your friend Goose a few moments of pleasure, I'm perfectly happy that he took it."

She sniffled. "Oh, that is the sweetest thing I've ever heard."

"And it's the absolute truth," Derek insisted. "I don't want you to spend another second worrying about it. The robe was quite old. I was going to buy a new one soon."

"See that, Becky?" Dad said, stroking Mom's hair. "It's going to be all right." Looking at Derek, he added, "She's got such a tender heart."

I slid my barstool closer to Derek and squeezed his arm lightly. The truth was, the bathrobe was brand-new, a Christmas gift from his parents in England. But it was easily replaced, unlike Goose's life.

We spent the rest of the meal speculating on what had happened to Goose. As near as I could figure, as soon as we'd all left for the Bistro, Goose must've gone wandering around the house. Derek's bathrobe had been hanging on a hook in our bathroom, so Goose had definitely given himself a thorough tour of our place. He took a quick shower, shaved his beard, and threw on Derek's bathrobe. At that point, he probably walked into the living room and surprised the intruder.

So in a way, Goose was a hero. I didn't know if the woman was after my books and I couldn't yet tell if anything was missing from the closet safe, but aside from that, nothing had been taken from our apartment. I figured Goose must have surprised the woman and she had fled the scene before she could accomplish her main goal of stealing one of my books.

There wasn't a doubt in my mind that stealing a book was her ultimate goal. I just didn't know *which* book she was after. And unfortunately, with Goose's body blocking the closet door that shielded my book safe, I wouldn't know the answer until the police came and moved him.

Had she been trying to get into the closet when Goose surprised her? The answer had to be yes. Why else would Goose be lying dead directly in front of the closet door?

Had she heard the elevator rising? Was

that why she ran out? Given the length of time we were gone from the house, she couldn't have been here more than a few minutes.

"I wish the police would hurry," I muttered.

As if I'd conjured them, there was a knock on the door.

"I'll let them in," Derek said.

Mom and I hastened to clear the table of breakfast plates, and a moment later, Inspectors Lee and Jaglow followed Derek inside.

Both of them stared at the body of Goose for a long moment.

"That's a nice bathrobe," Inspector Jaglow said. "Friend of yours, I assume?"

"No," Derek said bluntly. "He's an old friend of Brooklyn's parents. My understanding is that he's been living on the streets for quite a few years. They ran into him last night and brought him here in hopes that he would enjoy a night of untroubled sleep."

Jaglow gazed at my parents. "That was nice of you."

"I'm not sure he would thank us now," Dad said grimly.

Inspector Lee walked directly over to the body and began taking photographs with her telephone, capturing Goose's image from a number of different angles. I'd never seen her be so quiet and wondered if something was bothering her.

"Hey, Nate, help me move him away from the door so he's lying down flat," she said to her partner, finally speaking for the first time.

"Are you all right?" I asked.

"She's having man trouble," Nate Jaglow said, bending down to shift Goose's body.

"Nate, shush," she said mildly, clearly indicating she wasn't angry with him for speaking out of turn.

I didn't dare ask which man was giving her trouble, but I glanced at Derek meaningfully. He shrugged as if to say he didn't have a clue as to whether Crane had contacted her or not.

Now I had to wonder if maybe Inspector Lee had a boyfriend. I'd never bothered to ask, since we weren't intimate friends. But I was dying to know.

"Tell me more about this guy," Lee said, still looking at Goose.

"We knew him years ago," Mom said. "Back in the days when we were following the Grateful Dead."

"Did you keep in touch?"

Dad said, "No. Once we moved to

Dharma, we lost touch with a number of our old Deadhead friends."

Inspector Jaglow was busy writing down the information in his notepad. "And what's his name?"

"We always called him Goose."

"So you don't know his real name?"

"Sorry."

"We'll fingerprint him and try to track down his next of kin."

"That would be lovely of you," Mom murmured.

"Do you know where he grew up?" Jaglow asked. "Where he went to school?"

"No idea." Dad shook his head. "Sorry."

"Anything you can tell us about him that might help us put some pieces together?"

"He has a dragon tattoo on his butt cheeks," Mom said.

Lee's head jerked up. "Yeah?"

"Wow, Mom," I said. "Just how well did you know Goose?"

"Becky?" was all Dad could say.

"Oh, Jim. Don't tell me you've forgotten all the times we used to go skinny-dipping."

"Honey, I've never forgotten our skinny-dipping days."

"Then how could you miss seeing a full-blown winged dragon tattoo spread across a man's buttocks?"

172

"Good question," Lee said, trying to contain a smirk.

Derek didn't bother to hold back. He just started laughing.

Dad glanced at the other men in the room, then back at his wife. "This may come as a shock, but I rarely spend time checking out other guys and their buttocks."

"I suppose I should be happy about that," Mom conceded.

"I'd say so," Inspector Lee said. Then she flashed her partner a look of resignation. "Looks like we'd better turn him over and check out this tattoo."

"Let's do it." Jaglow positioned himself by Goose's head.

"Would you like some help?" Derek asked.

"I'd appreciate it," Lee said. "Thanks, Commander." She moved aside so that Derek could grab Goose's feet while Nate took hold of his head. With as much care as possible, they shifted Goose over until he lay in a prone position with his face pressed against the hardwood floor. As a result of moving him, the bathrobe flapped open and bunched up, leaving the dead man sadly exposed and the rest of us in complete shock.

"It's not him," Mom whispered.

Ten minutes later, Mom had recovered from her shock. "How did we conclude that this man was Goose?"

Dad shook his head, clueless.

"It could still be Goose," I said, offering another possibility. "Tattoos can be removed."

"I looked at it pretty closely," Lee said, then quickly amended the statement. "I mean, as closely as I ever want to get to a homeless guy's butt. Anyway, there's no way he ever had a tattoo there. Even the best tattoo removal job leaves a remnant of ink. This guy's got nothing."

"So how in the world did we mistake him for Goose?" Mom wondered again.

The two of them replayed the scene outside the Fillmore the night before. Dad finally decided that they'd simply bought in to their friend Stewart's comment when he said, "Hey, that guy looks just like Goose, doesn't he?"

"How's that for the power of suggestion?" Mom muttered gloomily. She shook her head in dismay. "This is such a fiasco. I feel so bad. You kids have put up with so much from us."

Derek tried to put her at ease. "We love having you here. It's terribly unfortunate that the man was killed, but it wasn't your fault. And I wouldn't dream of changing your generous nature and tender heart for all the money in the world."

My father actually *beamed* at Derek and I had never loved him more.

"And as gruesome as it sounds," I added, "this will be a visit we'll always remember."

Dad chuckled ruefully. "You can say that again."

"Do you still want to go to the wedding, Jim?" Mom asked.

"Of course I do and so do you, honey. It'll make us both feel better. And it's the right thing to do."

"You'll see so many old friends there," I said. "After a while you'll be able to relax and enjoy yourselves."

Dad said, "And a few of the wedding guests were with us last night when we thought we saw Goose, so maybe we can put our heads together and figure out how we all mistook this guy for our old friend."

Feeling better about the wedding, they went off to their room to get ready.

I found an old sheet to cover the body and that was when I remembered what I'd been itching to do for the last hour.

"I'm going to check my safe," I announced to the cops.

Inspector Jaglow came over and re-arranged the sheet cover. "Let's move this sheet closer to the closet door so in case there're any footprints to be found, you won't disturb them."

"Good thinking," Lee said.

The first positive sign was that the closet door was still locked. I pushed the jackets aside and knelt down to key in the combination numbers. The lock didn't look as though it had been tampered with. Another good sign.

After working the combination lock, I opened the door to the safe and breathed a huge sigh of relief. Pulling all eleven books out, I carried them over to the dining room table to make sure everything was as it should be. While the police did what they had to do, I spread the books out and in my detail-oriented brain, I listed the title of the book and the work I'd been commissioned to complete.

Poor Richard's Almanack — clean; resew cords; create storage box; write up an appraisal.

Dracula — clean soiled boards; regild spine; remove foxing if possible; talk to Genevieve regarding bleach.

176

One Flew Over the Cuckoo's Nest — repair torn book jacket.

The Grapes of Wrath — repair and resew text block; new cover (ask Genevieve if she would prefer leather, with original color illustration set into leather and beveled); regild title and flourishes on spine; regild front cover.

The Merry Adventures of Robin Hood of Great Renown — replace cloth cover because of considerable fraying along the head and spine and corners; replace second free endpaper to get rid of previous owner's unsightly signature.

The Maltese Falcon — loose front and back hinges (already repaired).

Lonesome Dove — another broken hinge and a fraying spine.

The Great Gatsby — general cleaning and do something about foxing, if possible.

Amo, Amas, Amat: A Little Book of Latin — this was a classic old schoolbook that Genevieve wanted refurbished. She said it reminded her fondly of her days in Catholic school, so she planned to keep it for herself. Both front and back endpapers were torn from the cover at the hinges so the papers would have to be replaced and sewn back into the book; a few interior tears needed repair; other minor cleanup work.

Songbirds in Trees — the Bird-watchers Society book I'd received from Jared Mulrooney. I'd almost forgotten about the charming little Audubon book with the bluebird on the cover. I wasn't sure what I would do to repair the damage from the wine spill, but I was fairly certain I would have to take the book apart and wash and press each page. But I might be able to get away with leaving the book intact, I thought, as long as I could effectively shield the leather cover from any liquid or solvent I might use.

And finally, Inspector Lee's art book for her mother — repair and reaffix torn pages; create a storage box with title plaque.

"Everything's safe," I announced, glancing at Inspector Lee.

"Thanks," she said with a brisk nod.

Derek gave my shoulder an encouraging squeeze. "That's good news, love."

"Yeah, glad to hear it," Inspector Jaglow said.

Discovering all my books safe and sound was a tremendous weight off my shoulders, despite the horrible scene that had taken place within inches of the closet door. I returned the books to the safe and locked it securely.

Two uniformed officers arrived to get

instructions for knocking on doors in the building. Inspector Jaglow moved into the main hall outside our apartment to search for any clues or footprints.

Two crime scene techs showed up soon afterward. One of them worked out in the hall with Jaglow and the other, a muscular man in his forties, stayed inside. He spent a few minutes talking to Inspector Lee and then unpacked his fingerprint kit and began to dust the doorknobs and -jambs for prints.

I let go of another sigh. I really hated fingerprint powder. It got all over everything and was so hard to get off again.

And wasn't it a little sad that I'd had so much experience with fingerprint powder? I tried to overlook that detail.

I walked into Derek's office. "Are you working?"

He looked up and smiled. "It's a little difficult to concentrate with all the activity."

"I know. That's why I thought I'd come and bother you."

"Come in and sit down. You're never a bother to me."

I sat in the chair next to his desk and leaned forward. "I feel like someone should mention to the police that there's an elephant in the room."

"Only one, darling?"

I blinked. The fact that he thought there was more than one elephant told me that Derek was thinking along the same lines as I was. "And that's just one reason why I love you."

"Because we're on the same wavelength?"

"Yes. Among other things."

He sat back in his chair. "So tell me about your elephants."

"Okay. First, there's Billy, Genevieve's cousin. I think we need to talk to him and maybe get a sketch of the guy who's been hustling him. Because I can't help thinking that there's some connection we're missing in all this. After all, everything started to fall apart soon after I took the books home from the bookshop."

"The guy who's been hustling Billy is a man, though. Our intruder was a woman. As far as we know." Derek did not look any more surprised that a woman had gotten through his security and past his well-trained associate than a man. We had both dealt with cold-blooded killers of both genders.

"They could be working together," I said. "One could be a lookout for the other."

"True."

"Or, even though our intruder from the other night was a woman, today's break-in

180

could've been done by a man."

He considered this, then said, "It's a bit of a stretch to think that we're dealing with two different thieves."

I shrugged. "I know, but stranger things have happened. In fact, stranger things have happened to *us*."

"True enough. We'll tell Inspector Lee about Billy and the hustler." He began to make notes on a legal tablet, then glanced up. "You have another elephant."

"Yes." I took a deep breath, then blurted out, "The other elephant is Jared Mulrooney."

Derek's eyes narrowed on me and I had a feeling he'd been considering the same possibility. "Go on."

"Am I the only one who thinks it's more than a coincidence that both Goose and Jared Mulrooney were killed in the same fashion?"

"Namely, a knife in the stomach?"

"Yes."

"You're not the only one, darling." He wrote something on the tablet. "It's entirely too coincidental to my way of thinking, but we can't make assumptions, either. It'll take a medical examiner to determine if the murder weapon was the same."

"So we'll have to talk to the police."

"Talk to the police about what?" Inspector Lee said. She quickly added, "I wasn't trying to eavesdrop, but I was looking for you. The medical examiner is here and wants to make sure everything is in order before he takes the body to the morgue."

Her words gave me a chill. It was the mention of taking Goose to the morgue. It was so . . . final. Not to mention the autopsy procedure, which was nothing but creepy. Necessary, of course, but creepy. So, in true *me* fashion, I forced that image out of my mind.

"I'm glad you found us, Inspector," Derek said. "We were discussing the similarities between the murders of Jared Mulrooney at the Covington Library the other night and our friend Goose here in our home this morning."

She considered his words. "Both took a knife in the gut."

"Exactly."

"I'll have the ME track those two CODs."

Causes of Death, I thought, and tried not to be too pleased that I had caught on to the jargon of violent death.

Lee leaned against the doorjamb and crossed her arms, getting comfortable. "But what do you think it means? What's the connection between the two?"

I knew she was asking Derek, but I had a possible answer. "The only connection is the book Jared gave me. It's in the safe, but it's nothing, really. I mean, it's worth a little money, but it's a book of bird paintings. I can't believe someone would kill for that little bird book when I've got books in my safe worth five or ten times more."

"Are you sure the bird book is the only connection?"

"To tell you the truth, until I saw how Goose was killed, I was sure the intruder was after the *Poor Richard's Almanack*. But now I don't know what to think. Is getting stabbed to death in the stomach enough of a connection between the two?" I brushed my hair off my forehead as I thought for a moment. "I did receive both books at the Covington that night, but that's hardly note-worthy."

"It could be," Lee said. "Tell me what happened."

"I ran into Genevieve Taylor earlier that evening." I backtracked to explain my relationship with Genevieve, the owner of the bookshop, then told her about our cryptic conversation in the foyer of the Covington, during which she'd handed me the *Almanack*. That was followed an hour later by my meeting with Jared and Ian when I'd been given the bird book. I'd carried both books in my purse the rest of the evening for safekeeping. And now two people had been killed and I was pretty sure it was because of one of those books. That thought was enough to give me another chill.

Always the skeptic, Inspector Lee said, "Okay, even though all that happened, there still might not be any connections to be made. Except for the fact that the two men died in a similar manner."

"True."

"A lot of people die of stab wounds," she muttered.

"Yes, so you could be right. There might not be any connection at all." Even though I doubted it, saying the words aloud made me feel a tiny bit better.

"It'll take a few days," Lee said, "but once the ME determines the actual cause of death and can verify the type of knife used in both killings, he'll pass the word on to me and I'll let you two know."

Derek's expression was somber. "I'd appreciate your contacting me as soon as possible, Inspector."

Lee pushed away from the doorjamb, no longer relaxed. "You got it, Commander."

I frowned. She sounded way too co-operative. Was I missing something? I was naturally worried that someone could still sneak in here and steal the book, but why were they both so tense all of a sudden? "What's wrong with you two?"

They exchanged a solemn glance.

"Think about it, darling." Derek reached for my hand. "If you're right and Goose's and Jared Mulrooney's murders are both connected to one of the books inside your safe, it means your life is in mortal danger."

CHAPTER EIGHT

Well, duh. Of course I was in danger.

But I stared at Derek and had to admit that the thought hadn't really sunk in until he said it out loud. So did that make me dumber than a stick? No! At least, I didn't like to think so. The fact was, I'd been working with books since I was eight years old, and my life had been wonderful — until a few years ago when I first ran into trouble and had to learn a hard lesson. That was when I found my bookbinding mentor dying in a pool of his own blood and began to realize there were people out there who were willing to kill or steal or blackmail or threaten others in order to get their hands on something rare and beautiful — and expensive. Namely, a book.

That trouble hadn't gone away. In fact, it had been snowballing since then. In many cases, I was the only thing standing in the way of one malevolent person and the rare book he or she desired more than life itself.

For me, an exquisitely bound book was no less than a masterpiece. A work of art. But while most great art was guarded and treasured and well beyond the reach of thieves and evildoers, a book was generally smaller, more portable, and easier to steal.

So nowadays I was always aware of the possibility of danger. And I was always careful.

Except for those times when I wasn't.

"I'll be more careful, I promise." I grabbed Derek's hand. "But if I'm in danger, then so are you."

"I can take care of myself, love." He sent Inspector Lee an imploring look, as if silently asking for backup.

"Derek carries a gun," she said, her tone blunt. "He knows ten ways to kill someone with a toothpick. You don't."

I scowled at both of them, mainly because they were right. I'd grown up in a loving, peaceful, rustic environment, running through the fields as free as the birds, my hair fluttering in the breeze and Birkenstocks strapped on my feet. I couldn't shoot a gun to save my life. And forget about toothpicks. "All right, fine. So what do I do? Besides double up on the self-defense lessons with Alex?"

"That would be a good start," Lee said. "But beyond that, I want you to be aware of your surroundings at all times. Be suspicious of everyone you see. I don't want you putting yourself in harm's way."

"I won't," I grumbled, ready to change the subject. "So what comes next?"

"First thing tomorrow I want to interview Billy at Taylor's Fine Books. Let's see if there's a clear connection between your break-in and this guy."

"Oh." I recalled what I'd heard during my eavesdropping session at the bookshop. "Genevieve might've already contacted the police."

"Good," she said. "I'll check with the Richmond District Station to see if anyone's been over there to see him yet. And even if they have, I'm going to pull rank and take over Billy's case. There's a fifty-fifty chance his hustler is linked to our murder investigation."

"That's great news," I said. "You're the best."

Her smile was dripping with irony, metaphorically speaking. "I won't argue with you this time."

It made me laugh, despite the gloominess of the conversation.

"If Billy's con man is associated with our

intruder," Derek said, returning to Lee's point, "there's your connection."

Lee scowled. "Can't get much clearer than that."

Minutes after the police and medical examiner left, I was able to get in touch with my old friend Tom and ask him to bring his team over to our place to clean things up.

It was an ugly little fact that when a violent death occurred and blood was spilled, a crime scene officially became a biohazard site. Tom and his guys had worked for me a few years ago when a man died inside my best friend Robin's apartment.

Tom and his two helpers showed up early that afternoon and four hours later, every surface of the living room and hall had been cleaned and disinfected. There was also no trace whatsoever of the dreaded black powder used for fingerprinting, and for that alone, I was grateful. I signed a few forms so that Tom could collect his payment from our homeowner's insurance. It was nice that, under the circumstances, no money had to change hands, but what I appreciated most about Tom was that he and his guys were always kind and empathetic toward whoever was left to deal with a friend's or loved one's death. Or in our case, a stranger's death inside our home.

Since it was Sunday night and tomorrow was a workday, Derek and I stayed home and had a quiet dinner of grilled chicken, asparagus, and roasted rosemary potatoes. I was beyond proud of myself for preparing and cooking the vegetables from scratch. Gazing joyfully at the way the veggies were artistically arranged on our plates, I was struck by the realization that I was getting to be a pretty darn good cook. Not as good as my sister, of course, who was a Cordon Bleu–trained chef and owned one of the top restaurants in the wine country. But hey, I could roast potatoes like a champ — if you overlooked those few chunks that were scorched beyond recognition.

We went to bed early, well before Mom and Dad got home from the wedding. But we both woke up when we heard the front door open and close. I checked the clock. Midnight. Must've been a fabulous wedding, I thought, and hoped they had had fun.

Derek went out to greet them and make sure we were all locked up for the night. I knew he was also making sure there were no surprises this time. No strangers spending the night. We didn't want a repeat of the horror of the evening before. I heard Mom and Dad wish Derek a good night's sleep and I dozed off soon after that.

The next morning, Derek and I woke up early, slipped on sweatpants and sweaters, and wandered out to the kitchen to start the coffee. I was surprised to see Mom and Dad already up and dressed and sitting at the kitchen counter, reading the paper and drinking coffee.

"Good morning, sweet people," my mother said, way too cheerfully for this early hour of the morning. Even for her.

But she'd already made coffee, so after I'd taken a few sips, I found I could handle her perkiness. "How was the wedding?"

"Oh, it was lovely," Mom said. "We had the best time."

Dad set down his coffee cup. "We talked to Stewart and a few of the other fellows who were outside the Fillmore when we met Goose."

"And what did your friend Stewart have to say for himself?" Derek asked.

Dad grimaced. "He was standing outside after the show and a homeless man approached him for money. Stewart thought he looked familiar and asked him, 'Goose, is that you?'"

"So the fake Goose decided to play along?" Since we still didn't know the man's name, I made the decision to continue calling him Goose until the police informed me of his real name.

"That's what we figure," Dad said. "So things went along from there and finally we offered him a place to stay for the night."

"We must've seemed so silly to him," Mom said, sounding sad and a little flustered.

Derek protested. "You don't have a silly bone in your body, Rebecca. And I'm quite sure the faux Goose was grateful to have a place to sleep, a shower, food. No doubt he felt very fortunate indeed to have run across you."

"None of this is your fault, Mom," I insisted. "Like Derek said, you made it possible for him to get a good night's sleep and a lovely shower. He probably felt better than he had in years, thanks to you. And I know it doesn't help much, but as far as I'm concerned, he died a hero."

"Oh, sweetie." She wrapped her arms around me and hugged me tightly.

We were all silent with our own thoughts for a long moment. Then I grabbed the coffeepot and poured more for everyone.

"What are your plans for today, Mom?" I

asked, determined to change the subject as I sat down at the counter.

"We're going to make you breakfast and then leave for home around noon." She gave Dad a pointed look. "Right, Jim?"

Dad wiggled his eyebrows at her and I started to get a bad feeling. "Righto."

"What's going on?" I asked.

Dad straightened and said, "Brooklyn, your mother wants to clear up any bad energy our visit might've stirred up."

"What?" My head bobbed up and I twisted around in my chair. "No, Mom. That's not necessary. There's no bad energy here. We had a cleaning crew in to wash it all away. Right, Derek? It's all good."

But Derek was fiddling with the toaster and pretending not to hear me. I could see his shoulders shaking, though, and knew he was laughing at my pain. What a coward!

Mom was gazing blissfully at nothing in particular and didn't seem to notice my panicked reaction. "The vibes are everywhere," she said, "so it's important that I perform a transformational cleansing ceremony before we leave. I hope neither of you has to rush off."

"Oh." Was my throat closing up? I had to struggle to swallow and to speak.

"Honey, you need a Heimlich?" Dad asked.

I waved him off. "I'll be fine," I whispered. My mother's spells and cleansings were always dramatic and sometimes they even worked. But they were bizarre and noisy and I was pretty sure she made them up on the spot.

I gave Derek a pleading look, hoping he would help put the kibosh to her plans, but his broad smile signaled he was about to betray me. He'd always had a soft spot for my parents, so I knew he wasn't going to be any help with this at all.

I tried anyway. "Um, Derek has to go to work."

"I can be a few minutes late," he said jovially. "I wouldn't dream of missing your mother's transformational cleansing ceremony."

I gave him a dark look, but he continued to grin unrepentantly.

"Wonderful!" Mom said. "Because when I woke up this morning, I realized I'd promised you my home-protection spell, and then in the rush of everything happening, I completely forgot."

"That's okay, Mom. You've been preoccupied."

"Boy howdy," she said with a nod. "We've

194

all had a tough weekend. But now I have some time and I owe you besides. I'll combine the protection spell with my ultra-super cleansing-and-purification ceremony to completely wash away the bad spirits and usher poor Goose's soul onto his next adventure."

"I've seen this one and it's a doozy," Dad promised.

"Oh gosh. I can't wait."

"Nor can I," Derek said.

"You'll be happier without that underlying scent of death in the house," Mom said with an off handed gesture.

Derek and I exchanged looks of horror. "Mom, the Haz Mat team was here yesterday. You can't possibly smell anything."

"Of course not. It smells as fresh as a daisy in here. But it's the psychic odor I'm referring to." She shrugged philosophically. "The memories stick in your mind and your soul. Think about it: a killer was inside your home. The scent of blood fills your nostrils. The picture of a body lying on the floor floods your mind. The aftermath, when police and medical technicians disrupt your lives. And let's keep it real, sweetie. If all that doesn't bother you, let's remember that Goose had some world-class pungent body odor going for him."

"Well, there's that." I shook my head at my mother's ability to get down to the nitty-gritty.

After that little speech, the fact that any of us were hungry was astonishing. But we managed to choke down a light breakfast of cereal and fruit anyway. Afterward, Mom steered us into the living room, where she had already laid out her equipment and supplies on the coffee table. Derek grabbed my hand and pulled me down next to him on the couch. Dad took the big red chair.

There was a round mirror lying flat in the middle of the coffee table. This was surrounded by twelve votive candles, all lit. In the center of the mirror was a small bowl of smoldering incense that wafted up and filled the room with an exotic, spicy scent.

Mom stood on the other side of the coffee table and addressed us formally. "Derek, Brooklyn, this ceremony is for your home, that we may keep out negative influences and bad people and also cleanse the souls of the departed so that they might find their way to the new frontier."

"Wonderful," Derek murmured.

"Oy," I whispered.

"So let us begin. Join with me in spiritual oneness here at my Wiccan Altar." She splayed her hands toward the coffee table to indicate its new role as Wiccan Altar.

I glanced at Derek, then back to Mom. "We're all in for you, Mom."

She pressed her hands together in a namaste pose and closed her eyes. "Pour all of your energy and intention into my words. If you believe it, so it shall be. And your new home will be safeguarded from negativity and evil and bad vibes." She cracked open one eye. "And, you know, annoying people and smells and stuff."

"I'm all for that," I said.

She gave a quick nod. "Then we begin." Picking up the thin, smooth branch that she'd whittled into a wand, she stood before the Wiccan Altar and bowed. Then she walked around the coffee table — er, Wiccan Altar — circling it three times as she repeated, "The mirror reflects the flames. The mirror reflects the flames. The flames cleanse the air. The flames cleanse the air."

I gazed around the room, watching the reflected candlelight flicker and bounce off our walls.

Mom stopped circling and raised both arms into the air. Pointing the wand toward the heavens, she began to chant.

"Oh, Goddess of the Solar Light,
Oh, Mistress of the Trees;

Great Goddess of the lunar skies,
And of the deep blue seas.
Here in this place with candles bright
And with this mirror shining;
Protect my loved ones with your might,
And send all scoundrels flying."

Mom lowered her arms, set down the wand, and grabbed a saltshaker from the table. Moving in a clockwise direction again, she began to shake the salt onto the carpet and the couch and the chairs.

"Um, Mom?"

"Salt purifies," she intoned. "It repels the negative forces. Leave it where it lies for twenty-four hours. Then gather it up and keep it in a tight-lidded jar in plain sight for as long as you live in this space."

"Will do," I muttered, thinking the vacuum cleaner would gather it up well enough.

Suddenly, she began to shout.

"Sacred Salt! Guard this house!
Keep it safe from thief and louse!
Protect all those who dwell inside!
Evil has no place to hide!"

She opened a little enamel box, pulled something out, and slipped whatever it was onto the fingers of both hands. She began to move her fingers together and a loud, rhythmic, clicking sound erupted.

Castanets? Oh my God. Where were the flamenco dancers? Or the mariachis? And as long we were going with that theme, where was my margarita?

"Repeat it with me!" she cried, causing me to jolt.

"Sacred Salt! Guard this house!
Keep it safe from thief and louse!
Protect all those who dwell inside!
Evil has no place to hide!"

She was dashing around the room now, repeating the chant as she moved more and more quickly and chanted even faster. We were all reciting it now and the castanets were clicking like extremely large, noisy crickets. "Listen!"

We stopped chanting and I could hear our breath heaving in and out from the exertion.

Suddenly, Mom cried, "Watch the light! Shatter the air! Cleanse it! Burn it! As you dare!"

She made her way back to the Wiccan Altar and was silent for a minute. Lifting her arms into the air, she began to sway and undulate to some music only she could hear. Then she started with another chant.

"Thank you, Goddess. You're the best!
Hold us tightly to your breast;
Light our way and keep us safe;
I am but a helpless waif,
Buffeted on a storm at sea;
But with your grace I am set free."

Once again, she couldn't stand still but began to dance with abandon, shaking her hips and smacking those castanets.

"Faster, faster!
Race against the devil!
Fly, my little wild ponies!
Let your spirit run free!
This is my will, so mote it be!"

She stopped shaking her hips and began to spin around in place, moving like a whirling dervish with her arms spread out and her eyes closed. Her head moved back and forth and I thought for a minute that she might pass out. But then she opened her eyes, grinned, and came to a complete stop. She wobbled a little and I didn't think it was part of the ceremony. No, I was pretty sure she was completely spent.

We all were, frankly. It took a full minute for me to bring myself back to calm reality.

"Wow," Dad said.

Derek nodded, looking a little dazed. "Indeed."

"I feel cleansed," I said, smiling at Mom. Though I still wanted that margarita.

She smiled back. "Me, too."

"Thank you, Mom."

"Oh, sweetie." Her eyes filled. "I want you both to be happy."

Dad stood and lifted Mom up in his arms. "You deserve a break, baby." He set her down in the red chair and she was asleep within seconds.

"She takes all those vibrations and energy into herself," he explained. "It wears her out. She'll be asleep for a while."

"A well-deserved rest," Derek said. "It was a fine ceremony."

I linked my arm through his. "A real doozy."

We let the candles flicker out of their own accord. Mom had once told me that you were never supposed to blow out a candle after using it for a spell or a protection ceremony. It was okay to pinch it or use a candle snuffer, but blowing caused all the good fire and air energy to be scattered and dispersed. And that was a waste, Mom said, especially after she had worked so hard to concentrate and focus all that energy to work on your behalf.

An hour later Derek took off for work. Mom and Dad left for home around noon, as they'd planned. So it was me and Charlie alone for the rest of the afternoon.

With the kitten curled up under the table, I got to work and for several hours was able to block out the events of the past few days. Eventually, though, the fact that we'd dealt with two attempted break-ins and two murders, plus the complication brought on by Billy being taken advantage of by some con man, plus my parents being there, well, it was too much to overcome. Giving up for the day, I tidied my workshop and put the books back inside the safe.

Now that the dust was beginning to settle, I could admit I was overwhelmed by what had happened. Someone had actually been killed inside our house. Poor Goose — or whatever his name was — hadn't had a chance against the professional intruder and thief who broke in.

And maybe it was completely ridiculous, but frankly, I was worried about Charlie. Had she been seen by this person? The killer? What if she had been hurt? The thought had me shivering. I bent down to pick up the kitten — who was no longer a kitten, I suppose, because she was getting bigger every day. She was almost eight months old now, not a kitten at all, but not quite a full-grown cat. The four pale orange spots on her back were more defined and slightly darker now, and she had the sweetest light tufts of marmalade fur on her cheeks. Otherwise, she was completely white and completely adorable.

"Hello, my sweetie pie." I held her against my neck and listened to her purr. "I won't ever let anything bad happen to you."

"Meow," she said, and licked my chin.

"Aw." I buried my face in her soft white fur and breathed in her soft kitten scent. I was so happy to have a pet who loved me as much as I loved her. I'd been a pet sitter for my neighbors' cats and I knew the pain of living with a cat who held you in complete contempt. Don't get me wrong. I loved Splinters and Pookie a lot, but they couldn't care less about me, even when I was the one feeding them. They were true snobs when it came to humans.

My hope was that Charlie had been hiding under the desk in my workroom when the intruder broke in. But what if she'd been out in the living room? What if she'd seen what the woman had done to Goose? What if my kitten was traumatized? How would I know?

A good friend of mine had once taken her cat to a pet psychic after a neighbor had tried to steal the poor animal. My friend insisted that the therapy had been successful and the cat had been able to heal from the shock of that incident. Charlie licked my chin again and I wondered if she was trying to calm me down. Was it possible that she could tell that my imagination had just gone into hyperspace? Was she trying to soothe my pain?

Or was I as big a wacko as I sounded?

"Get a grip," I muttered, and set Charlie back down on the floor. Looking her in the eye, I said, "Let's keep this little conversation between ourselves, okay?"

She stared up at me and purred, as if to say, *Sure, kiddo. Yeah. Whatever you say.*

That afternoon I received a phone call from an attorney who asked me to serve as an expert witness in a divorce case she was handling. She introduced herself as Trina Jones and told me she had seen me on *This Old Attic,* the television show where experts evaluated antiques of all sorts. The show traveled around the country and hired local experts in different fields. I had been lucky enough to work as their book expert for the two weeks they had spent in San Francisco last fall.

Trina wanted me to evaluate a first edition copy of *To Kill a Mockingbird* and promised to send the book to my house by messenger first thing tomorrow morning. Apparently, the couple was fighting over who would get custody of the book. My court appearance was scheduled for early the next week, possibly Tuesday, depending on how the trial was proceeding, so I put it on my calendar and spent a few minutes figuring out what to wear. I mean, the women on every television courtroom drama I'd ever seen had been dressed to the hilt in designer suits and high heels.

"Alex!" I said. She would be the perfect fashion consultant if I wanted to present a high-powered image to the court. I pictured myself in one of her stunning pencil skirts and formfitting jackets and started to laugh. Why would I do that to myself?

"Yeah. Never mind," I muttered. I admired Alex's style and she had even lent me an outfit or two for special occasions, but I would be so uncomfortable wearing what she wore every day. And let's face it, nobody in the world was going to care what I wore to appraise *To Kill a Mockingbird*. So that settled it. I would wear my black pants and maybe my burgundy sweater and be relaxed and happy. Or as relaxed as one could feel while being cross-examined by a hostile attorney.

Despite the possibility of a hostile attorney confrontation, I was thrilled to be hired as an expert witness. This was something new. I marveled at what a lucky choice I'd made when I first decided to work with books all those years ago. I'd been able to use my skills in so many different areas, and here was another one. And it was altogether different.

"You should be getting a visitor sometime this morning," Derek said the following morning as he poured me another cup of coffee.

"I know. The attorney's messenger is bringing me the book to appraise for the divorce trial."

"Ah. That, too. But I'm also expecting Gabriel to come by and give us an estimate of what equipment it will take to upgrade our security."

Derek owned his own international security company, but his expertise was in people and artwork, mainly. He dealt with heads of state and members of royal families, as well as rare works of art on display all over the world. He had the heads of Interpol and the FBI and Scotland Yard on speed dial and he was familiar with every piece of equipment and spyware on the market. But he relied on others to procure all that state-of-the-art equipment and satellite technology and drones and fun stuff. That was where Gabriel came into the picture. He was the tech guy.

"Oh, wonderful," I said. "It'll be so nice to see Gabriel. It's been a while."

"I just saw him the other evening." Derek said, clearly preoccupied as he broke eggs into a bowl to make scrambled eggs. There was something delightful about watching a gorgeous man whisking eggs for breakfast while wearing a thirty-thousand-dollar Brioni suit.

"Did he come to your office?" I wondered.

He grabbed the pepper grinder and twisted it a few times to spice up the eggs. "No, he was here."

I frowned at him. "What?"

He glanced up, and if I hadn't been watching him closely, I would've missed the reaction. His eyes flickered and his mouth opened in surprise and he immediately turned his back on me. "Or maybe it was last week. I can't remember. Wait. You're right. I saw him at the office."

"Oh my God, you're lying." Flabbergasted, I choked on my laugh. "And you're so bad at it," I added. "What is going on?"

"Absolutely nothing."

I was still laughing. "Come on, Derek. When did you see Gabriel and why are you lying about it?"

He made a sound of disgust and smacked his forehead with the heel of his palm. "Because I'm an idiot. A jackass."

I stared at him as though he were an alien being. "What's wrong with you?"

"Why did I open my mouth?" he muttered, shoving the carton of eggs back into the refrigerator.

"You're starting to scare me."

"Fine," he said, disgruntled. "I saw Gabriel out in the hall the other evening. He was heading for Alex's apartment. There. I said it. I told you, even though I promised myself I'd never breathe a word of it. But I couldn't help it, could I? Because I'm clearly a knucklehead, as my mother would say."

"You're the furthest thing from a knucklehead there is," I insisted. "But let's go back to the beginning. You saw Gabriel going into Alex's apartment? Why didn't you say something?"

"Because they don't want anyone to know they're seeing each other." He shook his head and mumbled, "I can't seem to stop talking. It's obvious that you've been a bad influence on me, my love. I fear I've become a veritable chatterbox and I'm not sure how I feel about that."

"Well, you can't stop now," I said, laughing. "You have to tell me everything."

He pointed his finger at me. "And this is why I wasn't going to say anything. Because you will get involved and you'll get your hopes up about them and when they split up, it'll break your tender heart."

"Oh, please. Now you sound like my dad describing my mom."

"That makes sense, doesn't it?" He took two pieces of sourdough bread from the bread box and dropped them into the toaster. "The two of you are very much alike."

I frowned. "I'm not sure that's a compliment."

"Believe me, darling, it is." He pulled me close and wrapped his arms around me. "Your mother is a lovely, thoughtful woman, and so are you."

I gazed up at him. "Thank you. And to defend myself, the only reason I would feel bad if Gabriel and Alex split up is that one of them would be hurt. And since I love them both, it would be painful to watch."

"Exactly my point."

My mind was buzzing as I tried to put together a dozen different pieces of a puzzle. "So when we saw them together after Robin's wedding, they were . . . together?"

"They were fighting."

"Tomato, to-mah-to."

"Darling, it's none of our business."

"You are so wrong." I sighed. "I'm already a little sad because they're doomed to break up eventually."

"Why do you say that?"

"Because. Um, well." I stared at my nails. "You know. Alex likes a type of guy that, well, Gabriel is *not*."

"Ah, the alpha-male-versus-beta-male question." He rubbed his forehead, probably feeling a headache coming on.

"Exactly." Alex had once confessed that she preferred mild-mannered, submissive men — or beta men, as she called them — to a more high-powered, take-charge kind of guy like Derek. Or Gabriel. In her previous relationships, she'd always been the high-powered, dominant one. "So what changed her mind?"

He shrugged. "That was then. This is now."

"That's all you can say?" I thumped his chest, still shocked that he'd known something was going on with our friends and hadn't shared the news with me. "You know a lot more than you're telling me, and that has to stop now. What's going on with them? Spill your guts, pal."

"Not bloody likely." He clamped his mouth shut.

"That's so unfair."

He pulled me close and I had to smile as I rested my forehead on his chest. "I promise I won't say anything about it unless Alex says something to me."

"I would appreciate that." He stepped back and tried to get around me to leave the kitchen. "Now I've got everything ready for your breakfast. All you have to do is cook the scrambled eggs. I've got to get going."

"What? No! Please, Derek. I need to know."

He caressed my cheek. "And I need to be on time for a meeting."

"But you're the boss."

"I love you," he said, and kissed me thoroughly.

"And I love you, too." I reached out and walked my fingers up his arm. "But this conversation isn't over."

My gorgeous British agent fiancé flashed

211

a determined smile. "It's beyond over, darling. It never happened."

Two hours later, the messenger arrived with the book I had been hired to appraise. With it, Trina Jones had included a letter stating what we'd already talked about, that I was to appear in superior court next Tuesday and testify as an expert witness in the case of Flint v. Flint. I was representing the wife.

Ms. Jones reminded me to keep track of my hours and reiterated our payment agreement. Essentially, my research or preparation time would be charged at a slightly lower rate than the time I spent giving my expert testimony to the court. When we spoke on the phone, she asked if I required an up-front retainer. I suppose I should've said yes, but I was new at this game, so I told her I would bill her. Obviously, I would have to do some research on expert witness fees so I would know what to say next time.

I decided to begin work on the *Mockingbird* right away and get it over with. The first thing I did was go online to find prices for the exact same book in terms of copyright date and amount of repairs needed. I compared that to the same book in pristine condition. The difference was over twenty thousand dollars, which obviously made this copy worth repairing.

Next, I examined the book, inside and out, under my strongest magnifying glass. I pulled out a notepad and began to tally up the costs of restoring the book to its most valuable state. I listed all the repairs that would be necessary to restore the book to its original splendor. There were the usual minor items, such as creases to the book jacket and minor wear and tear along the edges and spine. There was a round stain on the back of the jacket caused by someone resting a wet glass on the book (which made me want to scream, but I resisted the urge). The moisture had seeped through to the cloth cover and stained it badly as well. The boards were soiled and the spine was slanted badly. The front endpapers were tearing at the joint. The edges were chipped. I totaled up the costs of repairing the book.

I wrote out a more detailed list that I planned to read aloud in court, including other less tangible reasons why a book like this might be worth so much money. Some people didn't understand how a book could be worth so much, and I was always willing to educate them.

To Kill a Mockingbird was a perfect example of a book with quite a bit of sentimentality attached to it. The book had won the Pulitzer Prize the year it was published. The movie made from the book was a big hit and won a number of Academy Awards. The book was also named the best novel of the twentieth century by legions of literary reviewers as well as by one of the most prestigious publishing journals in the country.

I'd already checked the copyright dates to see if I was holding a true first edition of the book, and it was clear that I was not. While this book was dated the year the book came out, 1960, it stated on the copyright page that it was the "Eleventh Impression."

If this had been a first edition, I could've appraised it for over twenty thousand dollars, even with all the repair work needed. Still, this edition of the book was a keeper and would be worth at least five thousand dollars if the repairs were made. If no repairs were made, I estimated that the book would be worth twenty-five hundred dollars. Repairing the book would cost about six hundred dollars.

I hoped Trina and her client would be happy with that estimate. It was probably a good thing I didn't know the details of the divorce case. I didn't know whether the appraisal would be met with joy or with disgust. I didn't know if the couple really knew something about books or if this was a sentimental copy someone had bought on a whim. So rather than try to make anyone happy, I would simply have to give my honest opinion and walk away before the feathers started flying. It wouldn't be the first time a rare, valuable book had turned perfectly civilized, mild-mannered people into belligerent, bloodthirsty brutes.

I slipped the copy of *To Kill a Mockingbird*, along with my notes, into a sturdy envelope, then rushed out of my workshop to make a sandwich. Along the way, I hoped and prayed that the brutal images floating through my mind of Jared Mulrooney and poor Goose, the two latest victims of someone's blood thirst, wouldn't completely destroy my appetite.

CHAPTER NINE

"Oh, is that Brooklyn? Hallooo!"

I'd just returned from getting our mail downstairs when my neighbor Vinnie Patel called my name. She was stepping from the elevator, carrying a dozen packages and grocery bags.

"Hi, Vinnie," I said, meeting her halfway to give her a hug and help her with her bags. "It's been too long."

"I am so happy to see you, my friend!" she cried, her melodic Indian accent as charming as ever. She was petite with delicate bone structure and as pretty as her lilting voice. She offset the sweet image by dressing in clunky biker chick boots, torn jeans, and a black leather vest.

Vinnie and her girlfriend, Suzie Stein, lived almost directly across from me and we'd been friends since the first day I moved in. The two women were renowned chain saw artists who worked exclusively in burl. But not just any burl. The tree had to have already fallen in the forest before my friends would take it to use. Unlike a lot of other artists, they disapproved of chopping down a perfectly good living tree simply to turn it into a work of art.

Their favorite medium was redwood burl, but they had been known to sculpt everything from cherrywood to eucalyptus to pine, depending on the specific piece they envisioned.

Burl is an outgrowth, like a gigantic wart, on a tree trunk or a branch. I wasn't sure how the section of wood became deformed, but I knew that burl contained knots or rope-like tangles, making the wood very hard, and prized for the unusual veneers it produced. Artists everywhere sought out these unusual growths in forests all over the world.

"How's everyone doing?" I asked. "Derek was just saying that it's about time for us to have a party because we've been away so long."

"A party is exactly why I'm glad I ran into you. Since we were away in India for Lily's official birthday, we have decided to throw an impromptu party for our American friends to help us celebrate the anniversary of our darling girl coming to live with us. It is Sunday afternoon. I hope you'll be able to come. Lily misses you."

"Of course she does," I said, laughing. "Because eighteen-month-old babies are so aware of their neighbors."

Close to a year ago, Lily's parents, Maris and Teddy, were killed in a car crash. Their will had stated that in case of their deaths, they wanted their best friend, Suzie, to be Lily's guardian. The adorable baby girl had quickly become the center of Suzie's and Vinnie's lives. The women were also the pet parents of Pookie and Splinters, the cats who hated me for no good reason. But I didn't hold that against the parents.

Vinnie smiled. "Lily has a highly developed emotional response to certain people, and you are clearly a favorite of hers."

I was still chuckling. "I've missed you so much, Vinnie. And we would love to come to your party."

"I am so glad," she said. "Alex is bringing cupcakes."

"Not that we have to be bribed, but Alex's cupcakes seal the deal. We'll definitely be there."

"Wonderful. We can catch up on all the latest news then."

"Yes, let's catch up at the party." I could tell that she had heard my unfortunate news, but I didn't have the heart, just then, to go into the gory details of the death that had occurred in our apartment over the weekend. How could I make sense of the fact that some homeless man had been invited by my parents to spend the night and then some unknown intruder had broken into our place and killed him? It was too much information to take in during a quickie conversation with a neighbor in the hallway. Even *my* neighbors, who unfortunately were well acquainted with my tendency to stumble over death.

I knew she would hear everything eventually, of course. The rumor mill was alive and well in our apartment building, and Derek and I could always be counted on to provide plenty of grist. For now, though, Vinnie and I waved good-bye and walked off to our respective homes.

An hour later, the doorbell rang, and after checking through the peephole, I swung the door open.

"Gabriel." I stepped into the hall and gave him a giant hug. "It's so great to see you."

"Hey, babe," he said, wrapping his arms around me in a warm hug. As always, he was wearing his signature color: black. Boots, jeans, cashmere sweater, leather

219

duster, all in black. It suited him. He was outrageously sexy and very, very alpha indeed.

Gabriel had saved my life once upon a time and I would always have a warm spot in my heart for him. Happily, he and Derek were great friends, too, and had worked together on a few high-security projects.

He kept his arm around me as we walked into the house. "Heard you had a little trouble over the weekend."

"Oh, just a little," I said, my tone lightly sarcastic. But I couldn't keep up the pretense for long. "It was pretty awful."

"Derek gave me the details, so I can imagine what you all went through. Especially your mom. She must've been bummed beyond repair."

"She was. Me, too."

"Of course you were. Your home, your sanctuary, was breached."

"That's right. It still makes me sick to think about it."

"I know, babe. But we'll fix it so it never happens again."

"Thanks." I gazed up at him. "So, did you hear about the break-in from Alex?"

"No. From Derek." His eyes narrowed in on me. "Why would I have heard about it from Alex?"

When he looked at me like that, I couldn't lie. I was terrible at lying anyway, so what would have been the point? "Derek was pre-occupied this morning and I guess he wasn't thinking. Basically, he managed to blurt out a detail or two about you and Alex."

"I see. Unusual for Derek."

I suddenly clapped my hand over my mouth and squeezed my eyes shut. "Oh, shoot! I promised I wouldn't tell you. He was really preoccupied and I interrupted him and he just happened to mention that he saw you here in the hall. It's not his fault — it's mine."

"It's all right, babe."

"No, it's not." I shook my head. "I'm sorry. Just pretend I didn't say anything. I need to mind my own business."

"Too late for that." He sighed and folded his muscular arms across his chest, watching me cautiously. "So. What do you think?"

I gave him a bright smile. "I think it's wonderful."

"Oh yeah? That's it?"

"Well, not completely." I hesitated, then forged ahead. "I'm kind of afraid you'll end up hurting each other."

"I would never hurt her," he insisted, sounding insulted. "I don't hurt women."

"Oh, I know that," I hastened to say. "I

do. I meant emotional pain. I just want all my people to be happy and loved and, you know, sunshine and lollipops, okay? I know you would never hurt her. But . . . I'm afraid she might hurt you."

He held his arms out. "Come here." I stepped closer and he gave me another big hug. When he dropped his arms and we both stepped back, he reached out and gave my nose a little tweak. "You're sweet to care, babe, but I don't intend to get hurt."

"Okay. Good. Because I love you both and I don't want to lose any friends over this." Realizing what I'd just said, I quickly doubled down. "Because it's all about me, don't forget."

He chuckled. "I'll remember that." He glanced around the apartment. "Place looks awesome. You guys did a great job."

Relieved to have the subject changed, I followed his gaze. "Doesn't it look wonderful? Now we just have to make sure we can keep the bad guys out."

He winked at me. "That's what I'm here for."

"Have you heard from Inspector Lee yet?" I asked Derek over dinner that night. We were enjoying the amazing butternut squash ravioli my sister Savannah had made and sent

222

to us in frozen packets via my parents. I had managed to whip up a green salad and Derek had opened another fabulous bottle of Medoc from the Bordeaux region in France. Life was good.

"No, and I'm tempted to give her a call. I want to find out if she contacted your friend at the bookstore yet."

"I'm curious about that, too. I was thinking of paying a visit to Genevieve tomorrow to see what's going on."

Derek poured more wine into my glass. "I don't think that's a good idea, but I'm not about to tell you what to do."

"I appreciate that," I said, relieved that he was being so reasonable.

He sipped his wine. "But I'm going to go with you."

"Oh, Derek, that's not —"

"Necessary?" he finished. "You're wrong, darling. I mean to keep you safe."

I smiled. "I would love you to come with me. Even though I can take care of myself."

"Of course you can. But please indulge me."

I was always happy to have Derek around, but I had to admit to being a tiny bit miffed that he didn't trust me. I'd been taking self-defense classes from Alex, hadn't I? I was smart and capable. Never mind that I couldn't look at a trickle of blood without turning the color of chalk.

He reached across the table and took hold of my hand. It should've been romantic, but I knew better. "Darling, do you have any memory at all of the last conversation we had with Inspector Lee?"

"I recall something about my life being in danger."

"Yes, something like that." He gave my hand a gentle squeeze. "So if you're determined to put yourself in harm's way, I am determined to accompany you."

"I really do appreciate it."

"All right. Good."

"Shall I call Genevieve to let her know we're coming?"

He thought for a moment. "No. She might mention it to Billy and it would be better not to telegraph our actions."

"You're right."

"I never get tired of hearing that."

I laughed, as he knew I would.

"Darling, I'm not trying to run your life. I just want you to be safe."

"I want that, too. And I want the same for you."

He grinned. "Then we'll be protecting each other."

I sat back and stared at him. "I just realized you want to go see Billy as much as I do."

Derek paused to dredge a bite of ravioli through Savannah's delicious buttery wine sauce, flavored with bits of corn and sweet peppers. After another sip of wine, he pondered aloud. "You're right. We've had two murders that were both closely connected to you occur in the last week. I'm inclined to agree they're connected to one of those books you've got hidden in our safe. And since most of them came from Genevieve's bookshop, I'm interested in seeing what's going on there."

I took a sip of my wine. "I just wish I knew which book it was. If we could figure that out, then we could turn the book over to the police with lots of fanfare and publicity and then maybe we'd be safe."

"Perhaps our trip to Genevieve's shop tomorrow will bring us one step closer to solving the puzzle."

Early the next morning Derek and I were eating breakfast and discussing our plan of action for our trip to Genevieve's bookshop when Ian called from the Covington Library.

"Hope I didn't wake you," he said.

"Of course not."

"Good. The Bird-watchers have invited me to attend Jared Mulrooney's memorial service Friday morning. They're calling it a celebration of life. I mentioned that you'd met Jared the other night and they've extended an invitation to you, too. It's going to be held at their sanctuary overlooking Golden Gate Park."

"I would love to go." I briefly considered the ramifications of being at an event where a killer might be in attendance and added, "Do you think they would mind if Derek came, too?"

"I don't see why not. The more the merrier, if you'll pardon the expression. I'm sure Jared's family and friends would appreciate having anyone come who wants to."

Ian gave me the address and we promised to meet each other there. Then he signed off and I stared into space.

"What was that about?" Derek asked, looking up from the morning paper.

"Bird-watchers," I murmured.

"I beg your pardon?"

"I'm invited to the Bird-watchers Society tribute to Jared on Friday. Can you come with me?"

"Bird-watchers." He pursed his lips in thought. "Sounds intriguing."

"I think we should find out."

"Indeed, we should."

At ten o'clock, Derek lucked out and found a place to park a mere half block down from Taylor's Fine Books on Clement Street. The store was located in an area of the city known as the Inner Richmond, as opposed to the Outer Richmond, which extended all the way west to the Great Highway, which ran along the beach. While the Outer Richmond was best known for the fog that enveloped it on an almost daily basis, the Inner Richmond was packed with charming flats, a plethora of Asian restaurants, fabulous bistros and bars, lots of fun shops, and a general lack of parking spaces. The area was flanked by two massive, beautiful parks: the rugged, historic Presidio edging along the north side and Golden Gate Park, which constituted its southern border.

"Do we need a plan?" I asked, unbuckling my seat belt.

"I've a basic idea," he said, glancing up the street toward the shop. "If Billy's there, I'd like to engage him in conversation, treat him as if he's a book expert."

"I'll distract Genevieve if necessary," I said, then added, "I think you've touched on part of the problem with Billy. He's young and basically just a salesclerk, so I'll

227

bet the con man flattered him with attention, made him think he was more essential to the business than he is."

"And that's what I'll do," Derek said. "And on the off chance that we actually learn anything, we'll report it to Inspector Lee."

"Of course." I bit my bottom lip and worried. If Derek discovered that Billy had other secrets, Genevieve might be in danger as well.

With a semblance of a plan, we got out of the car and walked the half block to Taylor's.

Derek pushed the door open and ushered me inside. Once again, I breathed in the luscious scents of aged vellum and aromatic leather. And just like that, I was in my happy place.

For me, electronic readers would never take the place of a real book. The feel of vintage paper, the clean smell of a brand-new book, the experience of picking it off the shelf and making a new friend that would take you on a journey of discovery.

"You're getting that dreamy look in your eyes again," Derek whispered. "I like it."

I smiled at him. It was good to be understood.

Derek nodded toward the counter that ran

along the side of the store. Billy was standing near the cash register, writing something on a pad of paper. "Is that him?"

"Yes," I murmured. "I don't see Genevieve, but she might be in the back office."

"You go browsing," he whispered. "Try not to let him see you."

"Okay."

"Greetings, my good man," Derek announced in his best lord-of-the-manor tone.

I grinned as I slipped unnoticed into the Antiquarian Room, by far my favorite space in the store — except for the fact that I'd discovered the dead body of Joe Taylor in this very room. *Behind that very chair,* I thought, glancing over at the corner.

"Never mind," I muttered under my breath. "Just browse."

So I did, checking everything out while also trying to catch Derek's conversation with Billy. It wasn't a hardship to stare at the fabulous books available in the display cases of this room. I noticed that the nicely preserved copy of *The Little Prince* was the same one I'd seen the last time I was here over a year ago. The book had been signed by Antoine de Saint-Exupéry, the author, and was still priced at twenty thousand dollars. I'd thought it a little steep the first time and wondered if Genevieve had considered lowering it a few thousand. It was a sweet little copy, however, and the author's signature was a bonus. Maybe she was just waiting for the right buyer.

I strolled back to the archway leading to the main room and tried to catch snippets of Derek's conversation with Billy.

"I say, you must know quite a bit about books," Derek said, laying it on a little thick. "A friend recommended your shop rather highly when I mentioned that I was desperate to get my hands on some rare books."

"Are you looking for something in particular?" Billy asked.

"Excellent question. I knew you'd be able to help me. Yes, indeed, I'm very much interested in finding a first edition set of Ian Fleming's works. James Bond, you know. Personal hero of mine. Can you help me?"

"Oh, bummer," Billy said. "We just got a set of five books in last month, but they were snapped up immediately."

I rolled my eyes. By "snapped up," he meant "ripped off." Stolen by thieves that Billy himself had unknowingly aided and abetted.

I was being harsh, but honestly, Billy was the reason we were in this mess to begin with.

"Bummer, indeed," Derek murmured. "In

that case, let me put myself in your hands. Have you anything else along those lines that I might be interested in seeing? I could make it worth your while."

"Oh, you mean, like, on the side? Heck, that's not necessary. I don't . . . I mean, unless . . . uh, no. I'm here to help and that's all."

"Aren't you upstanding?" Derek declared. "I'm impressed. But I can't be the first person who's ever offered a finder's fee. It happens all the time, doesn't it?"

"Not here, sir."

Okay, I felt a little better to hear Billy fighting the urge to walk on the wild side. Although he was obviously tempted. I figured Genevieve must've drummed the fear of God into him. Or more likely, the fear of cops.

And speaking of cops, I watched out the front window as Inspector Lee pulled up to the curb and parked.

I might've let out a tiny shriek of surprise, but I covered it up by coughing loudly. That caught Derek's attention and he abruptly ended his conversation at the checkout counter and headed for the front door. I met him there and with my face averted from Billy's view, I pushed the door open and rushed outside. Derek followed closely behind me.

"Oh, come on, you guys," Inspector Lee groused as she approached. "This can't be a good thing."

"Good day, Inspector," Derek said, his accent still in *Masterpiece Theatre* mode.

We led her away from the bookshop, stopping two doors down the block so Billy wouldn't see us.

"You'd be so proud of Derek," I said, gushing a little. "He really did a number on Billy. But to the kid's credit, he didn't bite."

"He's scared to death," Derek said. "The entire time I spoke with him, his eyes were wide and fearful and he continually checked the front window. I can only hope it's because his cousin warned him and not because he's been threatened by his criminal friend."

"I just spoke to a guy over at the Richmond station," Lee said. "He told me that nobody's come by to get Billy's story yet. So his little friend is still out there."

"Which means you don't have a description of him yet," I said. "That's a drag."

"Wait a minute." Lee glared at me. "What are you doing here? What part of 'your life is in danger' don't you understand?"

"I've got my bodyguard with me," I said, tucking my arm through Derek's.

But Derek didn't look much happier than Inspector Lee. "I couldn't dissuade her from going out, so I insisted on accompanying her."

I scowled at both of them. "Sure. Throw me under the bus. I've been there before."

Lee jabbed her finger at me. "Under the bus is probably safer than being out in plain sight."

Derek nodded but wisely said nothing.

"That doesn't even make sense," I protested.

"Sure it does," she said, grinning.

"Oh! Wait," I said. "I'm starting to get an idea."

"That can only spell trouble," Lee muttered.

"What is it, darling?" Derek asked, instantly winning back my affection.

"Even if Billy gives you a description of the guy and even if he points out the guy to the police, you'll only get so far. You won't have fingerprints or a closed-circuit camera to nail the guy. You've got to catch him red-handed or else get a warrant and search his place. But you might not find anything because chances are he's already fenced the stolen books. Right?"

Derek nodded. "It's unlikely that he'd keep the books in plain sight."

"Go on," Lee said, reluctantly willing to listen.

"Okay. So suppose the guy saw me working in the store last week. Suppose he watched me walk out with all those books that Genevieve wanted repaired. He could've been curious, followed me home, and found out where I lived."

Derek's jaw clenched. "Possibly."

"And then suppose a day or so later, Billy told him about the *Almanack* and mentioned that it was being repaired. The guy might've imagined that I was the one who had it. So he scopes out our place, sees us leaving for the Covington, follows us, and is right there when Genevieve actually hands the book to me."

"You've got a lot of *supposing* going on," Lee said.

I held up my hand. "Bear with me for one more minute. *Suppose* he was tracking my movements around the Covington, waiting for the opportunity to steal the *Almanack* from my purse. Then he saw me talking to Jared Mulrooney and saw me slip something else into my purse. At least, that's what he thought he saw. Suppose he wanted to know what that was all about, so he followed Mulrooney into the back gallery and things went badly."

Inspector Lee and Derek stared at me, then exchanged glances. Both had skeptical looks on their faces and I had to mentally scan back through my words.

"Okay, that didn't make sense at all," I admitted.

Lee snorted. "You're right."

"But then, none of this has made sense from the start." I sighed. "My point is, the only way you'll trap this guy is with a book so phenomenal he won't be able to resist. And that's where I come in."

"Not going to happen," Lee said. "Look, you mosey on home and I'm going to go talk to Billy."

"You'll think about my idea and call me if you need me?"

"You bet I will," Lee said, laughing. "Be sure to wait by the phone."

"I think she was being sarcastic," I said on the ride home.

Derek squeezed my hand in solidarity. "You're nothing if not observant."

I shrugged. "I thought it was a good idea."

"Frankly, darling, I agree. It is a very good idea. Except for the part where you'd be putting your life in further danger."

"I know, but still." I squeezed his hand in response. "I have to say, by the way, that

235

your conversation with Billy was nothing short of brilliant."

"Thank you, love. I think my use of the James Bond connection was a minor stroke of genius."

"Absolutely." I nodded firmly. "We are both brilliant and Inspector Lee is going to call any minute, just as soon as she realizes how essential we are to her success."

"I expect to hear from her within seconds."

I leaned my head against the passenger window and stared at nothing in particular. And wondered if it was too early for a margarita. Chips and salsa would be good right now.

And suddenly Derek's phone rang.

The following afternoon, I walked into Taylor's Fine Books, clutching my satchel for dear life.

After talking to Billy yesterday, Inspector Lee had come to the conclusion that my half-baked idea could actually work. In fact, she thought it might be the only way to catch a thief — and possibly a killer — in the act.

Billy had been assured of complete immunity if he would tell them everything he knew and if he was willing to arrange a meeting at the store with his con man friend. He was eager to help catch the guy who'd made him look stupid, so when he got his friend on the phone, he explained that Genevieve's bookbinding expert would be coming into the store with the repaired *Almanack* at two o'clock that afternoon. If he wanted the *Almanack,* he would have to be there because the window of opportunity was about to slam shut. At least, that was Billy's story to him.

The story we'd made up for Billy to tell was that Genevieve was planning to mail the *Almanack* to a client in New York later that afternoon. If that happened, Billy's friend would never have the chance to own — or steal — a fascinating rare piece of American history.

The guy took the bait and promised to be there.

So here I was, in Taylor's Fine Books, preparing to put myself and the poor *Almanack* in jeopardy and shaking in my shoes. Luckily, they were my best running shoes in case I needed to make a run for it.

Naturally, Derek and half of his security staff were close by. Two of them were stationed inside the bookshop, casually browsing the back rows. They were to be as quiet as possible but still act normally so as not to scare off Billy's contact.

Two more agents were parked in different cars on the street in case they had to give chase. A couple of female agents were window-shopping along Clement Street.

Inspector Lee and Derek were ensconced inside the back office with Genevieve.

Despite all the security, I was freaking scared to death. If this was the same guy who had killed Goose — and possibly Jared Mulrooney as well — then he was dangerous to the max.

For the hundredth time that day, I thought to myself, *Why did I open my big mouth in the first place? Why did I have to volunteer to play the starring role?*

To stop a thief and avenge a homeless man's death, I said to myself.

Oh yeah.

Billy was the only one working the check-out counter, and he was wired for sound. I hoped that the store would be empty of real customers. I didn't want anyone to get hurt, including me.

"Oh criminy," Billy muttered. "Here he comes. Oh jeez."

"Deep breaths, Billy," I whispered. "Relax. Be cool. Don't blow it."

"Easy for you to say. You're always cool."

I almost laughed. Where in the world did

he get that idea? But I didn't have time to disabuse him of that preposterous and completely wrong notion because the front door opened and the bells above it began to chime. So I simply murmured, "That's right, Billy. I'm cool. Be just like me."

But *Oh criminy,* I thought. *Don't blow it.*

CHAPTER TEN

"Brooklyn, this is Micah Featherstone," Billy said, sounding as cool as a cucumber all of a sudden. He turned to the man and said, "Brooklyn's the bookbinder I was telling you about."

"I couldn't be more honored to meet you," Micah assured me as he shook my hand enthusiastically. "I really admire the work that bookbinders do, so this is a real pleasure."

"Thank you," I said. "It's nice to meet you, too." I didn't know what to think. His words seemed genuine, but then again, he was a crook, right? It followed that he was lying through his teeth, right? I would be a fool to trust one word he said.

I had to hide my surprise at finding him attractive. He was tall and slim, with startling green eyes, a charming smile, and a shock of white-blond hair that brought back visions of the punk rockers of my youth.

Somehow my imagination had conjured up a snarling, broken-nosed thug in a dirty trench coat, but Micah Featherstone was nothing like that. Of course, if all thieves were trolls, we'd be able to spot them at a distance, wouldn't we?

Billy reached under the counter and carefully presented him with a lush black silk book box. "Here's the *Poor Richard's Almanack* I was telling you about."

"Oh, oh," Micah whispered reverently, taking it in his hands. "This box is exquisite." He turned the box around to examine the side seams and edges, the fabric loop with its elegant pewter fastener. Glancing up, he said, "And you made this, right? It's amazing."

"Thank you." It was foolish of me to feel flattered, knowing it was probably the exact reaction he wanted from me. But since I agreed that the box was gorgeous — if I did say so myself — it was easy enough to play along.

"May I open it?" he asked, his fingers touching the miniature pewter sword I'd used as a button for the loop latch.

"Of course."

He set the box on the counter and slowly lifted the top. The inside bed was lined in the same black silk. For the inside of the lid, I had used a complementary shade of rich gray silk. For extra protection I had slipped the *Almanack* into a slim pouch made of the same gray silk. It was masculine and very elegant.

Micah frowned at Billy. "You introduced Brooklyn as a bookbinder, but she's clearly much more." His gaze panned across to me. "You're obviously a magnificent artist and I would venture to say you're also a master at book restoration."

"Yeah, she's really good," Billy said.

"Billy, Billy, Billy," Micah said, shaking his head in mock dismay. "Another pitiful understatement."

I chuckled. Yes, he was a thief, but come on, everyone loves a good compliment. "Thank you, but you haven't even seen the *Almanack* yet."

"I can't wait to see it," he said, lifting the box again and continuing to study it from every angle. "And yet I'm enjoying this feeling of anticipation building up inside me."

I almost laughed, but I took one look at his solemn expression and immediately quelled my reaction. He quietly oohed and aahed over every little feature with such rapt appreciation I didn't dare speak. I also didn't dare mention that the box he was gushing over was one I'd whipped up last

242

year for a completely different book. Last night I had taken an hour to futz with the inner walls so that they held the book more securely and I resewed the pouch to make it look as if it had been tailor-made for the *Almanack.* My trickery didn't take away from the fact that it was indeed a fabulous box. Again, if I said so myself.

Finally, Featherstone set the box down and picked up the gray pouch. He rubbed the fabric between his thumb and forefinger, then weighed the package in his hands. After carefully loosening the cord, he slid the *Almanack* out of its protective sheath.

"Ah." He took a deep breath and let it out, as if he were entering a cathedral and uttering a sigh of veneration. Taking his time, he scrutinized the *Almanack* much more seriously, more reverently, more closely, than he'd done with the box.

After several long minutes, during which Billy shot me at least three nervous frowns and I tried to remain serene, Featherstone finally glanced up. "You completely resewed the loosened threads."

"Yes. Several had come undone."

"And you obviously must have cleaned these self-wrappers."

"I did." I was surprised to hear him use the term "self-wrapper," which was what

Benjamin Franklin had called the pages of his *Almanacks.* It was a term that was both historically and factually correct, and I wondered where he had come up with it. Was he simply a quick study? Had he Googled everything there was to know about *Poor Richard's Almanack* in order to pass himself off as an expert?

"How did you track down the proper thread?" he asked, running his fingers over the linen strands.

"My job is to study the materials and techniques that were in use at the time a book was first created." I shrugged. "In good conscience, I wouldn't dream of using thread or cloth or a knotting technique that wasn't in fashion at the time."

"Did you read through the *Almanack* while you worked on it?"

"I did. It was truly enjoyable."

He seemed pleased with my answer. After holding the pages up to the light for a long moment, he set it down on the counter. "I've seen a number of these *Almanacks* before, and this one is in better shape than any of them."

"It is now," I said.

He grinned at my minute correction. "The historical significance of this particular volume is breathtaking."

"Yes, indeed."

"Which renders it beyond priceless."

I nodded. I'd had the same thought while working on the *Almanack,* so I found it interesting that he agreed.

He gazed at me with his piercing green eyes and I had to fight to remain unaffected. It occurred to me in that moment that he was wearing contact lenses. Did he wear them to deliberately unsettle his opponent? I would bet money on it.

When he turned back to inspect the pages, I surreptitiously studied his white hair. Was he wearing a wig?

Frankly, the man confused me. Under normal circumstances, I would have been flattered by his compliments and his admiration for my work. I would have been disarmed by his charm, his rakish grin, and that twinkle in his eye. He listened to me, laughed with me, and essentially treated me as though I were the only person in the world he wanted to talk to and spend time with. I should have been intrigued by his extensive knowledge of bookbinding. Not a lot of people were familiar with the sort of esoteric details that bookbinders handled on a daily basis, but this guy was. And he made sure I knew it. It made me wonder what his real background was. Was he a bookbinder? A bookseller? Or was he just an uncommon thief and a really good scammer?

Featherstone switched his attention to Billy. "How much are you selling it for?"

"Y-you want to buy it?" Billy said, clearly thrown off by the quick switch in conversation.

"Of course I want to buy it."

"I — I'll have to ask Genevieve. She's, um, not here right now."

Micah smiled patiently. "I'll be happy to come back, but I want the *Almanack* and the box. I'll leave you a deposit of five thousand dollars. Will that be enough to forestall it being mailed to New York?"

"I'll make sure of it."

Featherstone pulled a hefty money clip from his pocket and peeled off five thousand dollars in hundred-dollar bills and handed them to Billy. He still had a thick wad of bills when he slid the clip back into his pocket.

As Billy counted the money and wrote out a receipt, the man took my hand and shook it gently. "I hope we'll have a chance to talk again. It's been such an honor."

"Thank you very much. I hope you enjoy the *Almanack*."

"I will cherish it, and the book box as well."

Billy handed him the receipt for his deposit and Featherstone walked out of the shop.

Billy sagged against the back wall. "I think I'm going to throw up."

"You did great," I said. "You sounded surprised when he wanted to buy it."

"I was." He scratched his head, bewildered. "I still am."

"Do you mean he's never bought a book here before?"

"No, never. Whenever I've seen him at the pub, he talks about coming into the store to buy something, but he never has. I thought it was because . . . well . . ."

"Because he broke in and stole them?"

"Yeah."

"That's interesting," I said, mystified as to why Featherstone was so willing to buy the *Almanack* today if he'd never done so in the past. "But you did great, Billy. I'm really proud of you."

He grinned. "That was kind of cool."

I smiled and patted his arm. "Totally cool." But as I walked to the back office, I was more confused than ever.

"So maybe he's not the thief," Genevieve

247

said from where she sat cross-legged on top of her office desk. "Maybe he's not the one who stole the James Bond set."

"You think it might be a coincidence?" I asked. "One day he was asking Billy about those very books and it just so happens that three days later, they were stolen?"

Gen grimaced. "It's so not a coincidence."

"Probably not," Inspector Lee said. "But we can't arrest someone without hard evidence."

"Can you search his house?" Derek asked.

Lee scowled. "We don't know where he lives."

"But Billy has his phone number," I said. "Can't you track him down through the phone company?"

"We tried. It's a burner," she said in disgust.

Gen blinked. "He uses a disposable phone? That proves he's disreputable, doesn't it?"

"Wait." I pointed toward the front of the store. "He just left a few minutes ago. Someone should follow him. Derek and I can try to catch up with —"

"Cool your jets, Wainwright," Lee said mildly. "I've got a car following him."

I took a deep breath and let it out. Derek had agents watching Featherstone, too.

"Sorry to freak out, but I really want to catch this guy. What if he's the one who killed Goose?"

"Did he strike you as a killer?" Derek asked.

"Good question," Lee said. "You just spent twenty minutes with him, Brooklyn. What's your take?"

I hid my surprise. The fact that she would ask my opinion was another heady moment for me, since that didn't happen too often. "I was expecting someone less polished," I admitted. My feelings were still percolating in my mind, but I tried to express them the best I could. "He knows a lot about books and bookbinding, and that surprised me. He came across as erudite and charming, frankly."

"What does he look like?" Derek asked.

I glanced up at him. "Not quite as tall as you. Sort of attractive, but very intense. Green eyes, white-blond hair. But I think he was wearing contact lenses and I'm pretty sure his hair is dyed. He's thin. I know Alex thought she saw a tall, thin woman at our door, but I'm wondering if it could've been Featherstone. He's tall and really thin and could probably masquerade as a woman. That's another long shot, though."

"Yeah," Lee muttered as she made notes.

"He seems to love books, but if that's true, how can he justify stealing them?" I stared at the skeptical faces in front of me. "Okay, I'm being naive, but it just seems wrong. Anyway, despite him putting on a very charming act, I thought it was just on the surface. I saw something else in his eyes besides the contacts. He was very controlled, but once or twice I caught a flicker of pure, raw anger. Underneath the shiny, smooth veneer, I would bet he's a bubbling cauldron of rage. He could flip out at any moment. I wouldn't want to be around if he did. His eyes . . ." I shivered. "His eyes were like pinpoints, staring right into your brain. I think he picked that shocking green color on purpose, just to freak people out."

"Sounds creepy," Gen said.

"It was." I stretched my jaw and rubbed my cheeks.

"What's wrong?" Derek asked.

"My facial muscles ache, probably from trying to keep this fake smile on my face. I was tense the whole time, but trying to be cool and calm."

"You're not the only one," Genevieve said. "I've been uptight all morning."

I gave her a sympathetic look, then turned to Inspector Lee. "I know I'm not a psychiatrist, but I think Micah Featherstone could be a sociopath. He's naturally charismatic and really manipulative. He had Billy wrapped around his little finger. And what really bugs me is that if I hadn't been warned about him ahead of time, I might've fallen into his trap, too."

Lee nodded and kept writing.

"I wish I could be more specific," I said. "If I remember anything else about the conversation that might help, I'll give you a call."

"You seem to have remembered quite a bit," Derek remarked.

"And don't worry about it too much," Lee said. "We had Billy wired, so we'll be playing back the tapes later today. If I have any questions, I'll call you. You've been a big help."

"I'm glad," I said. "I just hope the guy following him can find out where he lives. I don't like not knowing whether he's the thief or not."

"Or the killer," Derek added.

"Yeah," Lee said, frowning. "That, too."

"I wouldn't have been surprised to see Featherstone try and steal the book box before our very eyes."

Instead of driving home, Derek and I

251

decided to take a stroll down Clement Street to enjoy the crisp, clear San Francisco weather. With all the colorful shops and restaurants lining the street, it was always a treat to window-shop. And this close to lunch, I was practically drooling over the intoxicating aromas that emanated from the plethora of Asian restaurants we passed. It made me hope I could talk Derek into stopping for a meal somewhere nearby.

"Listening to the conversation from inside the office," Derek said, "we were all rather shocked when we heard him pay the deposit. I think Inspector Lee had a moment where she was unsure whether to call off the sting or not."

"I'm glad she didn't. I think he could be the thief."

Derek pondered the situation. "Perhaps he sensed he was being set up."

"Maybe." I frowned. "Can you believe he paid cash? Five thousand dollars. Who walks around with that much money these days? I don't know why he creeped me out so much."

Derek held my hand as we walked. "That sort of obsessive-compulsive behavior can be alarming and confusing up close."

"I definitely felt confused." I gazed up at him. "I think you're right about him being obsessive-compulsive."

"Either that," he said casually, "or he's a stone-cold psychopathic killer."

"Comforting," I muttered.

He squeezed my hand. "Time for you to let this go, if you can." Scanning both sides of the street, he said, "How would you like to have lunch at one of these places?"

My stomach did a victory lap. "There you go, reading my mind again."

We walked another half block and picked a restaurant at random. But as we passed the shop next door, I glanced in the window and stopped. "I have to run in here for one minute."

"You're going shopping?" he said.

"I just need one thing. It's too perfect." I quickly found what I was looking for and paid for it. Five minutes later, we walked into the restaurant and were quickly seated at a comfortable booth. And with my first bite of delicately wrapped Burmese samosas, I began to relax.

We chatted about nothing in particular while sharing a bowl of rich seafood stew and a dish of riotously flavorful Singapore-style noodles. The service was wonderful and I was happy.

But the joyful food-fest couldn't last forever, and when we finally walked outside,

I was reminded that I lived in a world where someone as disturbingly enigmatic as Micah Featherstone could intimidate me enough to make me search the faces of the people around me to make sure he wasn't nearby.

"He shouldn't have bought the book," I murmured as we crossed the street. "It makes me question whether he's our thief or not, even when I know in my gut that he is."

"He obviously came prepared to pay the money," Derek mused. "Perhaps he realized in advance that he'd been made."

"Do you think Billy could've telegraphed it somehow?"

"Certainly. He's a nice kid but clearly a weak link."

"Poor guy. He was so nervous."

"And Featherstone is a pro," Derek said flatly. "Billy's no match for him."

"I figured as much before, and now that I've met the man, I know it's true. So he brought five thousand dollars with him, just to psych us out?"

"Perhaps. The sociopathic types I've run into tend to enjoy playing mind games with their intended victims."

Scowling, I said, "I refuse to be his victim."

"You'll never be his victim," Derek said,

wrapping his arm around me. I was glad of it; the fog was rolling in and I was starting to get chills. "I was referring to Billy and Genevieve."

"We can't let anything happen to them."

"Inspector Lee promised them an hourly patrol for the time being." He pulled the car key from his pocket and pressed the button, and the doors of the Bentley unlocked. I stared at Derek across the roof of the car. "Featherstone will return with the rest of the money and pick up the *Almanack* as soon as Billy calls him with the price. Shouldn't we stick around?"

"No. From here on, Inspector Lee will take charge."

We drove a few blocks in silence, and then I said, "What's still confusing me about Featherstone is how much he knew about bookbinding. Is he really a bibliophile or just a very smart thief? I mean, he didn't have to give Billy any money. Even if he knew he'd been set up, he could've walked away. Is he so invested in this deal that he'll pay out that much money?"

Frustrated, I pounded my fists together a few times and continued my rant. "And if he's just a simple book lover, then who is the real burglar who's been breaking into Taylor's Fine Books? And who broke into our house and killed poor Goose? And why? Were they after the *Almanack*? Are they connected to Jared Mulrooney? We know there must be a connection because of the similarity in the way they both died. So it's got to be connected, but how? Is Featherstone working for someone else? What in the world is going on here?"

Derek turned onto Geary and headed east. "We ought to sit down tonight and make a list."

I was so irritated, it took a few seconds for the words to sink in. And then I smiled. "You know I love making lists."

"Of course I know." He grabbed my hand and held it the rest of the way home.

Derek and I had found that the best way to deal with those myriad questions swirling around was to sit down and make a list of suspects and motives. Of scenarios. Of means and opportunity. Building a list of all those items helped us to focus in on what was important. We could break things down. Work things out. Clear away the mental muck, so to speak.

The fact that we found ourselves making these sorts of lists with alarming regularity was why we now made sure we did it with a nice bottle of wine nearby.

Meanwhile, since it was almost three

o'clock when we arrived home, Derek decided to finish up the workday in his home office. I went to my workshop in hopes of starting the restoration of the next book from Genevieve's shop, the small Latin primer *Amo, Amas, Amat.*

Since both the front and back endpapers were badly torn at the fold, I went ahead and cut them all the way through. Then I set the cover aside and took hold of the text block. With the spine facing me, I tore off the original headbands, those small decorative fabric bands attached to the head and foot of the spine. The headbands, besides being pretty, served to cover up any remnants of loose threads and glue that might otherwise be visible after binding. Ideally, they also add strength to the spine itself.

I carefully picked and peeled away the old glue from the spine and from the super, which is a very stiff strip of woven cotton that also adds strength to the spine.

In a book this age — I saw that it was copyrighted in 1927 — the adhesive used by the bookbinder was almost sure to be animal glue derived from animal protein. This type of glue had its uses, but bookbinders rarely used it anymore because it tended to turn brittle on paper and darken and shrink with age.

I picked off as much of the old glue as I could and then brushed an even coating of methyl cellulose over the spine. The methyl cellulose would soften the original animal glue and make it easier to remove.

It took a few minutes for the methyl cellulose to do its work, so in the meantime, I picked up the old cover and began removing the original endpapers from the cover boards. For this task, I used a thin stainless steel tool called a micro spatula that could be wedged between the endpapers and the cloth turnover to lift and separate and tear away the paper from the boards. As much of the endpaper had to be removed from the boards as possible, after which I would sand away any bits that remained in order to create a smooth surface for the new endpapers.

Meanwhile, the methyl cellulose had softened the old glue, so I returned to the text block spine and used the micro spatula to scrape away more glue. The combination of glues was extremely sticky and I had to continually scrape at it to get rid of it all.

Once everything was removed and all of the surfaces were sanded and smooth, I picked up the text block and tapped it gently against the surface of the table several times to straighten and realign the sewn signatures.

For the new endpapers, I had chosen two sturdy pieces of acid-free paper with a nice pattern of forest green swirls. I folded each of the pieces in half, lined the text block along the fold, and trimmed the paper to size.

Starting with the back of the book, I brushed the edge of one of the endpapers with PVA glue and attached it to the back edge of the text block. Once the glue was dried, it was time to actually stitch the new endpaper to the first set of signatures of the text block, using linen thread and lining up the original needle holes. I reinforced the kettle stitch knots with tiny dabs of glue and then slipped a sheet of wax paper between the sheets. Then I placed a heavy metal weight on top of the text block to press it until it was set.

I repeated the same procedure with the front endpaper. Once this was done, I glued a new piece of the stiff super to the spine, smoothed it down with my bone folder, and weighted it until it was dry. I added new headbands to the ends of the spine because they would make the book look professional and pretty.

Now it was time to reattach the cover to the text block. I wrapped the cover around the text block to test that everything fit nicely and used a blade and a steel ruler to make one tiny trim to the back endpaper.

Slipping a piece of waste paper between the sheets to keep the glue from going onto the other pages, I coated one side of the endpaper with PVA, evenly spreading it in the direction of the grain of the paper. Otherwise, the paper would stretch as well as buckle.

Removing the waste paper, I carefully pressed the cover of the book down onto the glued paper. I checked that it fit together nicely — there was still time to tweak it before the glue dried — and made sure that the edges of the endpaper ran evenly along the inner cloth rim of the book. It looked really good and straight, I thought, so I opened the book and smoothed down the endpaper with the edge of my bone folder to get rid of any minute bubbles or ripples. Then I used the tool on the outside cover to further define the hinges.

After repeating the gluing process with the front of the book, I surveyed the finished book. Genevieve was going to be very happy with her newly restored Latin textbook. And that, in turn, made me happy. As a final step, I slipped a piece of wax paper between each of the front and back endpapers and placed a weight on top of the book until the glue was completely dry.

A quick check of the wall clock told me it was almost time to start dinner. I cleaned up my worktable, put away my supplies, and rushed out to the kitchen to start dinner. In other words, call in an order for pizza.

After we polished off a lovely sausage-and-veggie pizza served with an antipasto salad, Derek poured each of us another glass of wine and I got out my legal notepad.

I always felt the need to justify what we were doing by insisting that we would never actually act on our suspicions — although we usually did. By which I meant that we called Inspector Lee to run our theories by her. But as far as making these lists went, it was just a way to organize all the information floating around in our heads. If we sensed a pattern emerging, that was when we would call the police.

I liked to look at our list-making as being proactive and helpful. And it was a lot better than sitting around waiting for the other shoe to drop. Or the next body to fall. That was my story, anyway, in case Inspector Lee ever got wind of our list making.

"I'll start with our suspects," I said, and began to write names. Three seconds later, I looked up, frowning. "I've got Micah Featherstone, although I'm not sure why he would try to break into our house and steal the *Almanack* when he showed up at the store and bought it."

"True, but he's suspicious nonetheless."

I picked up my pen to write down a second name but couldn't think of one. "I'm sure one of the bird-watchers could've killed Jared, but I don't know any of them."

"Won't we meet them tomorrow at the memorial service?"

"Yes."

Derek sat back in his chair and casually swirled his wine. "Maybe we should start our list tomorrow night."

Even though our list-making ability was hampered by our lack of suspects, we stayed at the table and talked out a few scenarios and possibilities anyway.

"We know both Jared and Goose were stabbed," I said, "but we don't know if the same knife was used."

"If it was, then the same person killed both men," Derek said. "If not, we are dealing with two separate cases."

"And what are the chances of that?" I wondered.

"Slim to none," he murmured.

I frowned. "If these are two separate cases,

then they must involve two different books."

"Very good thinking, darling."

"It's too bad we can't start with the books. I've assumed all along that the thief was after the *Almanack*. But what if they were after something less obvious, like the *Robin Hood*?"

"Or *Dracula*," Derek added.

"Right. Or *The Maltese Falcon*, which is worth somewhere around ninety-five thousand dollars."

He raised one eyebrow. "That much? Why didn't you mention that before?"

I shrugged. "To tell the truth, even though it's worth the most money of all the books from Genevieve's shop, it's not the most historically significant. That would be the *Almanack*. But since Featherstone just bought it, it's officially off the table."

"In other words, it doesn't seem like a motive for murder."

"Exactly." I took a quick sip of wine. "But then, neither does *Songbirds in Trees*, the book that Jared gave me to repair. So maybe we're missing something."

"I have no doubt of that," he muttered, and studied our scant suspect list. "How does Jared Mulrooney's death fit with Goose's murder?"

"Well, I did spell out one possible scenario

yesterday, where the killer was following me from Taylor's Fine Books to home to the Covington. What did you think of that idea?"

He thought for a moment. "It was a good one, but unfortunately, now that Micah Featherstone has bought the *Almanack,* I'm afraid that part of your theory might not be viable anymore."

I pouted a little. "Oh well. It was pretty flimsy to begin with, but still."

"Darling, can you think back and perhaps recall whether you might've seen Featherstone at the Covington that night?"

I thought of the man I'd met at the bookshop today. Micah Featherstone, with his deep green eyes and oddly intense demeanor, was definitely unforgettable, and not in a good way. I would've recalled seeing him before. "No, I would've remembered."

"There were a lot of people there."

"I know. And he might've been in disguise."

"That's possible."

"I definitely believe he's capable of killing someone over a book. So if it turns out that he was there, I would have no trouble believing that he killed Jared."

"I'm willing to go along with your instincts

about him."

I stared at the list for another minute, then flashed Derek an optimistic smile. "How would you feel about calling Inspector Lee?"

"To ask about the autopsy results?"

"I'm always amazed when you read my mind." I quickly added, "But if you don't feel like calling her, then we can just sit and chat and drink our wine and have a nice, quiet evening."

His lips twisted wryly. "I'll call her right now."

See why I loved him?

The conversation was casual enough. Derek thanked Inspector Lee for treating me so kindly after my ordeal with Mr. Featherstone. He listened to her lengthy response, reaching over to stroke my hand as she spoke. The gesture made me wonder what in the world she was saying. But maybe Derek just wanted to make contact with me, to somehow bring me into the conversation through his touch alone. I turned my hand over and held on to his.

Finally, he responded, "Thank you, Inspector. I always appreciate your insight. By the way, have you heard anything from the medical examiner as to the weapons used in both of the recent murders?"

I couldn't hear what Inspector Lee was telling him, but I could tell from the frown he wore that it wasn't the cheeriest of news. After another minute, he thanked her for the information and hung up.

"What is it?" I asked, almost afraid to hear the results.

"The murder weapon in both cases was a curved knife with a six-inch blade."

The very thought of knives sent a quick shiver racing up my arms. My sister the chef had been accused of killing a fellow chef with a fish knife, but that weapon had been much bigger. She was not guilty, of course, but Savannah remained much more at home with knives than I would ever be.

"So the medical examiner thinks the same killer was responsible for both murders?"

Derek nodded. "Yes. Not only was the weapon the same, but the angle of the thrust was the same."

A knife was not a clean and easy way to kill someone. You had to get up close and personal and plunge the knife, hard, into your victim's body. You had to be willing to feel his death on your hands. To see his blood seeping from the wound. It wasn't a dispassionate way to kill. And the fact that someone had carried a knife like that into the Covington Library the other night, and then into our home three days later, made me realize that not only had the same person killed both men, but also both of the murders had to have been premeditated. Or if not planned out, per se, the murders were certainly not unanticipated. He — or she — had come prepared to kill.

And once again, I had to face the fact that I was connected to each death. I had known and spoken to both of the victims only hours before they died. The thought made me a little seasick.

I wasn't crazy enough to blame myself. That would be ridiculously egotistical and shortsighted, not to mention nightmare-inducing. This case wasn't about me. This was about someone who was willing to kill over a book. Again. Which meant that, well, it was sort of all about me, since the book in question was undoubtedly among those sitting in my closet safe at this very moment.

Honestly, when I had first begun to study with my old mentor, Abraham, I believed that the world of bookbinding was a pleasant, creative, safe, *insulated* career choice. These last few years had been anything but. On the other hand, if not for becoming a bookbinder and stumbling on Abraham's murder, I never would have met Derek. So, no matter how crazed my life had become, I wouldn't change a thing. And yet . . .

"I'm so sick of this."

"I know, darling." He stood and circled the table. "Come here." Pulling me out of my chair and into his arms, he held me for a long while in his comforting embrace. I sagged against him, confident that he could hold me upright, if just for a minute. It felt so good to let go.

With a final, gentle stroke of my hair, Derek released me and we sat down again.

He tore a piece of paper off the legal pad and quickly sketched a picture of a curved dagger. "The ME said that the blade was almost two inches wide." He added more detail to the drawing, improvising a fancy carved design along the hilt.

"It could be a cooking knife of some kind," I said. "Except for the curved part. And it's too short to get much leverage on a big piece of meat." I realized I'd gone off on a cooking bent, forgetting I could barely boil water. I waved my words away, saying, "Never mind. I'm hardly one to talk about a chef's preferences."

He stared at his drawing. "I've seen a number of these types of knives in parts of India and Asia, and soldiers used to bring them back from Vietnam."

"But who carries around a knife like that

these days?"

"Someone who means to kill."

That was unfortunately true. "But why?"

"That's what we've got to find out."

After showering the next morning, I dressed in my best funeral attire. Black pants, black sweater, black boots, and the beautiful black trench coat Derek had bought me on his last trip to London. I added a thin burgundy wool scarf for a slight touch of color and I was ready to go.

Derek and I parked on Cabrillo Street, a block away from the National Bird-watchers Society building, and walked down Twenty-third Avenue toward Golden Gate Park. As we got closer to the park, the sound of birds chirping and chattering and singing grew louder and louder until it was all I could hear, even above the traffic noise. The bird-watchers couldn't have chosen a better location for their meeting place than directly across from this heavily wooded section of the park near the corner of Twenty-third and Fulton Street.

The society was headquartered on the second floor of a beautiful, spacious three-story Mission Revival building with its dramatic parapet and arched doorways and window frames. We walked upstairs and found the door open, so we strolled inside to find the large space filled with people chatting, drinking coffee, and munching on some kind of coffee cake. Wide plate-glass windows lined the wall overlooking the park, giving members an extraordinary view of dense thickets of eucalyptus, pine, elm, and Monterey cypress that formed a veritable forest in the middle of the city.

We both greeted Ian and then separated to meet and mingle with the bird-watchers. Derek headed for the windows, and I turned in the opposite direction. On the wall before me was a display of black-and-white photographs showing all sorts of birds in dramatic action. An owl lifting its wings to depart from its nest. A heron standing in a marsh with the Golden Gate Bridge in the foggy distance. A cute, fuzzy, fat bird sitting on a branch, looking more like a miniature Buddha than a winged creature.

"That's so cute," I said, leaning in close to study the detail.

"Bushtit," a man behind me said.

I turned to see a tall, grizzled man staring at the same photograph. "I beg your pardon?"

"That bird you're looking at," he said, pointing at the photo. "It's a bushtit. Sweet little thing with a warble that'll melt your heart."

"Did you take this photograph?" I asked.

"Yep. Took 'em all."

"They're beautiful."

"They ought to be. Took me long enough to set up the dang frames. Birds are not the most willing creatures, in case you didn't know. Downright stubborn pains in the butt is what they are."

I grinned at him. "I'm Brooklyn Wainwright."

"Socrates McCall, at your service." He extended his arm and we shook hands.

"Are you from Scotland, Mr. McCall?"

"Aye, you caught a whiff of my brogue, did you?"

"I did." I smiled. "It's charming."

His cheeks turned pink and he frowned. "Haven't seen you around here before."

"I met Mr. Mulrooney at the Covington Library the night of the Audubon opening."

He made a face. "Same night he died."

"Yes. I'm sorry."

Socrates glanced around, then lowered his voice. "I figured he was there to steal the book and got himself killed."

It was my turn to frown. "What book is that?"

"The big one," he barked. "The one

everyone was gabbing about. The big bird book."

Was he kidding? I couldn't tell. Besides being massive, the Audubon book was more closely guarded than anything the Covington had exhibited in years. Not since they'd hired Derek to secure the Winslow exhibition a few years back had the place been so fortified. It would be impossible to steal something so valuable and well secured.

But how else could the head bird-watcher's death be explained? I watched Socrates carefully, unsure if he was pulling my leg or not. "You don't honestly think Jared was planning to steal it, do you?"

He lifted both hands and shrugged. "How should I know? He talked about it, though. Thought it should be a law that all the Audubon books be kept here, under our jurisdiction. Jared Mulrooney was an odd bird." He chuckled at his inside joke, then frowned again. "Drank too much for my taste, but to each his own. Ran the society well enough. Not sure if the next in line will be able to hold it together."

I'd known plenty of Scotsmen and I'd never heard one of them complain of someone drinking too much. And besides that, I wasn't sure what drinking had to do with anything, mainly because I myself enjoyed a nice glass of wine and the occasional cocktail. But then again, Jared had damaged the bluebird book by spilling the wine he'd been drinking. So maybe he couldn't control his liquor. I still wasn't sure what that had to do with stealing the big Audubon book, though.

"Who's next in line to be president?" I asked.

"Marva Pesca." He pointed toward the banquet table at the end of the room. "That's her over there, the pushy one in black, running everyone ragged."

I glanced in the direction he indicated and saw a short, heavyset woman in a black-and-yellow horizontally striped dress, telling others how to rearrange the table, impatiently moving casseroles and platters here and there herself when her minions didn't react quickly enough. She reminded me of a meddlesome bumblebee.

"Bossy old cow," Socrates muttered.

I watched her for a moment, then asked, "Did she get along with Jared?"

"As well as anyone, I guess. But she sure was anxious to take over once he was dead. Don't ask me why. It's a thankless job with too much responsibility and none of the fun. You've got to answer to the members and deal with the city and the state, and the national society, and every environmental group under the sun, and PETA, and everyone else on the planet."

"It sounds important."

He rolled his eyes. "As long as you're willing to suck up to the Audubon theorists, you'll get along fine."

"Theorists?"

"Yeah. I'm not one of 'em." He lowered his voice and leaned closer. "I'm a Wilsonian myself."

"Wilsonian?" I was beginning to feel like a mynah bird, repeating everything he was saying. "What's a Wilsonian?"

He straightened to his full height. "Alexander Wilson was only the greatest bird lover of all time. He was a true ornithologist and a Scotsman to boot. He was the first to write and illustrate a book on birds."

"He was?"

"Way before Audubon. Wilson had more knowledge and understanding of birds in his little finger than Audubon ever had in his life. But Audubon had an ego and he was determined to beat Wilson at his own game." He shrugged. "I suppose he was a decent enough painter, although I still believe he copied Wilson's best works."

"You mean, copied his paintings?"

"That's exactly what I mean. Audubon

certainly had a flair for art. I'll give him that. But Wilson had the smarts. It's a tragedy he died so young."

"I'm sorry."

He blinked as if he'd come out of a dream, then glanced around furtively. "Guess I got carried away."

"Was Jared Mulrooney a Wilsonian?"

"No way," he scoffed. "He was your typical Audubon apologist. To be honest, very few Wilsonians can put up with the fanatical adoration most bird-watchers have for Audubon. It's all I can do to stomach some people's attitudes around here, but my wife likes coming, so what's a man to do?"

Did Socrates McCall dislike Audubon aficionados so much that he might have killed one of them? I couldn't see it. "But you said you thought Jared was a good society president."

"Good enough. But then again, there was the drinking." He screwed up his mouth and wrinkled his brow, indicating he was thinking really hard. "Perhaps Jared was hiding some deep dark secret. And then drowning his sorrows."

"Do you think so?"

"It's a possibility."

"Maybe he was a closet Wilsonian."

Socrates blinked, then burst out laughing.

"That's a good one, lass. But no, there's not a chance in the world."

But he had me wondering. Just because Jared liked to drink, it didn't mean he was hiding some deep, ugly secret. On the other hand, he *had* been hiding a secret: he had ruined the society's most valuable treasure, the *Songbirds in Trees* book. So maybe Socrates had the right idea about him.

I glanced around at the motley crowd. Did someone here know about the damaged book? Had they confronted Jared Mulrooney at the Covington that night?

I shook my head in disgust. I'd forgotten that the same person who killed Jared Mulrooney had also killed Goose. So how in the world could Goose's killer be one of these bird-watchers? Unless Jared had told someone I had the book and they'd decided to come looking for it. With a dagger. Wearing a mask.

Stranger things had happened, but that theory seemed far-fetched, to say the least. Didn't mean it didn't happen that way, though.

Socrates announced he was making a break for the food table and waved good-bye to me. I glanced around for Derek and Ian and saw both of them talking to different people, so I wandered over to the near-

276

est window to check out the view.

It wasn't long before I heard the sound of high heels tip-tapping against the wooden floor, and they were moving in my direction. Turning, I saw Marva Pesca approaching.

"Hello," I said.

"You don't look familiar."

Well, that was one way to greet a visitor, I thought. *Bossy old cow* might have been an apt description.

"I'm just visiting," I said cordially. We introduced ourselves and I practically had to force her to shake my hand. "I met Jared at the Covington Library the other night and he told me about your organization. I'm so sorry for your loss."

She scanned me slowly from head to foot. "I specifically told people not to wear all black. I hate funerals. I wanted this to be a celebration."

I hated to be rude, but I really didn't like Marva Pesca very much. And besides, she was wearing black, too, so who was she to judge me? Okay, she also had big yellow stripes to break up the black, but really, who died and made her the arbiter of all fashion? I looked down my nose at her and said, "I was invited by the head of the Covington Library. He didn't mention a dress code."

"Fine," she said. "Whatever."

And yet she stayed by my side. Since she wouldn't walk away and leave me alone, I decided to try to get some information from her. "How did Jared die? If you don't mind my asking."

"He was killed in the line of duty," she said somberly. "He died protecting the beautiful Audubon book on display that night."

I blinked. "The line of duty? Really? Was someone trying to steal the book?"

"That's what the police told me."

So Marva Pesca thought Jared was protecting the book, and Socrates thought he was trying to steal it. Was one of them correct, or were they both crazy?

Marva sighed and patted her chest. "It was just like Jared to put himself in harm's way like that. He loved birds, even the ones in books. He was such a special man." She began to sniff and gulp and her eyes teared up.

"Oh dear. You're going to ruin your makeup." I grabbed a napkin from a nearby side table and handed it to her.

She wiped her eyes and blew her nose. "I haven't stopped crying for days. Jared was a good person. So devoted to birds."

"He did seem like a nice guy." And so Big

Bird–like, I thought. "But is it true he had a drinking problem?"

She gasped. "What a terrible thing to say!"

She was right and I felt bad, but I had to try to shake her up a little. Since she was clearly unwilling to discuss it, I changed the subject quickly. "I couldn't help noticing that the glass display case over there is empty. Is there usually something inside it?"

She was still sniffing, but from outrage this time. Yet she managed to spit out an answer to my question. "Yes. There's usually a very special book on display in that case, but right now it's being appraised by our auditors and will be returned in the next week or so. You'll have to come back and see it."

I didn't believe her invitation was sincere, but I left it alone. "It must be a book about birds."

"Yes, it is. It's filled with beautifully painted Audubon birds, similar to the big book on exhibit at the Covington, only much smaller. And simply delightful. Audubon is such a genius."

Clearly, she wasn't a Wilsonian like Socrates McCall.

"I'll look forward to seeing it," I said. "Thank you so much for spending time with me, Ms. Pesca."

She nodded regally. "Do enjoy the cake."

An hour later, Marva gathered the members and visitors together on the spacious balcony, where a cold breeze rustled the branches of the tall trees lining Golden Gate Park. She instructed us to hold hands and share our memories of Jared. It took a few minutes to get the ball rolling, but finally one lady said, "He did love the birds."

That was followed by a few titters and snickers and I wondered if it was a double entendre. Did Jared like the ladies as well as the occasional alcoholic beverage?

"Jared was a great president and the life of the party."

"He was tall. I like that about him."

"I miss him so much," a soft-voiced woman in the back said.

"Remember his crazy laugh?" another said. "It always reminded me of the plaintive cry of the red-footed booby."

A few people chuckled softly at the sentiment and someone added, "After a few drinks, he walked like a booby, too."

"Jared devoted his entire lifetime to searching for the small-headed flycatcher," one man said reverently. With that, a few people sniffled.

"Waste of damn time," Socrates muttered.

"Everyone knows there's no such thing as a small-headed flycatcher."

"Oh, cram it, McCall," the other guy said. "Just because your precious Wilson never saw one doesn't mean the thing doesn't exist."

"You cram it, Harold," Socrates griped. "You know darn well Audubon never saw one, either, but he went ahead and painted it anyway. He was just a big faker."

"And Wilson was a loser," Harold said.

"Audubon was a thief! He stole the idea of an illustrated book of birds from Wilson."

"Wilson was lazy."

"Audubon was a draft dodger!"

"Wilson was a bore!"

"Don't you say one more word about Wilson," Socrates shouted, shaking his finger in Harold's face. "You're not good enough to utter his name."

"Ah, shut up, you old goat."

Socrates raised his fists and started to rush toward Harold. A woman screamed and Derek and Ian jumped between the two men to hold them back.

Another old guy shouted, "Fight! Fight!" A few others joined in, clapping along. "Fight! Fight!"

Marva stomped her foot to little avail. "Gentlemen! I insist you stop fighting right

281

now. This is neither the time nor the place for squabbling. Poor Jared is barely in his grave and you —"

Before she could say another word, Socrates managed to pull away from Ian and he shoved Harold hard. The old guy fell back against a very large wooden box, and the box began to quiver and shake.

A young man dressed in a red sweater vest ran over and grabbed hold of the box to steady it. "Oh, dear Lord, now you've done it!"

The box took on a life of its own, shaking so much that it began to move across the balcony floor. We could all hear something inside, like a beating pulse or some kind of motorized engine. It grew in decibels. It was alive.

"It's too late now," the young man cried. "I can't hold them back!" And he yanked the lid off the box. Hundreds of white doves rushed out and went flying into the sky.

"Oh," I whispered. "That's cool." *Except for the part where they were all stuck inside that box for a few hours,* I added to myself.

There was a chorus of oohs and aahs as the graceful birds filled the sky.

"So pretty," one woman said.

The two fighters were instantly distracted and stared up, watching the birds fly in formation, zigging one way and then zagging the other. It was beautiful, really. If only their premature takeoff hadn't been brought about by two bickering old coots. But thinking of the fight made me wonder again who this Alexander Wilson person was. An ornithologist, according to Socrates. A competitor and a contemporary of Audubon's, clearly, but why had I never heard of him?

Marva stomped her foot again. "I had a whole speech prepared and you two geezers ruined it."

Harold waved his hand at her. "Who cares about hearing a speech anyway?"

"Yeah, cut to the chase, Marva," Socrates said, scowling.

At least they'd found something they could agree on.

"Fine." Marva took a deep breath and struck a pose, once again looking like an industrious bumblebee in her striped dress. "May he rest in peace. Amen."

"I need some fresh air," I said. "Can we walk in the park for a few minutes?"

"I don't think that's a good idea," Derek said, glancing up and down the street. "You're not out of danger yet."

"Just for a few minutes?" I said. "What

can go wrong with you by my side?"

He flashed me a suspicious look. "We'll make it a very short walk."

We jogged across the street and entered Golden Gate Park using a narrow pathway. It meandered through the tall trees and scrub brush until it opened up onto busy Crossover Drive.

"A four-lane highway running through the park?" Derek said. "So much for fresh air."

"I thought we would end up closer to the lake," I said, glancing around. "I give up. Let's go home."

On the way out of the park, Derek said, "What did you learn today from the bird-watchers?"

"Some people thought Jared had a drinking problem, and I suppose I would agree, seeing as how he ruined the book by sloshing wine on it."

"It could've been an accident."

"True," I said. "It doesn't mean he was a lush. Anyway, according to the members I talked to, either he was killed because he was trying to *steal* the big Audubon book, or because he was trying to *protect* it from someone else who was trying to steal it."

"Interesting," Derek said. "Neither is true, of course."

"Of course not. There was no way anyone

could steal from the Covington. But I think they all want to believe his death was somehow connected to the Audubon book." We crossed Fulton and strolled back to the car along Twenty-third Avenue, where we could enjoy the pretty trees growing on the median strip. "I know in my heart that he was killed because of some connection to the book he gave me. How could it be anything else?"

"Tell me about the other books you're working on," Derek said.

I named them off.

He gave me a puzzled look. "There are quite a lot of bird titles in that list."

"What do you mean?"

"Not all of them, of course," he said, coming to a stop at Divisadero Street. "But see here. You've got a *Cuckoo* and a *Robin,* and a *Dove* and a *Falcon.* Even *Dracula* turned into a flying creature."

I gaped at him. "That's just bizarre. Why didn't I ever notice that?"

"Because you're too close to the books." He squeezed my hand. "It doesn't mean anything. Simply something I picked up on as you named them."

"And the book from Jared is literally all *about* birds, so there's one more."

"You're for the birds, darling."

"Thank you," I said, rolling my eyes. "You sound like Socrates McCall with his little bird joke."

"I do like his name, even if he is a curmudgeon."

"He was a real character. I learned about another ornithologist who was apparently a competitor of Audubon's." I gave him a brief recap of what Socrates had told me.

"Fascinating. Is that what those two old rascals were arguing about?"

"Yes. Oh, and Socrates is one of the members who considers Jared a big drinker. Of course, I don't think Socrates drinks at all, so we'll never be close."

"Some teetotalers consider one drink to be too many."

"He did sound pretty strict on the subject. Kind of odd for a Scotsman, but it takes all kinds. Thank goodness nobody knows how that book really got damaged." *Demon Wine,* I thought. "And according to Marva Pesca, the book is at the auditor's office being appraised."

"So she doesn't know the truth," Derek murmured. "Do you think anyone in that group knows the real story about the damaged book?"

I thought about it. "Someone must know. It just makes sense that Jared's killer is one of the bird-watchers. Who else would care that much about a little book?"

"Someone cares a great deal," Derek mused, his expression growing darker as his jaw tightened. "Because after they killed Jared, they broke into our home and killed Goose."

"That's right," I said, clutching his hand tighter. "I think it's time we got to know those bird-watchers a lot better."

CHAPTER ELEVEN

Saturday morning, I drove to Alex's gym, located in a modest minimall in Hayes Valley, north of Market Street and a few blocks west. I had been working out with her for a few months before I took a break to relocate to Dharma. Today I knew my muscles were going to suffer because of all that time away, and as soon as I walked into her no-frills gym, Alex confirmed it.

"We'll be starting from scratch," she said, handing me a long piece of rubber tubing with handles on each end. It looked like a pink jump rope, only stretchy.

"Is that necessary?" I asked. "I did a lot of walking in Dharma." I was hoping she'd give me credit for something.

"I'm glad to hear it," she said. "Walking is aerobic, so that means you're breathing a lot and moving your muscles. It's really good for you."

"So why are we starting from scratch?"

"Because you probably didn't practice a lot of self-defense moves, right?"

I hung my head. "I didn't."

"And that's what you're really here for, right?"

"Right." I held up the pink rubber thing. "So why am I holding a jump rope?"

"First of all, it's not a jump rope. It's a resistance band. In a few minutes I'll show you how to use it and you're going to love it."

"Love is an awfully strong term."

"There's another reason we're starting from scratch," she continued, effectively ignoring me. "The ability to defend oneself begins with a healthy body. Balance and co-ordination are essential. Building some muscle mass is essential, too. It's great that you did a lot of walking. I hope you keep it up. But today I want to incorporate some stretching and isometric exercises. I want to show you how to breathe. And I want you to do all this stuff at home, every day. We'll work on the self-defense moves you've already learned and get you back up to speed. And then when you come in next weekend, we'll move forward. Okay?"

"Okay. Sounds good. I can do that."

"Of course you can. So as I said, today we'll concentrate on the balance and breathing, but I want to throw in a few of those self-defense moves to get you back into the habit of thinking about your surroundings and reminding yourself that there are people out there trying to kill you."

"Thanks. I love you for that."

She laughed. But only for a millisecond. After that, my black-belted friend was all business, and for the next ninety minutes, she systematically kicked my behind from one side of the padded-floored, mirror-lined, utilitarian room to the other. There was no friendly chitchat, no talk of men or food or shopping or movies. There was just the serious business of creating a stronger body for me. It wasn't pretty or fun, but it was effective. And I really did like my new pink stretchy band so much that she gave it to me to use at home. I was pitifully grateful for her help, even if it was hard to say so at the time. Mainly because I'd completely lost the ability to catch my breath.

Later that afternoon, after soaking in a hot Epsom salts–infused bathtub to ease my aching muscles, I got all dolled up for Derek's office party. Thanks again to Alex's guidance, I'd recently gone shopping to buy several outfits for dressy occasions and had actually found a few that I liked. This was a big change. I'd never enjoyed shopping because I didn't have a clue what looked good on me. My best friend, Robin, another fashion expert, had joined forces with Alex to finally drum some basic style and fashion guidelines into my head.

I was to follow five rules: number one, employ the store's personal shopper whenever possible, since I didn't have a clue where to find anything or what to try on; number two, alternatively, go shopping with Alex or Robin whenever possible; number three, always buy well-designed undergarments that fit perfectly and feel fabulous — and wear them while shopping; number four, with every outfit you try on, picture Derek's expression when he sees you wearing it; number five, have fun and laugh a lot.

Rules to live by, or at least to shop by. And they seemed to have worked for me.

Tonight I was wearing what Alex called an LBD, a little black dress. It was so sexy and cute — if a dress could be both — that it still shocked me to look at myself in the mirror. The dress was short but not appallingly so, and it somehow made my legs look a mile long. Derek seemed to like it. I mean, a lot.

I added a single twisted gold chain, earrings, and a pair of shiny black heels. Not stiletto heels like the ones Alex wore, because I'd tried them and they were just too hard to stand in, let alone walk in for any distance. I was willing to sacrifice a lot to look fabulous, but I had long ago decided that my shoes had to feel right or I just wouldn't have a good time.

When it came to shoes, Robin had washed her hands of me, convinced that my years of wearing Birkenstocks had molded my feet into the shape of a hobbit's. Alex, however, was willing to work with me, and after watching me try on most of the shoes in the Nordstrom shoe department, she suggested that I settle for a pair of lovely three-inch heels with a half-inch platform, which gave the illusion that they were higher than they really were. She then insisted I buy them in five different colors, including two in black, just to be on the safe side. But since I spent most of my time wearing Birkenstocks, I compromised and bought one pair in black and one pair in red. Alex approved.

So, here I was, fluffed and dressed and only slightly aching after my torture session with Alex. Derek was very happy with the results. And he looked simply spectacular in his gazillion-dollar suit, white shirt, and flashy silver-and-black-striped tie. Gazing at him, I decided it was really fun to play dress-up once in a blue moon.

Derek had suggested that he and Crane arrive at the party half an hour late so that things would get rolling more easily without the boss and guest of honor standing around, waiting and watching. I thought it was a brilliant strategy and wondered if it had actually been his assistant Corinne's idea.

We parked in front of the four-story building that was designed in the classic Mediterranean style and located on California Street near the top of Nob Hill. As I walked into Derek's offices, the first thing I noticed, as always, was the room itself. I really loved this place with its high ceilings and exposed brick walls. The city views from the massive plate-glass windows in the wide-open two-story reception area were spectacular.

Corinne and her husband, Wallace, were the official greeters, and they'd stationed themselves by the wide archway leading into the reception lobby, where a lively scene was already happening. The couple was in their fifties and so down-to-earth and friendly, I had glommed onto them the first time I ever met them.

Two years ago, Corinne had accompanied Derek from his London office to help set up the San Francisco office. She and Wallace had fallen in love with the city and had emigrated without a qualm, settling in the Sunset District near Golden Gate Park. They were close enough to the ocean to get a hint of a sea breeze every afternoon. They also lived in the famous Fog Belt, but Corinne didn't mind a bit.

"Reminds me of London, doesn't it?" she'd said, the last time we talked.

Corinne and Wallace both gave me hugs and I relaxed instantly.

"Everything looks perfect, Corinne," Derek murmured.

"Thank you, Derek," she said, nodding. "I'm glad you approve. Otherwise, heads would roll and it would become quite messy with bloody brains and bits flying everywhere."

"Exactly," he said. His wink belied the ruthless businessman demeanor and Corinne was chuckling as we strolled into the party.

He stopped a wandering waiter and grabbed two champagne flutes, handing me one and clinking my glass with his. "Thank you for being here," he said.

"I wouldn't want to be anywhere else," I murmured, and we both took a sip of the rich, bubbly liquid.

"Time to mingle," he whispered in my ear. "Are you ready?"

"As ready as I'll ever be."

"That's my girl."

We turned and faced the crowd of people. I recognized most of them, but there were a few new ones here and there.

Derek's partners and several of his long-time clients greeted us both effusively. I was grateful that most of his employees were lovely, smart, and helpful. I was doubly thankful that he'd managed to cull some of the snarky women I'd met at the first party. The "mean girl" clique was no longer operational and I couldn't be happier.

Please understand me. Those women didn't have to be culled because they were mean. They had to be culled because they were stupid. Because think about it: a group of haughty women standing around, loudly dissing their boss's new girlfriend at a company party? Stupid, stupid, stupid.

Since that first time, things had improved. I mean, maybe the women in his office still hated me, but they knew better than to voice their feelings in front of me. I still enjoyed watching people trying to impress Derek or just trying to get close to him. I couldn't blame them, because objectively speaking, Derek was awesome. The role of the boss, or CEO, or Commander came naturally to him. He was intelligent, confident, strong, and fiercely loyal to the people who were loyal to him in return. He had a wonderful sense of humor, he could handle constructive criticism, and he rewarded innovative thinking.

And of course, he was always the most handsome man in any room he walked into. Why would I want to be anywhere else?

We'd been mingling and chatting for about fifteen minutes when I noticed George Thompson walk into the room. I nudged Derek and we both went to greet him.

"How are you feeling?" I said, concerned that I hadn't seen him since he left for the hospital with the two police officers last week.

"I'm completely fine," he said. "Nothing to worry about. Except for the residual humiliation factor."

"Please don't feel that way," I said. "Turns out, we're dealing with a pretty ruthless creep, so I'm just glad you weren't injured too badly."

"Thanks, Brooklyn. I heard about the fellow who died in your house. I'm sorry." He glanced at Derek. "If there's anything I can do, boss, just call me."

"Thanks, George," he said. "There's no one I trust more than you."

He seemed overwhelmed for a moment. "I really appreciate that."

A moment later, George excused himself to get a drink and that was when Derek glanced toward the front of the lobby. "Ah. Here's Crane."

I turned in time to see the second-most-handsome man walk into the room. He, too, wore a beautifully fitted business suit and once again, each woman in the room had her gaze fixed firmly on him as he crossed the wide lobby to where we were standing.

"Perfect timing," Derek said, shaking Crane's hand with enthusiasm. "Glad you could make it."

"Thank you so much for doing this," Crane said. "I'm grateful. And now I suppose it means I owe you."

Derek chuckled. "I'm happy you understood that."

"Absolutely. Goes without saying." Crane laughed. "But seriously, you'll both come to Beijing and I'll treat you like royalty."

"I'd love to visit Beijing," I said.

He flashed Derek a cocky grin, then turned to me. "Well, if the old man can't make it, I'll be happy to show you a good time."

Derek glared at him. "I'll be there."

He sighed. "Always ruining my fun."

It was great to see everyone smiling and ready to enjoy the evening. Derek picked up a fork from one of the nearby catering stations and tapped it against his glass to get everyone's attention.

"Thank you all for coming," he said. "It's an honor to have my oldest and dearest friend, Crane, visiting this week. I can't think of a better excuse for a party, and I knew that a friendly gathering like this would be the perfect way to introduce him to all of you. I hope you'll take the time to stop and talk with him, because I know everyone here, including me, can benefit from his unique outlook and expertise in the Asian markets. Besides that, he's a great guy, even if he does cheat at poker."

Everyone laughed and Derek had to shout out his last sentence. "Please help me welcome Crane."

There was roaring applause and shouts of "Welcome."

With his hand over his heart, Crane gave slight bows in three directions. "Thank you so much, Derek. Thank you all."

Within seconds, he was surrounded by Derek's partners and clients and some of the other businessmen Derek had invited to the party.

"That was a lovely speech, Derek."

I turned and saw a woman I didn't recognize standing too close to my fiancé.

She was a tall, willowy, and very beautiful Eurasian woman with a melodious voice and a bewitching smile that seemed designed to promise ineffable pleasure.

"Thanks, Lark," Derek said. "Are you enjoying yourself?"

"Oh, very much. I so appreciate being invited."

"You're part of the team now, so of course you belong here."

"Really, I'm so grateful. I won't ever let you down." As she said the words, she touched the lapel of Derek's jacket.

The room began to shrink as I focused on her delicate hand. On his very expensive jacket.

I felt my eyebrows rising and my teeth clenching. Was I going to have to kill her? I'd never been jealous in my life until I met Derek. No, that wasn't quite accurate. It was only when he started taking me to his office parties that my hackles would go on red alert. These women were ruthless!

I watched as Derek glanced down and Lark slowly removed her hand. He looked mildly irritated and she smiled innocently.

Or tried to, anyway. I was pretty sure she didn't have an innocent bone in her body. But her smile really was lovely and I wondered what she would look like with her two front teeth punched out.

Alex would be proud to know I was considering using some of the moves she'd taught me.

"Let me introduce you to Brooklyn, my fiancée."

It was the first time he'd introduced me in public as his fiancée, and I had to admit, I loved the sound of it.

Lark, on the other hand, looked about as thrilled as if she had just swallowed a live frog. I couldn't be happier.

"Oh, uh," she said, gulping as she shook my hand. "How do you do?"

"Nice to meet you, Lark." I shot Derek a sympathetic smirk as he made a swift retreat. "Did you just start working here recently?"

"Yes, just last week. I'm so lucky. It's a wonderful company."

"I agree. It's a fabulous place to work."

"You used to work here?"

"No. I've just met a lot of the people and of course I know Derek. Everyone seems very happy here, so I know it must be a good work environment."

She seemed puzzled and I wasn't sure why. Was it because I was giving my opinion of the company without having any actual experience working there? Did that disqualify me from expressing my feelings?

I was glad I wore heels, because even though Lark was tall, I was now an inch taller. Was I imagining it, or did it really seem to bother her that she had to look up at me?

"What do you do?" she asked politely.

"I'm a bookbinder."

A look of confusion flashed in her eyes. "A what?"

I knew she didn't care about any of this, but she had to be nice to the boss's fiancée. And now I'd confused her with my occupation, so that was another point against me on her imaginary scorecard. "I'm a bookbinder. I restore rare books and I also work as a book artist."

"So you . . . paint books?"

I bit my tongue but managed to smile. "No, not exactly."

She glanced around as though there might be someone more important for her to talk to. But of course there wasn't. "So, how did you and Derek meet?" she asked.

I searched my brain for an innocuous way to answer her, because she seemed to be taking my words a little too literally. "We met through our mutual love of books."

"Oh." She seemed completely flustered by that explanation.

It was true. Sort of. Derek and I had met when I took a rare and important book from my dying mentor's hands and slipped it inside my jacket. Derek pulled a gun and accused me of stealing the book and killing the man. So yes, there were books involved in our first meeting. Lark didn't need to know all the details.

"What do you do, Lark?" I asked, changing the subject.

"I'm an analyst," she said robotically. "I work with numbers and determine risk versus return."

Now it made sense. She dealt with numbers and had no clue how to deal with people. Except men. She seemed to deal with men just fine.

"Sounds fascinating," I said. "Do you specialize in any particular area of risk analysis?"

"Um, specialize?" She frowned. I was pretty sure she thought I was too dumb to comprehend what she'd just said. "I specialize in risk analysis." She said it slowly and even raised her voice slightly, as if I were a particularly dimwitted second grader.

I wanted to laugh at this completely nonsensical conversation, but I was sure she would have misunderstood my amusement. She seemed to lack the ability to recognize irony.

"It was nice meeting you, Lark," I said, giving her an out. She took it and dashed away. Within seconds she was swallowed up by another group over by the bar.

I watched her interact with the others for a minute or two and detected an edgy streak to her mannerisms. That, and her mini seduction scene with Derek, made me vow to steer clear of her for the rest of the night.

I was about to turn away when I noticed her entire attitude changed. She extricated herself from the group and moved in a direct line across the room to meet Crane. They shook hands and I watched him say a few words to her. Her response was sultry and flirtatious. Some men would have been bowled over, but Crane didn't seem particularly impressed or interested. I had to wonder why. She was one of the most beautiful women I'd ever seen, but he looked almost . . . bored.

Was it horrible of me to say that Crane's reaction made me like him even more?

It suddenly occurred to me to wonder if Crane was married or not. I didn't think so, given his reaction to Inspector Lee — not that that would necessarily mean anything. But Derek hadn't mentioned anything about him having a spouse back in China, either. So I had to assume he was unmarried and simply not attracted to the provocative Lark.

A few minutes later, I was chatting with Corinne and Wallace when we all noticed a slight rise in the noise level over by the entranceway. I turned and saw Crane's brother, Bai, walk into the room.

I quietly explained to Corinne who the man was.

"Oh, isn't that nice that his brother was able to make it?"

"It is," I said. At least, I hoped so. I hadn't enjoyed our brief introduction at the Slanted Door the other night, so I was wondering what this meeting would bring. I tried to relax and think good thoughts. If nothing else, the man was definitely attractive. He was your classic bad boy, a type that usually appealed to women.

He saw me and grinned and waved, but didn't stop to talk. Instead he headed straight for his brother. I watched Crane's reaction to seeing his brother and saw him frown for the briefest moment, then smile broadly as though this was a happy surprise.

Maybe it was, despite that frown I'd seen. Maybe he was hopeful and happy that Bai had made an appearance at his party with all these influential people. Maybe he dreamed of his brother turning into a good friend and a loyal family member. Or maybe he'd been burned too many times before and was just hoping Bai would behave himself in front of these important business-people. It was hard to tell, but *hopeful* was a heck of a lot better than *hopeless*.

They spoke in whispers for a moment and Crane shook his head. His lips were pressed together in a frown. Was he disappointed in something Bai said? I couldn't tell. But almost immediately after that, Crane grinned and grabbed his brother's arm as he turned to the assembled group. In a loud, clear voice, he announced, "My brother, Bai, has done me the honor of crashing your lovely party."

Bai laughed and many in the crowd joined him, including me.

"I hope you will welcome him as you have welcomed me," Crane continued. "Thank you all so much for your generosity."

There was cheerful applause and Bai bowed once. "Thank you, brother. I'm honored as well. Thank you, everyone." He waved, then turned and whispered one more thing in Crane's ear. Crane gritted his teeth and tried to smile. Bai chuckled, then wandered off to get himself a drink and mingle.

I was talking to one of Derek's partners and his wife when Bai approached our small group. I introduced him and we all talked for a few minutes. When the partner and his wife walked away, Bai leaned closer. "I'm glad to see a friendly face tonight among all these uptight suits."

I was momentarily speechless but quickly found my tongue. "Everyone here is really nice and very supportive of your brother. Not only that, but they represent important business opportunities for Crane and for your country."

He shrugged. "That's got nothing to do with me."

"No, I guess not." I had to grip my hands together to keep from smacking him. I searched my mind to change topics. "So, are you living in San Francisco now?"

"Temporarily. I'm working on a project that could wrap up any day now, but I'm enjoying myself so much that I hope it lasts awhile longer."

"It's a fun city, isn't it?"

"I love it."

I nodded. "San Franciscans love anyone

who loves their city." Whether they deserved it or not, I thought.

"There's a lot of energy here," he said. "But it's kind of dirty."

Really? He was going to criticize my city? I was itching to grab him by the lapels and shake him, but I refrained, barely. I noticed his glass was empty. "Looks like you need another drink."

He held up his glass. "Are you offering to get me one?"

"No, I'm sorry," I said with a tight smile. "I'll let you do that while I track down Derek."

"Nice talking to you," he called as I walked away. I ignored him, taking deep calming breaths all the way across the room. When I reached the wall of windows at the far end of the space, I turned and watched him walk to the bar to order another drink. Before I could see how it happened, he came face-to-face with Lark. He smiled and introduced himself, and she appeared to answer politely but didn't say more than a few words to him. I had a feeling she had sort of planted herself in his path, and yet now she seemed to be disinterested. And so did he. It was mystifying to me because they were both so gorgeous and toxic, you'd think there would be an automatic attraction. Who could figure out these things?

Bai mingled for another twenty minutes and seemed to cause sparks with everyone he spoke with. Then he reconnected with Crane, chuckled about something, patted his big brother on the back, and took off.

"Your reaction?"

I turned to find Derek standing inches away. "Honestly?" I said. "I feel awful to say it, but he's horrible. Did Crane invite him?"

"Yes. He asked me if I minded and of course I couldn't refuse him. He truly thinks Bai has mended his ways. I was surprised he stayed as long as he did. This really isn't his kind of crowd."

"Not at all," I muttered. "He thinks we're all uptight."

"Some of us are," Derek admitted with a shrug, "but that doesn't mean he's allowed to insult my people."

"I was watching him, and judging from the reactions of some people, I think he just went from group to group spreading turmoil."

"I'm sure I'll hear stories on Monday."

"I'm sure you will."

He gazed across the room to where Crane was chatting and laughing with several of Derek's partners. "For now, I just hope Crane was happy to see him."

"He seemed to be."

Derek glanced around, then whispered, "Are you ready to go home?"

"I'll stay as long as you want to."

He took hold of my hand. "I want to go home."

"What about Crane?"

"Will and his wife are going to take him out to dinner, wine and dine him, as you Yanks say." Will was one of Derek's most valued partners. He had moved here from London last year and we had spent a few fun evenings with him and his wife.

"Then he's in good hands," I said. "But you know as soon as you leave, the party will break up."

"Darling, I'm the boss. As soon as I leave, the party will finally get started."

I chuckled. "Then I guess we should leave so people can start having fun."

He squeezed my hand. "Let's get out of here."

The next afternoon, Derek and I walked across the hall to Vinnie and Suzie's apartment for baby Lily's party. There were already about thirty people mingling in the wide-open space they'd turned into a combination workshop and gallery for their sculptures. Their work was always revelatory, but their newest sculpture was phenomenal. It was a ten-foot-tall woman made entirely of thin pieces of wood curled and shaped into this stunning human form. I admit I ignored everyone in the room to stare and study it for a good fifteen minutes.

"So, what do you think?" Suzie said.

I blinked a few times and turned to look at her. "Are you kidding me? It's sensational. You guys are geniuses."

"It's a remarkable work, Suzie," Derek added.

"How do you do it?" I wondered.

She gave each of us a tight hug. "That's all I wanted to hear. Thanks, Brooklyn. Derek. Come and have one of our signature cocktails."

"You have a signature cocktail? That's pretty fancy."

She grinned, grabbed hold of both my and Derek's arms, and led us past the long buffet table covered with delicious-looking goodies and over to the open kitchen, where a cocktail bar had been set up, complete with bartender. "We call it Lily Vanilli and it's delicious. Very sweet, in case you didn't catch the drift."

"I caught it," I said, laughing. "I'll try one, but I might have to switch to something else afterward."

"That's probably the safest thing to do."

The creamy concoction was made with vanilla ice cream, of course, along with vodka, cream of coconut, almond liqueur, and a cherry on top.

The party was a lavish affair and the guest of honor — adorable in a fluffy pink dress with matching shoes and a bow in her hair — was thrilled with all the attention. Especially when Gabriel walked in, crossed the room, and picked her up. She just stared at him and made an adorable cooing sound. What girl wouldn't when Gabriel was holding her in his arms? The two of them had bonded early on, the first time we ever met Lily. It was a dark and stormy night, naturally, but Lily warmed our hearts immediately.

We all mingled and chatted about everything under the sun. Vinnie cornered me to ask about the murder. Just as I had suspected, everyone in the building knew about the attempted break-in and the subsequent death of Goose.

"You poor thing," she said, and hugged me.

"It was pretty awful. I feel so bad for that man."

"Your parents actually thought they knew him?"

"Yes. They were mortified and guilt-ridden when they found out the truth."

"Your parents have such generous souls. They should not take the blame for bringing this man into a warm home if only for one night."

"That's what I told Mom."

"Good." She glanced around, caught Suzie's gaze, and nodded. "Will you help me, Brooklyn? I want to gather everyone into the living room to open presents and have cake."

"Sure." I moved around the room, telling each cluster of friends that it was time for presents and dessert.

I was excited to have them open my gift.

Vinnie lifted the package out of the bag. "How charming. It's a nursery mobile made of origami cranes."

"That's so cool," Suzie said.

"It's a do-it-yourself project," I explained. "So first you do the folding and then you hang them."

"It's so clever," Vinnie said.

"There's a handmade book in the bag, too, but it might be a little too delicate for Lily right now."

"It will go on her shelf in a place of honor," Vinnie said.

"Thanks, you guys," Suzie said. "Lily's

going to love gazing up at the cranes. They're good luck, aren't they?"

"They're thought to be immortal," I said. "And magical."

Vinnie beamed. "How wonderful."

It was indeed pure luck that I'd seen the origami mobile in the window of the Chinese gift shop on Clement Street the other day. After talking to Crane about my cutout pop-up book of *Alice in Wonderland* and having him describe the much older Chinese art of paper folding called *zhezhi,* it almost seemed like fate when I saw it in the window.

"I hope she has many sweet dreams with cranes flying above her bed," I said. Seeing the gleam of happy tears in Vinnie's eyes, I knew my work there was done.

Monday morning I received the call from Trina Jones, the lawyer in the *Mockingbird* case, as I had started calling it. She confirmed that I would be needed in court the next morning. That afternoon, a messenger delivered a subpoena duces tecum to my house. Trina had explained that they always served a subpoena to any experts hired to appear in court. It was a matter of form and a necessary part of any trial. It basically ordered me to appear before the court and produce documents or other tangible evidence for use at the trial.

I put the subpoena in my file folder and went back to my notes. I wanted to double-check everything, including the list of repairs necessary to bring the copy of *To Kill a Mockingbird* up to the level of the comparable versions I'd found online. I made four copies of the comps I was using: one for each attorney, one for the judge, and one for me.

Tuesday I dressed in the outfit I'd planned out last week, put my notes and the book in a small folder, and slipped it into my satchel. Then I drove over to the Civic Center and the Superior Court Building on McAllister Street.

Two hours later, I was sitting on the stand and swearing to tell the truth, the whole truth, and nothing but the truth. It was all very exciting but frankly stressful, until I started talking about the book. Then I calmed down and did what I'd been born to do: talk about books. I read my findings into the microphone, improvising here and there when I thought it was necessary to expand on a particular thought. The judge was attentive and Trina kept nodding with encouragement, so I was pretty sure things were going well.

"Objection!"

I jolted in my chair. So much for relaxing. The opposing attorney had a bellowing voice that echoed off the walls. If I wasn't mistaken, his client, the husband, seemed to be egging him on. I suppose it made sense, since the husband appeared to be a book collector of sorts, that he would have opinions about such things. But whatever the lawyer was objecting to, he was wrong and I was right.

"Hearsay!" the guy shouted.

Trina, representing the wife, stood at her podium. "Your Honor, when an expert gathers comparable prices for a particular item, it's not considered hearsay."

"Of course not," the judge said. "Cool your jets, Mr. Slocum."

"Yes, Your Honor," the husband's attorney muttered.

The husband looked furious, so I avoided eye contact with him. The wife didn't look too happy, either, but I couldn't blame her. She'd been married to that guy for way too long.

After explaining all the sources I'd used to determine the book's value, and giving my own evaluation of the cost involved in bringing the book up to a higher value, I finished by announcing my appraisal price. I just hoped they would be happy with the amount. But in the end, their happiness didn't matter. I was there to do a job, and I'd done it to the best of my abilities.

Ten minutes later, after a brief, inconsequential cross-examination, the judge thanked me for my testimony and excused me. I walked out of the courtroom and waited in the hall for a few minutes, unsure what to do next.

The door to the courtroom swung open and Trina scooted out.

"I'm sorry I couldn't appraise it for more money," I said immediately. "Your client didn't look very happy."

She waved off my concerns. "That's the way these things go sometimes. My client is thrilled to be getting rid of that jerk and that's all that matters. So thank you. Send me your bill and I'll get a check out to you immediately."

"That's it?"

"That's it," she said, grinning. I gave her the book to return to the divorcing couple. Then we shook hands and I walked out of the courthouse and back to my car, feeling very righteous and Perry Mason-y.

That night I had a few minutes to double-check my figures on the comps I'd presented in court that morning. It was probably silly to dwell on it, but this was the first time I'd ever appeared in court, so I was a little fixated on the process.

I powered up my computer and went directly to my favorite rare-book sites. I searched *To Kill a Mockingbird* as usual, and the first book that came up was one I hadn't seen online before.

I stared at the book and read and reread the description. I studied the seller's name, Books by Bryce. I'd never seen it before, so I Googled it.

Books by Bryce, after further digging, turned out to be operated by Bryce Flint. Flint was the name of the divorcing couple in the case I'd testified for that morning. Bryce Flint was the husband!

The copy of *To Kill a Mockingbird* that he was selling online was in pristine condition. There were no creases or rips in the dust jacket. It was clean and bright, unlike the copy I had examined. There was no rubbing along the back cover, no hideous water stain on the back, the cloth was like new, and the spine stood straight and tall. There was no tearing along the front joint, and the edges were smooth and straight. No chipping anywhere.

What was going on here?

And then it hit me. Holy cow, the guy was trying to cheat his wife. He'd somehow come across a mediocre copy of the same book and that was the one I'd been given to appraise. But the real book, the one they were supposed to sell in order to split the profits, was this immaculate one I was viewing right now, from Books by Bryce.

This copy was worth at least ten times more than the copy I had appraised. The husband would get the entire amount of this book's sale price. He wouldn't have to split it fifty-fifty with his wife. No, all they would be splitting was the lesser amount of the inferior book.

What a creepy cheater!

And nobody would ever guess, because very few people knew what I knew about books: that to some people, they were worth lying, cheating, stealing, and killing over.

The next morning, I called Trina Jones to report the husband's larcenous behavior. She was shocked by the news, but quickly turned gleeful. "I knew that jerk couldn't be trusted. The judge is going to kick his ass across the courtroom."

"I hope so," I said, angry because I'd been lied to as well. "If you need me to explain the details to the judge, just let me know."

"You bet I will. Thanks again, Brooklyn."

■ ■ ■ ■

Derek called from his car a few hours later. "I'm on my way home, love."

I glanced at the clock and smiled. "It's barely noon. That's good news."

"Not exactly. I've got to fly to Los Angeles this evening."

"Oh. Not-so-good news. What's going on?"

"We've got an errant client who needs a lesson in deportment."

"Not again."

"Yes. He doesn't seem to think his stalker is all that serious."

"But didn't the woman get inside his house and try to poison his dog?"

"Yes," he said darkly.

As far as I was concerned, anyone who would harm a pet like that belonged in prison. And I wasn't the only one. Derek was determined to catch the woman and make sure she spent a long time behind bars.

"So can't he see that she's escalating?"

"He can't see beyond his inflated ego. He's like a petulant child with no boundaries."

It figured. Their client was a rich, good-looking "minor celebrity" who just couldn't get a break in television or movies, but had somehow caught the attention of a deranged fan anyway. Now he was being stalked and tormented by her. But he wasn't willing to listen to the advice of the security team he'd hired. I wondered if maybe he was enjoying the attention a little too much.

"Paul seems to think he'll listen to me," Derek said. "So I've got to get down there before he gets himself killed."

Paul was Derek's partner in charge of the case, but Derek was the boss. Some clients only responded when the boss was the one doing the talking, which meant Derek had to make these out-of-town trips on a regular basis.

People were so stupid sometimes. This guy in Los Angeles was in danger. He was the one who had contacted Derek's company, but now he was balking at every little turn. He hated having to go around town with bodyguards. He hated being advised to stay close to home until his stalker was caught. He didn't like having his phone calls monitored.

And how did he feel about dying? I wanted to know. Derek had to deal with these types of people all the time.

And all of a sudden, I was staring at

myself in the mirror, metaphorically speaking. I was doing the same thing that his childish client was doing. Both Derek and Inspector Lee had warned me to be careful, not take chances, and not put myself in danger. And yet I hadn't really taken their advice.

I felt sick to my stomach. Was this how Derek saw me, as a petulant child with no boundaries?

On the other hand, his clients were wealthy and used to being indulged. I wasn't like that.

Derek was the absolute best at calming down an errant client. But that meant he had to take an unscheduled trip out of town every so often. Like today.

I didn't want him to have to calm down his errant girlfriend. I vowed at that moment to follow his advice and be careful.

He made it home quickly and grabbed the small suitcase that was always packed and ready to go.

"I'll be back Friday afternoon," he said, kissing me good-bye at the door.

"Be safe," I said, trying to keep it light.

"You be careful," he said sternly. "Promise me. I don't want you taking any chances."

"I promise. I swear I'll be careful. I won't go out of the house unless I have someone with me. I'm sorry I worried you."

He gave me a perplexed smile. "What's wrong with you?"

"I don't want to be like your errant client. I know I'm in danger and I assure you I'll take every precaution."

He stroked my hair. "Darling, you're nothing like my errant client. You're smart and clever. I admire your courage and I love you very much."

I sniffed back a tear. "I love you and miss you already."

"I love you." He kissed me and then grinned and assured me he'd call when he landed. I stood in the hall and we waved at each other until the elevator doors closed. Feeling completely goofy and truly missing him already, I stepped back inside and went to work.

An hour later, I was just about to start work on the next book when I received a call on my business line. Happy to know that business was booming, I grabbed the phone.

"Hello?"

"This is Bryce Flint," the caller said. "And you're going to be sorry you ever opened your big fat mouth."

Furious and frightened, I slammed down the phone without responding. As soon as I did, I started trembling.

How dared he try to scare me! He really was as big a jerk as Trina said he was. No, he was even bigger. She had no idea how big. But I was about to tell her. I picked up the phone again and called her office. She wasn't in, so I left a message, letting her know that I'd just been threatened by her client's lying, cheating husband.

CHAPTER TWELVE

In order to take my mind off that ugly phone call from Bryce Flint, I buried myself in a frenzy of work.

I pulled all the books from the safe and laid them out on my worktable. I had already completed two of the books, the ones that required the least amount of work. So I immediately started work on the *Cuckoo's Nest* book jacket repair, first whipping up a batch of wheat paste. I cleaned and brushed the pages of another book until the paste was ready to use.

The dust jacket came out looking fabulous, if I did say so myself.

Next, I tackled Inspector Lee's art book, repairing the torn pages first. I'd promised she wouldn't be able to tell that they'd ever been removed from the book, so that became the challenge.

The problem with this book, as with many art books, was that the thick glossy paper would not respond well to moisture. So using a semiliquid glue and rice paper wasn't going to work.

But the good news was that little five-year-old Inspector Lee had managed to tear the pages out of her mama's book right along the inside seam, or the gutter. So I was able to use a transparent, pressure-sensitive archival mending tape that was as thin as a piece of rice tissue and was nonyellowing, with a neutral pH.

I nudged the torn page into place so that it lay perfectly even against the inside seam and then stretched the tape down so that it overlapped the page and the seam. With a bone folder, I gently flattened the tape to get rid of any tiny folds or wrinkles and then ran the tool back and forth to burnish the tape and stimulate and strengthen the adhesive. When I was finished, the tape was invisible and the page was affixed in the place where it belonged.

I repeated the process for all eight torn pages and was thrilled with the results. I hoped Inspector Lee and her mom would be equally thrilled.

I planned to construct the book box tomorrow or the next day. Now, though, it was finally time to deal with *Songbirds in Trees,* the book I'd received from Jared

Mulrooney. I'd been avoiding it because I knew it would take a lot of delicate, complex maneuvering to repair it, and even then, I wasn't sure I could bring the pages back to the life they'd known before being drowned in wine.

But I owed it to Jared to give it a try.

The phone rang, jarring my nerves. This time I stared at the screen. I didn't recognize the number and I was unsure whether to answer it or let it go to voice mail. I didn't want to hear Bryce Flint's threats again. But if it was him, I was going to let the police know.

I realized on the other hand that the call might have something to do with actual business, so I grabbed the receiver and said hello.

"Brooklyn, dear. This is Crane."

I almost dissolved into a puddle of relief. "Oh, Crane. How are you? I hope you had a nice time last weekend."

"The party was a huge success from my point of view. I couldn't be more grateful to Derek and his partners for showing me such a good time and introducing me to some extremely important contacts."

"That's great. I'm glad it's working out for everyone. And it was nice to see your brother show up."

"Yes, that was an unexpected highlight. But now I just spoke to Derek, who told me he was called out of town on business. I imagine you're all alone, drowning your sorrows, so I thought I'd take the opportunity to invite you to lunch tomorrow. If you're available."

I laughed. "That's so nice of you. I'd love to join you for lunch."

"Good. We can gossip about Derek and flirt shamelessly."

I laughed again, as he must've known I would, and we arranged a time and place to meet. I hung up the phone, feeling much better than I had when it first rang.

But thinking of telephones ringing reminded me of Bryce Flint. I decided that if he called again, I would get in touch with Inspector Lee to let her know I had been threatened. What was the use of having a cop on speed dial if I didn't take advantage of it every so often? Not that I expected her to do anything about it. No, I figured the best person to handle Bryce Flint would be the divorce court judge. I didn't think he would appreciate hearing that one of the expert witnesses was being harassed. Flint deserved to be thrown in jail for contempt or something.

I went back to studying the wine-damaged

book. As I carefully separated the stuck-together pages, I was struck by what an exquisite book it really was — despite its wrinkled, sticky clump of pages. Every page I was able to open contained a beautiful color illustration of a bird resting on the branch of a tree.

"Duh," I whispered. No wonder the title of the book was *Songbirds in Trees*. I marveled that even the tree branches were beautiful, decorated as they were with delicate blossoms and vibrant leaves.

It occurred to me as I studied the book that as far as I knew, no one from the Bird-watchers Society knew I had this book in my possession. I had a passing thought that I should take a lot of pictures in order to justify getting paid, since they weren't aware that I would be doing all this work.

It didn't matter. If it came to that, I'd donate my work as a charitable contribution to the organization.

But the point was, I really had no idea if one of the bird-watchers was aware that I had the book in my possession. After all, someone had killed Jared Mulrooney, and soon after that, someone had broken into my home and killed the homeless man we called Goose. Was it a bird-watcher? Did someone from the society know I had the book?

I made a mental note to remind Derek that as soon as he was back in town, we needed to check those bird people out.

Concentrating on the book now, I knew what I would have to do. I'd had plenty of experience working with water-damaged books, although the damage usually occurred during a flood or in the aftermath of a fire when water was poured onto the house or sprinklers were set off in a building. Often, the water did much more damage to the books than fire or smoke.

In those cases, the books were thoroughly soaked, the structure was weakened, and they were often filthy, covered either in soot and ashes or dirt and refuse carried along by the floodwaters. It was important to support the books at all times, carefully transferring them into towel-lined tubs before taking them to be rinsed.

But in the case of *Songbirds in Trees,* the sturdy leather cover had helped to protect the structural integrity of the book. The spine was intact. The adhesives hadn't been affected. It was just the central pages that were mottled, wrinkled, and sticky. The only good news in all this was that Jared had spilled some kind of pale white wine and it hadn't left a stain. Since a buttery chardonnay would've left its mark, I was guessing that Jared had been drinking a Pinot Grigio. None of this was good, but it was a much better scenario than if the poor book had been thrown into a vat of Cabernet Sauvignon.

I knew I couldn't separate the sticky pages without risking more damage. I might tear the page right out of the book, or maybe even peel the illustration off the page, which would constitute a clear case of malpractice on my part. I came to the conclusion that I would have to very lightly redampen each affected page and then proceed to carefully separate it from its neighboring page. After that, I would separate each dampened page with thin card stock to absorb the moisture and to encourage the pages to flatten. Finally, I would use the book press to compel the entire book to return to its original shape.

Since I couldn't do worse to the poor book than what Jared had already done, I took a few deep, energizing breaths and forged ahead.

Rather than spray water directly onto the pages and risk creating an environment where mold could form, I used short spurts of my portable steamer to urge those errant pages apart. It didn't take much effort at all to detach them from one another, and the result was excellent. They were no longer stiff, nor did I detect an overabundance of dampness. Now they were supple enough to be manipulated back to the flat, even state they'd been in before they were drenched with wine.

Before any of the pages could dry completely, I slipped a thin sheet of card stock in between each of them. I was momentarily worried that the addition of the card stock would cause the book to bulge and throw off the binding, but the stock was thin enough that it wouldn't be a problem.

Altogether, there were forty-two pages affected. Within the hour, all the pages had been steamed apart and separated by thin stock. I breathed a sigh of relief that the first two steps seemed to have been effective and prayed that my luck would hold.

After wrapping the entire book in protective paper, I slipped it into the book press, securing it with a few turns of the large wheel. Then I said a quick prayer to all the book gods in heaven and on Earth and let it sit overnight.

The next day, I drove half a mile over to the Mission District and found a parking spot on Valencia, then walked a block up to Eighteenth and two blocks over to Tartine Bakery on the corner of Eighteenth and Guerrero. I glanced over my shoulder constantly and stared down everyone I passed on the sidewalk, but it was worth it. This was one of my favorite spots for a casual lunch and also for buying the most awesome bread and baked goods in the world. I was pleased that Crane had chosen it over one of the fancier restaurants in town.

There was usually a line out the door, so I was surprised to see him waving at me from a small table inside.

He stood as I jostled my way over to the table and sat. "How did you get a table already? You must've gotten here hours ago."

"No, I just got lucky."

I didn't believe him for one minute, but I wasn't going to complain. I figured some woman working there took one look at Crane and immediately offered him a table, free coffee, and maybe a drink later.

"I love this place," I said, joining him at the table. "I start salivating as soon as I get within a block, the smells are so intoxicating."

"I've never eaten here, but it was highly recommended."

"I know we're here for lunch," I said, "but

you might want to order the croissant, just to experience heaven. It's just the right amount of crunchy on the outside and buttery perfection on the inside."

"So, a croissant appetizer. It sounds perfect. We can split it."

I smiled. "Thank you so much for inviting me out."

"I thought it would be a nice chance for us to get to know each other a little better."

"I agree."

"But first, let's decide what we're having."

It was a good idea, since we had to order at the counter and sitting around with no food on our table would quickly generate animosity among our fellow diners. I took a glance at the menu, but I already knew what I wanted. "The Niman Ranch ham and Gruyère on country bread, and a side salad."

He stared at the menu. "Niman Ranch is a good place?"

"I think so. Their methods for raising livestock are humane and sustainable. They don't feed their animals antibiotics or hormones. Their cattle are grass-fed and their chickens are free-range."

"All good things."

I shook my head. "You'd never know I subsist on junk food half the time."

With a laugh, he set the menu down. "Would you like something to drink?"

"I think I'll try the Belgian ale." Beer for lunch? I was living dangerously. But why not?

"Excellent idea. I'll go place our order and be right back." He made his way to the counter while I watched people nearby. It was one of my favorite activities, although today it served two purposes: entertainment and security. I particularly enjoyed the table of four women, each with a different luscious dessert in front of her, taking one bite and passing it to the next person. Those were my kind of friends.

Crane returned shortly with a numbered card. "She said it would take about fifteen minutes." He folded his arms across his chest and grinned. "So, Brooklyn. Tell me your life story. You have fifteen minutes."

I obliged and gave him the shortened version — raised in an arts commune, wine country, big family, bookbinding, etc., etc. "Now I want to hear about you."

"I've told you so much already."

"Tell me more about your family." I loved hearing about other people's families. Maybe because my own was so . . . interesting. I loved my family. A lot. But no one could say we fit into anyone's version of "normal." Not too long ago, I'd met one of Derek's brothers and I was looking forward to a trip to London soon so I could meet the rest of his family. I had a feeling it would be a fascinating time.

Until then, I'd make do with learning more about Crane.

"What would you like to know?" he asked.

I couldn't help myself. "Tell me more about your brother. Are you getting along? Will he be going home to see your mother? You said she was ill."

Crane smiled sadly. "It would be more accurate to say she's sick at heart, rather than actually sick. She has not seen Bai in many years. But at the party the other night, I was able to extract his promise that he would come home with me when I leave at the end of the week."

But now he was frowning.

"You don't look optimistic," I said. "Do you think he'll follow through?"

"He has a girlfriend," he said irritably, and sighed. "He claims it's serious. That always changes things."

"But he doesn't have to stay in China forever, does he? Just long enough to see your mother."

"This woman. This girlfriend of his." He shook his head and scowled. "Pardon me for sounding like an old crow, but she is not good for him."

"How do you mean?"

"She is . . . a failure. I have had to bail her out of jail."

"Jail?" I hadn't been expecting that. "For what? Drugs?"

"Shoplifting," he said with a heartfelt sigh. I felt almost guilty for bringing any of this up. I hadn't meant to upset him. "She said it was a misunderstanding. She's very beautiful and manipulative. And my brother, who can also be manipulative, is an idiot. It's a dangerous combination."

"Men behave strangely around beautiful women," I murmured.

"Yes, we do," he said, smiling. "As you well know, of course. Because you are one of them."

"One of what? Oh." I shook my head back and forth like a wet dog. Absurdly pleased and also a lot embarrassed. "No, no. I'm not one of them. Good grief. I'm completely normal."

He tossed back his head and laughed. "What you are is a gem of priceless value. My friend is a lucky man."

I could feel myself blushing, so I changed the subject. "Will you be coming back to San Francisco again? It's such a pleasure to see you and Derek together. He's always laughing when you're around."

"I know you mean he's laughing *with* me."

Our conversation continued in that light vein and our orders were brought to the table a few minutes later.

"You ordered the pizza," I said. "I was going to recommend it."

"I had to try it. I've read about it and it's actually the reason I wanted to come here for lunch."

"You'll see that everything you've read about it is true. The chef has been written up in every major magazine about his revolutionary process for making pizza dough."

As we took our first bites, the table grew silent except for the groans and yummy sounds we both made.

"I have eaten in the finest restaurants in the world and I've never had anything quite like this," he admitted.

"It's pretty darn good, isn't it?"

"That is a gross understatement, my dear." He took another bite, followed by a sip of the red wine he'd ordered for himself. "I hope your sandwich is satisfactory."

"It's absolutely mind-bending," I said. "I confess, I order this same thing whenever I come here."

"It looks delicious."

We continued to eat and chat about little things. I waited patiently for him to return to the subject of his brother, and finally he did.

"You asked me if I'd be coming back to San Francisco, and the truth is, I'll be back very soon if I cannot convince my brother to come home with me."

"But you said he agreed to go."

He paused with his glass in the air. "Did I mention how manipulative he can be? He'll say he's coming, but I won't believe it until I see him on the plane with me."

"Do you think his girlfriend might find a way to keep him here indefinitely?"

"It is my greatest fear." He paused. "No, my greatest fear would be Bai insisting on bringing the woman with us to meet our mother."

"Oh dear."

He seemed to weigh his next words before he finally spoke. "I told you about my ancestor Sheng's connection to Audubon."

"Yes."

"Bai has taken this to heart, and not in a positive way. I found out he started going to the Covington before the Audubon exhibit even opened. He applied for a special educational pass to study the private documents that arrived as part of the exhibit. Now he's claiming that James Audubon stole our ancestor Sheng's paintings."

I found his accusation hard to believe. "That's a serious charge."

"It is outrageous," he said bitterly. "Bai is determined to get his hands on the big Audubon book. He thinks he'll be able to tell up close which paintings are actually Sheng's and then he'll demand that the world accept the fact that Audubon wasn't the great master everyone thought he was."

Bai was beginning to sound like Socrates McCall. Both of them seemed eager to take Audubon down a notch or two.

"He won't be able to get his hands on the book," I said, knowing Ian and the level of security at the Covington. "Do you think he's right?"

"It doesn't matter," Crane insisted, lowering his voice. "We have to look at the way things were back then. England was not an easy place for a Chinese man to survive and thrive. Our ancestor was grateful for the opportunity of working beside a master artist like Audubon. I have read his journals and I feel certain he wouldn't have wanted this sort of unpleasant publicity stirred up on his behalf. He was a humble man."

"I would imagine there were a lot of

creative people who were taken advantage of back in the old days."

"That is undoubtedly true," he said.

"And who would've believed your ancestor if he had tried to claim that Audubon stole his work? Nobody would buy it. He might have been thrown in jail. Audubon was an important, acclaimed artist."

"And he was white."

My lips tightened at the problematic truth. "Yes. Sorry to say, but that would've been a major factor back then."

I liked to think that things had changed for the better nowadays. But in the case of Crane's ancestor, there was every chance that Bai was right.

Crane sighed in exasperation. "Honestly, Brooklyn, this story of Bai's is not based in reality. My ancestor had talent, it's true. But it was his job to work as a colorist for Audubon. He was very proud of his association with the great painter. It brought honor to him and to his family."

"I hope that's true."

"Frankly, I believe this potential brouhaha is just another way for Bai to make himself feel more important. He could've been one of the finest artists China has ever produced, but instead, he wastes his time with conspiracy theories and nonsense. What if he does find out he was right? What will it matter? None of it means anything." He shook his head. "But if Bai can bring some attention to the story and to himself, he'll try to make a buck off of it. Maybe he'll file a lawsuit."

Crane sat back and threw his hands up as if to say *Who knows?* "He's doing it all for the chance to bask in the residual glory that rightfully belongs to our esteemed ancestor Sheng."

Leaning forward again, Crane stared into my eyes and I couldn't help noticing the frustration etched on his face. "And the worst part of all this is that the woman Bai is seeing is the one who's urging him on, pushing him to make trouble, make waves. She seems to thrive on controversy."

"I hate to exaggerate, but she sounds a little like a modern-day Mata Hari."

"That is the perfect description," he exclaimed. "I tell you, Brooklyn, the sooner I can drag Bai back to China, the sooner I'll be able to breathe easier."

"I'm so sorry. But on the somewhat brighter side, I doubt if he would be allowed to look at the big Audubon book up close. Not while it's on exhibit."

He smiled. "A small ray of sunshine. Thank you."

"I'm sorry you're going through this."

"No, I'm the one who is sorry. I shouldn't be burdening you with my family's problems."

I shrugged. "I don't mind at all. Families are so complicated, it's nice to have someone to commiserate with once in a while."

He smiled. "You've said that about families before. Something tells me you know of what you speak."

"I have five siblings, remember?"

He laughed. "How could I forget? Your poor mother!"

"No, no. She loved having all of us kids underfoot. She still does."

"She sounds wonderful."

"I would love to have you meet her someday. And my father, too. They're the best people in the world."

"It's charming to hear the way you talk about them."

I smiled, took one last bite of my salad, and set down my fork. "I can't eat another thing."

"But you must. We've got to have dessert."

That was when I remembered his croissant appetizer and reminded him. "Did you change your mind?"

"I've decided to wait until after lunch and buy a few on the way out to take back to the hotel. But we must have something sweet now. It's the law, isn't it?"

"Yes, it's the one law I always obey, even when I'm stuffed." I rubbed my full stomach.

"I'll just order a little something and you can take one bite."

"If you insist," I said, giving in to the inevitable. "Since it's the law and all."

He grinned as he stood and walked back to the counter. A few minutes later he returned with a slice of rich dark chocolate cake topped with layers of caramel and chocolate ganache. Oh, Derek had wonderful friends.

"Oh jeez," I mumbled, grabbing my fork. "Good choice."

He laughed and picked up his own, and we didn't speak until the plate was empty.

"I'm happy you only wanted one bite."

I would've laughed, but it hurt too much. But seriously, in my own defense, there wasn't a woman alive who would have said no to that dessert. "Now I'm truly stuffed. That was so delicious. And I've had so much fun talking to you."

"We were supposed to gossip about Derek," he complained. "But I've spent the entire meal spilling my spleen instead."

I stared at him, baffled. "Do you mean guts?"

He frowned. "Is it guts? Are you sure?"

"Yes."

"Then guts it is," he said with a grin.

I drove back across town on Sixteenth Street and replayed some of the funny moments with Crane. I'd had so much fun with him and was sorry that Derek couldn't be there to join us. I recalled how much I enjoyed seeing Derek laughing and joking with his old friend. Derek had plenty of friends, but Crane was different. He provided something extra. The two men had a history together, and that made their friendship even more special. Not everyone was lucky enough to have a person like that in their lives.

I still thought it was a little odd that Derek had never mentioned Crane before. Derek knew everything about me, including my friends, but I knew very little about his life, except for the fact that he had four brothers and a very patient mother. It was just one more thing that made us so different from each other. He was "secret agent man with a gun" and I was "peace and love and country living." But somehow we made it work.

The thought made me smile, but it also made me realize again how much I missed

Derek. And why did that make me feel so infinitely stupid? I guessed it was because I now had to worry whether or not I had grown completely dependent on him after barely two years together. *When did that start?* I wondered.

Had I given up all my girlfriends? Was I content to spend time with Derek to the exclusion of everyone else? For heaven's sake, no. I wasn't dependent on Derek. I just loved being with him and really missed him when he was gone. Perfectly reasonable feelings, right?

"Right," I insisted aloud. I had plenty of girlfriends. True, I didn't see as much of my best friend anymore, but that was because she'd moved back to Dharma and married my brother. We still tried to see each other as often as possible, aside from that little geographic stumbling block.

Vinnie and Suzie were dear friends as well, but they had baby Lily now. And to be honest, Derek and I had been out of town for almost three months, so of course we hadn't seen them in all that time. But now that we were back, we would get together more often. We had already attended Lily's party last Sunday, so that was a good start.

I had plenty of bookbinder friends and librarian friends and book collector friends

I didn't see very often, but whenever I taught a class at Bay Area Book Arts or went to an event at the Covington, I would run into some of them and we would plan lunch or drinks together.

I didn't find it necessary to scurry home to Derek every night instead of going out with old friends.

And I couldn't forget my newest friend, Alex. I considered it my great fortune that she had moved in across the hall from me and Derek. The woman had saved my life at least once and was teaching me defensive skills that would help me save my own life one of these days. She had come to visit me in Dharma while I was there. And now that I was back in town, we would see each other more often. She and Derek were friends, too, so the three of us got together pretty regularly.

Maybe I would stop by to see her when I got home. Maybe she had some cupcakes she needed to get rid of. Not that I could eat one more bite right now, but I would be happy to take one for later.

As I turned left from Sixteenth onto Bryant Street, my mind drifted from cupcakes back to my worries that I was becoming too dependent on Derek. I missed him too much. I loved him like crazy.

So what was wrong with that? Did I really need to freak out about this? Of course I missed him when he was gone. Of course I loved him. But he loved me, too, and I was sure he missed me when he was out of town. Why did this have to be all about me?

Good point.

But just when I was figuring it all out, something else occurred to me, and it wasn't a good thing. With all the times I'd stumbled across murder victims, I had to wonder again if I was doing something to attract that negativity into my life. And the bigger question was, if it continued, would my friends be in danger? Would they start avoiding me?

"Good grief," I said out loud. "Don't be silly."

Right. I quickly and completely disregarded that horrible possibility. I had to stop thinking that way or I would drive myself crazy.

But my initial dilemma still gnawed on me. Had I forgotten how to be happy alone? I used to pride myself on my ability to live alone and thrive. What had happened to that girl? Where was that spirit? Would I be able to sleep alone in my bed tonight without Derek?

Wait, I thought, as I turned down Fourth

Street and made a quick right onto Brannan. Why didn't I ask myself the opposite questions? Namely, was it okay to need him? Was it okay to want to be with him? Could I maintain my individuality and keep my friendships flourishing with Derek in my life?

I pulled into my parking garage, parked the car, and sat for a time alone in the silence. And after a while, the answer came to me like a voice from a cloud. "It's all okay. You can need Derek, and want him, and miss him, and cherish him. And you can do the same with your friends. It's not an either/or proposition. It's both. It's the fullness of life. Enjoy it. Don't make such a big deal about it."

I glanced around, wondering where that voice came from, and felt silly. Because it had come from within me, of course. My smile grew slowly as I realized how much that voice sounded like my father, the original laid-back dude.

"Thanks, Dad," I whispered, and went upstairs to find Alex.

CHAPTER THIRTEEN

"Knock, knock," I called through the narrow open door. "Are you alone?" I wasn't about to walk into Alex's apartment uninvited. I'd learned my lesson the first time I walked inside and found a naked man sitting on her couch, his hands cuffed behind his back and a piece of tape over his mouth. Luckily, when I asked him if he needed me to call the police, he wiggled his eyebrows and made it clear that he was doing just fine and I shouldn't worry. So yeah, I didn't need to see that again. Especially if the naked guy happened to be Gabriel this time.

Oh dear.

"Hi," Alex called from somewhere behind me. I whipped around and watched her approach from down the hall.

"You startled me," I said, patting my heart. "I wasn't expecting you to come from that direction." It didn't help that I had been in the middle of visualizing a naked

Gabriel at the very moment she called out. No wonder I was jumpy.

"Sorry if I startled you. I just ran down to pick up the mail and left the door open."

"I'm so glad you're home," I said. "I thought I'd take a chance and stop by to say hello."

"I'm happy you did. Come on in."

She pushed the door open and led the way inside. The first thing that hit me was the intoxicating aroma of freshly baked cupcakes.

"I had a frustrating meeting with a client this morning," she explained as she reached down to remove her four-inch heels. "So I came home early and started baking."

"Can I have this client's name so I can call and thank him?"

She laughed, then sobered as she studied my demeanor. "What's wrong?"

I blinked. "Nothing. What do you mean?"

"Come on, let's sit at the kitchen counter." She pushed a tall stool toward me and I sat and watched her putter around the kitchen, fixing two cups of coffee and arranging two small plates with forks and napkins on the counter. "Do you want red velvet or mint chocolate?"

I moaned. "I just had a big lunch and dessert."

"Are you serious? You're not going to have a cupcake?"

"Give me ten minutes to digest the meal. Then I think I'll go for the chocolate mint."

"That's more like it." She grinned as she added cream to the coffee. "So, what's up? Don't pretend there's not something wrong. I know you."

"There's nothing really wrong. Well, except for the usual."

"The usual? You mean, dead bodies, suspect lists, police investigations? Is that what you're talking about?"

"Yeah." I grimaced. "Unfortunately, all of that really is becoming 'the usual.' "

"I'm sorry, Brooks." She patted my shoulder before sitting down with her coffee cup and a delicately frosted red velvet cupcake.

"Derek's spending the night in Los Angeles," I said, and immediately wondered why I'd said it.

"Are you lonely?"

"No. Well, not really. Oh brother." I pushed hair back from my face and tried to relax. "Okay, yes, I miss him, but am I lonely? I've never been lonely before, so why would I be lonely now?"

"Because you've gotten used to having him around."

"Yeah. I had a long talk with myself on

the way home just now, about whether I've turned into a complete wimp and given up all my girlfriends now that I'm living with a guy."

"It's the age-old dilemma," she said. "Lots of women lose touch with their girlfriends because our identities become tied to the men in our lives."

I smiled. "My mom used to talk about her women's studies classes in college where they actually tried to teach female empowerment. This was in the sixties when it was still a man's world. That's when things started changing for a lot of women. More of us went to college and joined the workforce. We had more choices, more control."

"True."

I frowned. "Now it feels like some of that forward movement is regressing, you know?"

"I sure do." She took a sip of coffee. "I had to deal with this client today who has a really low opinion of women. He excused his attitude by calling himself 'old-school.' Like that suddenly gave him carte blanche to slap my secretary's rear end and later try to corner her outside the ladies' room."

"You're joking."

"I'm not. The guy is thirty-two years old.

He's not 'old-school.' He's just an entitled jerk."

"What did you do?"

"I grabbed him by the collar and shoved him into a wall." She sighed. "It was wrong, but it felt so right."

"I love you so much," I said, laughing. "Did he fire you?"

"No. His smarter, more enlightened partner dragged him out of there and called me later to apologize."

"Good," I said, righteously indignant on her behalf. "He's got to realize you could slap a harassment lawsuit on his partner that would make his head spin."

"Oh, he does. I told him I wouldn't be working with his partner again and he understood." She got up and poured herself another half cup of coffee and poured one for me, too. When she returned to sit down, she gazed at me. "So, aren't you dying to ask about me and Gabriel?"

I gulped. "I don't know what you're talking about."

"You're funny," she said, laughing.

I hesitated for another half second and then blurted, "All right, fine. What the heck is going on? You told me you prefer submissive men, and Gabriel is about as submissive as a barracuda. In a good way, I mean.

The only man more alpha than Gabriel is Derek. So what gives?"

She smiled and gave a soft shrug. "I guess he wore me down. He kept insisting that we were right for each other and I fought him for weeks and weeks. But then . . . what can I say? He's incredible. Intuitive. Gentle. Sexy. And yet completely in charge when he wants to be. He just doesn't care about power trips and egos. He's so different. And it's amazing how much we have in common. Sometimes we spend half the night just talking."

She could've been describing Derek, I thought. And halfway through her description I realized there was something else going on here. "You're in love with him."

Her eyes widened and she waved her hands in protest. "No, no, no. Let's not jump right to the *L* word. I'm still working my way through all this unfamiliar territory."

"Okay." I jumped up and gave her a fierce hug. "But something tells me you're already there."

Back home an hour later, the phone buzzed several times, meaning there was someone at the door downstairs. Wary, I picked up the phone. "Hello?"

"Hey, it's me, Janice, um, Inspector Lee. Can I come up?"

"Absolutely," I said, and buzzed her into the lobby. Her visit was completely unexpected, even though I had left a message for her the day before, letting her know that her mother's book was ready.

I heard the freight elevator groaning its way to the top floor, and a few minutes later, Inspector Lee — Janice — knocked on the door.

"Hi," I said, ushering her into the house. "Do you want a glass of wine?"

"No, I've still got to drive home."

I walked into the kitchen. "How about a cupcake?"

She stopped in her tracks. "You have cupcakes?"

I pushed the platter toward her. "Alex baked them. She is the cupcake goddess. You need to try one."

"You're right. I do." She stared at the platter Alex had lent me to hold the six beautiful cupcakes she had insisted I take home.

"There's red velvet and chocolate mint. Here's a plate and a fork. Sit down while I get your book."

"These are gorgeous," she said, following my orders to sit and eat.

A minute later, I returned with the book

to find her mouth full of chocolate. "Good, huh?"

She had to wait to finish the bite. "Holy sugar rush. Those are amazing."

I sat across from her and took a sip of my wine. "She is the best neighbor ever."

Lee laughed. After she had polished off the cupcake, I took her fork and plate and set them in the sink.

"You don't have to wait on me, Brooklyn."

I looked at her for a long moment. "Can I call you Janice?"

She almost flinched, she was so surprised by the question. "Of course. Don't you call me that anyway?"

"I don't think I've ever called you by your first name. Maybe once, but it didn't stick."

"Yeah, well, we do tend to meet under unusual circumstances."

I nodded. "Crime scenes, you mean."

"Yeah." She shrugged. "Not real conducive to developing friendships."

"Well, next time we have a party, you're invited. So that means we're friends."

She gave me a lopsided grin. "Okay, it's a deal."

I slid the package across the counter. "Here's the book. If you want me to change anything, just say so."

"Cool." She unwrapped the thick white paper I'd used to protect it and pulled out the book box. "Wow, that's beautiful."

"I told you about the papers Derek brought back from Hong Kong. I wanted something with an Asian feel to it. Because of the nature of the book. I hope you like it."

"I'm blown away," she said, studying the box from every angle. "It's really gorgeous. This plaque looks perfect."

"I thought so, too. Well, open it."

"I'm almost afraid," she muttered, but unlatched the hook and lifted the top. "Oh wow." She carefully brought the book out and set it on the table. After a moment, she opened the cover and glanced through the pages. "You're right. The crayon mess doesn't look half as bad as I remember. And I can't tell which pages I tore out."

"Good. Hopefully, your mother won't be able to tell, either."

"Man, I knew you were good at this stuff, but this is really exceptional." She lifted the book and placed it gently back inside the box. "I appreciate this, Brooklyn. I think my mom is going to love it."

"That's all that matters." I couldn't help beaming as I took the box and wrapped it up again in the white paper. Inspector Lee

— *Janice* — had no clue how much her words meant to me and how happy I was that we were finally friends.

The next morning I woke up bright and early. I glanced around, slightly disoriented, and then realized why. Derek wasn't home and I'd slept straight through the night anyway.

Charlie leaned against me and purred, so I stroked her soft fur. "Good morning, Charlie."

After a few minutes with Charlie, I climbed out of bed, giving myself a mental "Attaboy." So much for all my worries and whining that I'd be so lonely without Derek that I wouldn't be able to sleep. Of course, I woke up on Derek's side of the bed as if I were draped across his gorgeous chest . . . but that didn't mean anything.

"Crazy girl," I muttered on my way to turning on the coffeepot. I glanced with fondness at the tray of the four beautiful cupcakes that were left after Janice — it felt so weird to call her that — and I had one each last night. It was great to have good neighbors, especially ones who baked.

I was glad to be getting an early start on my work today. My main goal was to finish *Songbirds in Trees* and move on to the next project. If my plan was successful, I would be able to clean up the book and make any other small repairs necessary. By the end of the day, I wanted to be able to drive over to the Bird-watchers Society and return their missing treasure to them. I had a feeling they would be happy to see the beautiful book back where it belonged, in its display case. Even if they had no idea what had happened to the poor book in the first place.

I had to admit, though, that the thought of facing the unpleasant Marva Pesca was not a cheery one.

Nevertheless, after coffee and a breakfast of granola, bananas, strawberries, and a cupcake, followed by a quick phone call from Derek, I cleaned up the kitchen and headed out to my workshop to get the ball rolling.

I approached my book press with some trepidation. I was pretty sure I'd gotten all the dampness out of the book, and the card stock would help absorb the rest of it. But what if the pages were still wrinkled? What if they were now stuck to the card stock? What if the press had screwed up somehow? It happened once in a while; the press would tug at one end and the book would end up bent or catawampus. Or one page would get tweaked and end up torn or otherwise damaged.

I'd given the book two days to straighten itself up. All I could do now was examine it and hope that my idea had worked out. I slowly unscrewed the wheel and pulled the book out from under the heavy wooden press. I'd also used two thin five-pound brass-plated book weights to ensure that even pressure was applied to the entire book.

I unwrapped the book and stared at it. And let go of the breath I didn't realize I was holding. I turned the book over a few times and held it up to study the spine. It looked good. Straight and even. I carefully opened the book and skipped through the pages, removing the sheets of card stock as I went. Nothing was stuck, everything was flat. It was beautiful. I was overjoyed.

"This one's for you, Jared," I said aloud. "You oddball bird-watcher, you."

With a quiet laugh, I thought of Socrates McCall and Marva Pesca and the others I'd met last week at Jared's memorial celebration. There was an entire roomful of oddball bird-watchers, come to think of it. I hoped they would all be very happy with their pretty new book.

But could one of those strange *birdfellows* be a cold-blooded killer? I set that thought

360

aside for now, with a mental note to remind Derek that we needed to revisit that group.

With the pages repaired, I took the time to examine the book more closely. I remembered thinking it was a sweet little book the night Jared gave it to me at the Covington, although looking at it now, I saw it was slightly bigger than I'd originally estimated. Just to be certain, and to be completely obsessive about it, I pulled out my measuring tape to double-check. It was just over eight inches tall, five inches wide, and an inch and a quarter thick. Still sweet, but not quite as little as I'd originally thought.

Setting the tape measure aside, I examined the book further. The brown morocco leather was rich and lustrous. The book itself was well made and now even more structurally sound, thanks to two days in the book press. I opened the book to check all those items I always made a habit of inspecting. Copyright date, country of publication, author name, any dedications, possible author signatures, odd watermarks in the paper. And of course, illustrations, lithographs, woodcuts, or other artwork that might add to the value of the book. In this case, the artwork was all there was, the book's raison d'être. And the illustrations were glorious.

Audubon truly was a talented artist, I thought, as I paged through the small book. I had gotten close enough to the big Audubon book to wonder how an artist could actually capture the emotion an animal was feeling in that frozen moment.

Did I dare say the paintings in this book were even more amazing? The colors were more vibrant, the animals more alive, if that was possible. The branches of the trees were made with more delicate brushstrokes than I'd noticed in the paintings of the larger book. I pulled out my powerful magnifying glass to study them more closely.

A snowy owl looked so real I could've counted the individual feathers in its wings. So soft I was tempted to stroke the downy fluff beneath its outer plumage.

A gorgeous yellow-tailed bird studied a purple flower bud with such deliberate concentration he might've been preparing to write a thesis on its exquisite form. It was uncanny. Even a small worm crawling toward the tip of the thin branch had enough detail to almost make me think it was alive.

A family of brightly colored parrots appeared so realistic I wouldn't have been shocked to hear them start squawking and talking. They perched on slender green bamboo leaves that shimmered in the background.

Maybe it was the fact that Mr. Audubon was creating on a smaller canvas that made these illustrations seem so much more delicate. Maybe he had to use different brushes or give more attention to finer details than with the larger paintings.

It took a few more minutes, but I managed to pull myself out of the book. It would be easy to spend hours studying the illustrations. No wonder Audubon had won international acclaim.

Since reading all about him at the Covington exhibit, I knew Audubon had been a prodigious writer as well as an artist. His journals were studied alongside his illustrations.

He wrote about his travels, his journeys with the Shawnee and Osage Indian tribes, frightening earthquakes, floods, and wars. He went bankrupt and was thrown in jail. He had successes and setbacks; he discovered two hundred of his drawings were eaten by rats. He traveled back and forth from Europe to the United States even though he was prone to seasickness and his ship was once attacked by pirates.

The large Audubon book on display at the Covington had an extended introduction and biography included in the front of the book. Each plate identified the bird or animal shown. Occasionally, it included the Latin name. So for instance, the purple gallinule was also identified as *Gallinula martinica,* more commonly known as the purple swamp hen.

But this small illustrated book had no writing in it. No introduction by Audubon, no foreword written by another artist or ornithologist, not even a short biography. And no names identifying the birds themselves. It was all artwork, and it was wonderful, but where were the attributions?

I had the strongest urge to go to the Covington to do more research. I also wanted to compare this smaller edition's painting style with the large elephant folio on display. Even though Jared hadn't asked me to appraise the book, I wanted to know more about it before I returned it to the National Bird-watchers Society headquarters.

I checked the time. It was only one o'clock. And since Derek wouldn't be home until later that evening, I decided to go for it.

An hour later, I was standing in the main hall of the Covington. I only had to wait a few minutes before I was able to use the interactive computer set up next to the large

Audubon display, on which you could call up a photograph of any page. Along with the paintings, you'd find Audubon's notes on the animal and cross-reference to when and where he had drawn the pictures. I was just about to pull the smaller *Songbirds* book from my satchel when I heard a voice behind me.

"Well, look who's here."

I whipped around and came face-to-face with Crane's brother. "Bai, what a surprise. What are you doing here?"

He looked uncomfortable despite the grin. "Didn't Crane tell you this is my new hang-out?"

"He mentioned that you were doing some work here. And if you've got to have a hangout, what could be better than the Covington?"

He frowned. "I'm not sure my brother would approve of that theory."

"Oh, sure, he would," I said genially. "It keeps us off the streets, right?"

My remark startled a laugh out of him. "Yeah, I guess so."

"And since I make my living with books, this is my natural habitat, so to speak."

"At least you have a reason to be here," he grumbled. "He wouldn't say the same for me."

"I can't believe that," I said with a smile, trying to keep the conversation casual. But I was dying to ask him why he was in such a crabby mood. "Crane says you're one of the best artists in China, and since this building is filled with wonderful artwork as well as books, I can't imagine him disapproving."

He looked taken aback but recovered quickly. "Thank you." He gave a slight bow. "You are as wise as you are beautiful."

I raised my eyebrows. "And you are full of it, but thank you just the same."

That surprised another laugh out of him, but he instantly sobered. "I know you feel close to Crane because of your relationship with Derek, but please accept this friendly warning."

Wary, I took a step back. "What is it?"

"Crane is not the paragon you think he is. You shouldn't believe everything he tells you about me."

I tried to appear clueless. "What do you mean? He told us about your incredible talent, but other than that, he's only mentioned that your mother is anxious to have you return to China."

"Yes, she is," he said darkly. "But only because Crane frightens her. I have always been a buffer between the two of them."

I started to question him, but he jerked abruptly. Pulling his cell phone from his pocket, he murmured, "Sorry. I've got it on vibrate, so it's always a shock when it goes off."

"I know what you mean."

Wearing a fierce scowl, he walked away, whispering into his phone.

As I watched him go, I had to admit that I was still confused by him. He couldn't be serious about Crane, could he? True, I didn't know Crane very well, but Derek did, and I trusted his opinion beyond anyone else's. This had to be another case of Bai trying to undermine his brother and maybe even turn me against him.

So nothing had changed. Bai was still poised to fight Crane every step of the way. I wondered if he understood his own brother's feelings at all, or if he was similar to a few other cosseted younger siblings I'd known, whose worlds seemed to revolve around themselves. They rarely took the time to consider anyone else's feelings and were surprised when you pointed out the obvious to them.

Now that I knew Crane a little better, I had serious doubts that he would criticize Bai for hanging out at the Covington. At least, under normal circumstances. But in this case, Crane was clearly afraid that his brother would wreak havoc if he found out that Sheng's artwork had been mingled with the Audubon paintings.

As Bai disappeared down the hall, I happened to glance up. A woman dressed entirely in black stood alone near the wrought-iron railing of the third-floor balcony. She caught and held my gaze for two seconds, then whipped around and vanished down one of the narrow aisles of books.

I didn't recognize her, so I shrugged and returned to the interactive computer screen. Reaching for the *Songbirds* book, I enjoyed myself for a while, comparing and contrasting the illustrations in the two disparate Audubon books, looking up particular birds and judging which was prettier or more interesting. Not that I was any judge, but I was having fun.

After a while, I realized that a line had begun to form behind me. I sighed and slid the smaller volume of *Songbirds in Trees* back into my satchel.

"Sorry," I murmured to the next person in line as I moved away from the exhibit. I wasn't really sorry, though. I'd been having a blast. Call me a nerd, but I couldn't believe how lucky I was to be able to play with books and artwork all day. I had to be one of the most fortunate people in the world. Or at least one of the top ten.

I spent another hour meandering through the other Covington galleries before I finally walked back to my car. As I drove home, I thought about stopping off at the Bird-watchers Society headquarters and leaving the book with them. But to be honest, I wasn't ready to part with it. Since they didn't know I had it anyway, it wouldn't be a problem if I were to hold on to it for another day or two. Besides, I wanted to show it to Derek. He'd be able to appreci-ate the beautiful drawings as well as the elegant book itself.

I stopped at the market on the way home to pick up some essentials. I was parked at the end of the row, and as I fumbled with a full bag of groceries and my car keys, I noticed a blacked-out BMW sedan revving its engine and pulling out of its parking space one aisle over. It headed toward the store, going way too fast for safety.

"Jerk," I muttered, and dropped my keys. There was something sinister about auto-mobiles with blacked-out windows. I didn't like it and wondered why it wasn't against the law.

"It should be," I grumbled, reaching down to grab my keys. I heard the car's tires screeching around the corner of the next aisle on the other side of mine. I stood up and saw the black car whizzing along toward the exit. But instead it swerved into the perimeter aisle where I was parked. It was going too fast — and it was headed straight toward me!

Without another thought, I dashed around to the front of my car. The BMW shrieked past me and kept going.

"What the —"

The car veered out of the parking lot and disappeared around the corner. I had to set my shopping bag down on the ground and lean against the front of my car to catch my breath.

That driver would've hit me if I hadn't moved. There was no doubt in my mind. Now I had to figure out if it was simply some jerk out for a joyride, or if I had just been the target of a killer's rage.

"Did you get the license number?" Inspector Lee asked.

I had to think. It wasn't easy. But I closed my eyes and pictured the car and remembered that detail. "There was no license plate in front," I said tightly. "They must've removed it. I was too rattled to see if there was one in back. So, no, I didn't get a number. But I can describe the car."

"Go ahead," she said, flipping her small notepad open and waiting with her pen.

"Black BMW, blacked-out windows, medium-sized. Not the sporty one and not the great big one."

"Maybe a five series?"

"Maybe. It looked almost new." I shook my head in disgust. "Sorry. Not much of a description."

"That's okay. Was the front windshield tinted?"

"Yes. How did you know? I couldn't see who was driving as they came straight at me." I scowled. "That should be against the law, by the way."

"It is," Lee said. "I'll call it in and maybe we'll get lucky."

"So why do people tint their windows if it's against the law?"

"Because people are stupid."

I snorted a laugh. "No kidding."

"It's just the front windows that matter," she explained. "And auto shops are well aware of the law. If we pull a driver over, we'll give him a ticket and we'll ask where he got it done. Then we slap a fine on the company who did it."

"Good."

She scrutinized me. "You gonna be okay?"

Sure, I thought. Except for wanting to cry. "Yeah, I'm okay. I was just shaken up. And I'm mad. But I'll get over it."

"Mad is good," she said firmly. "Mad will keep you alive. Hold on to that feeling. And go straight home and stay there."

"I will. Thanks for coming out. I wouldn't have called you, but I thought, well . . ."

"I know what you thought, Brooklyn, and you did the right thing. Call me if you remember anything else."

Derek got home later that night and I was pretty sure I'd never been happier to see him. Then again, I was always happy to see him.

We had a casual meal of pasta with chunky marinara sauce lightly covered in fresh Parmigiano Reggiano, and a salad. Derek poured us glasses of an earthy yet elegant Brunello di Montalcino and after dinner we sat at the table talking for a full hour.

He was furious when I told him about the parking lot incident. But since I couldn't say for sure if I was the actual target or if I had just been in the way of some feckless stranger showing off for his girlfriend, there wasn't much we could do. But he was glad

372

to hear that I had contacted Inspector Lee, just to be safe.

"Oh, I ran into Bai at the Covington Library earlier today," I said, and related the conversation to Derek. "I wonder, is he negative in general or is he simply jealous of Crane?"

"Both. I've known Bai for years," Derek said, a pensive frown marring his forehead. "And I've been willing to play along when Crane said he thought Bai had changed for the better. But he hasn't changed. I remember back in school, he would alter his entire personality when it suited him, saying all the right things to the right people. But his underlying essence has always been quite negative. It may sound harsh, but I think he may be a borderline sociopath."

It was surprising how many sociopaths we'd come into contact with recently and I wondered if we were tossing that word around too freely. All I really knew about Bai was that he seemed extremely insecure and narcissistic at the same time. He was manipulative and his sense of entitlement was off the charts. I thought again about my conversation at lunch the day before. "I worry about Crane."

"I do, too," he said, still brooding. "Did he tell you about the nickname Bai came up with in school?"

"No. What's that all about?"

He shook his head at the recollection. "When Bai found out that Crane had a rather cool nickname, he began telling everyone that he had a nickname, too."

"Just like Crane. Hmm. So what was Bai's nickname?"

"It's *Què*." Derek pronounced it "Cheh." "Crane told me his mother really did give Bai that nickname. The problem was, Bai told everyone at school that the word meant 'eagle' in Chinese, and he wanted them all to call him Eagle from that moment on."

"I'm almost afraid to ask what happened."

"First of all, nobody would call him Eagle. It just doesn't suit him."

"No, it really doesn't."

"And when Crane got wind of it, he nearly laughed his head off."

"Why?"

"Because *Què* in Chinese actually means 'magpie.' "

"Magpie. The bird?" I tried not to snicker, but it was hard. "Magpie is kind of a silly nickname."

"Only in our culture," he said. "In Chinese culture, the magpie is honored for all the joy it brings. It symbolizes happiness and luck. When a magpie nests on your property, it's supposed to attract marriage and children. It can also attract money. It has other meanings as well, and they're all quite joyful."

"So his mother's nickname for him was a wonderful bird, too," I said. "It just doesn't translate quite as well in English as Crane does."

"No, not at all." Derek smiled. "I remember Crane tormented him by calling him Magpie in public. Bai honestly looked as though he wanted to kill him."

I gazed at Derek and repeated myself. "I worry about Crane."

"I do, too, but I know he'll be fine." After a few seconds, he tried for a lighter tone. "You had a good time at lunch?"

"A wonderful time," I said. "But I'm really concerned about his brother's obsession with the Audubon exhibit at the Covington."

"Yes. Crane said that Bai calls it the Audubon shame."

"That's ridiculous."

Derek gave a brusque wave of his hand. "Yes. But this is what I'm talking about. Bai's always been this way, stirring up trouble where he thinks he can get something out of it."

I rubbed my stomach. "That's how I felt

when he told me about their mother being afraid of Crane."

"I hate hearing that," Derek said, clenching his teeth. "That's exactly what I'm talking about. That's why I still don't trust him. I have great affection for Crane, but he has a blind spot toward his brother. I wish I could convince him that Bai has not changed for the better."

"If nothing else," I said, "Bai is hurting his family, especially Crane."

"Hurting Crane was always Bai's greatest joy," Derek said.

"But why?"

He shrugged. "For being born first."

I couldn't understand it and wondered if it had to do with cultural differences again. "It's such a waste of emotion. Crane can hardly help being born first."

"No, of course not, but there you go. He was also jealous that Crane was born in Hong Kong and has dual citizenship."

"How did he get dual citizenship?"

"It's because his mother is half English and has dual citizenship herself. So since Crane was born in Hong Kong, she was able to obtain the same for him. But Bai was born in China, so he received no special treatment."

"What does it matter, though?" I wondered. "He has money. He can still travel all he wants."

"He wants whatever Crane has."

I had to pause and let that sink in. "That's just sad. So Crane has prestige and friends and respect at all levels of society and —"

"And Bai doesn't want to work for it or earn it, as Crane has done. He wants the shortcut. He's constantly trying to get it by causing trouble. That way he gets attention, which in his mind translates to a twisted sort of prestige."

Derek poured a touch more wine in each of our glasses, and I took a small sip. "I'm surprised to hear how you feel about him because you've never said a word to Crane about anything you just told me."

Derek shook his head. "It would hurt him too much."

I reached out and squeezed his hand. "You're a good friend."

He sighed. "I just think the sooner Crane can get his brother back to China, the better off things will be for him."

I wasn't so sure Crane would be able to convince Bai to go, especially after our conversation at lunch yesterday. "I'm a little worried about Ian, too. What will he do if Bai stirs up controversy over this imagined insult to his ancestor's honor?"

"Ian can handle it, don't you think?"

I smiled. "Ian does love publicity, even if it's scandalous. But I just can't see Bai's endgame." I fiddled with the stem of my glass, working out the theory. "To be fair, the story could be true. James Audubon could've used Sheng's talent to his own benefit. I imagine it used to happen all the time."

"Of course it did."

"And I wouldn't blame the family for wanting Sheng to get his due credit. But then, why not write an article for a journal or something? Why is Bai interested in attacking the Covington?"

"Because by hurling ugly accusations at a revered institution, he'll get more attention."

I exhaled in frustration. "But it all happened such a long time ago. I mean, it was two hundred years ago, and it was in England. How can Bai truly prove anything? What does he hope to accomplish?"

"We've been over this before," he said. "He wants to create havoc. It's what he's good at. It's what he did at Eton and he's never stopped."

"So a leopard doesn't change his spots?"

He smiled. "I know it's a cliché, but in this case, the old saying still applies."

Which only made me worry more for Crane.

Derek and I spent a domestic weekend together, just the two of us, cleaning and doing other chores around the house. There were errands to run and Derek insisted that he do them himself rather than have me expose myself to some homicidal maniac bent on running me over.

Happily, I was able to convince him that I would be safe inside a huge furniture warehouse store as long as he was there to protect me. The place was miles outside the city, so we took a nice drive and then shopped for furniture for our new rooms.

Since we'd already furnished the bedroom my parents had stayed in, we decided to set up the second new bedroom as a sitting room with bookshelves and a comfortable couch and chairs. The couch would pull out to a bed in case we needed the extra sleeping space.

Derek and I chatted and laughed all the way home over our new domestic-bliss lifestyle. Somewhere near Walnut Creek, Derek noticed a black BMW following us. When he sped up, the other car did the same. This continued for several long miles until the BMW took the Berkeley off-ramp and disappeared.

"False alarm," he muttered, but the incident reminded us that we needed to be vigilant at all times.

Despite that momentary dark cloud, we both admitted we were having fun and we vowed to spend at least one day a week doing all those little things that made life worth living.

And I further vowed to hire a cleaning service, because as far as I was concerned, *that* was a major key to making life worth living.

Monday, Derek went back to work and so did I. I had plenty of books to work on, but I wanted to make one more pass over *Songbirds in Trees.* Something had been niggling at my brain over the weekend. Something I'd barely noticed at the Covington on Friday. Now I needed to double-check my facts.

I wasn't happy that it was Bai who had caused me to reexamine something I normally would have taken into consideration from the very first time I looked at the book. But these weren't normal circumstances.

I paged through the beginning of the book and found the copyright page. There was no author attribution, which was unusual.

There was a publisher, of course, although I'd never heard of it. Under the publisher's name was the city of publication, Edinburgh, Scotland. And there was a copyright date of 1857. I wondered how many copies had been published at that time.

Ordinarily, one of the first things I would do was check the copyright page of any book I was working on. But with *Songbirds in Trees,* I had just assumed it was an Audubon book because Jared Mulrooney had said so. Also, the damage to the interior of the book had been so extensive that I'd been hesitant to open it until I actually started working on it. Even then, I hadn't glanced to see when the book was published. I accepted full blame for the oversight, although I did concede that I'd had way too many distractions lately.

But staring at the date made me wonder if the book might be much more valuable than I'd originally thought. Yes, supposedly it had been illustrated by Audubon — according to Jared — but I still hadn't considered it to be particularly rare because Jared had also mentioned that it only had sentimental value to the National Bird-watchers Society members.

With no author credit listed, why had Jared Mulrooney attributed this book to

Audubon? Had the bookseller told him so? Or had Jared researched the book's provenance?

I did a quick search on the computer and found out that Audubon died six years before the publication date. That didn't mean anything in particular, of course. His sons or his publisher might have been responsible for having the book assembled and published. But I could find no record of this particular book being a part of the Audubon bibliography. In fact, I could find no record of this book anywhere. None of my rare-book sites had it listed in their inventory. That fact made me wonder again how many copies had been published.

The fact that it was published in Scotland was notable because several of Audubon's paintings were first engraved in Scotland. He then went to London to work with Robert Havell, a well-known engraver who had helped produce Audubon's first publication.

I was beginning to see that Bai's theory might have some credence. Besides all the contradictory information surrounding the publication and authorship of the book, I had personally found a number of distinct differences in the painting styles of the larger Audubon book versus the smaller one in my possession.

And according to Crane, his ancestor Sheng had spent some time working in Scotland. Had he illustrated some of the birds in this smaller book? And despite his contributions, had the work still been attributed to Audubon? The problem was that I had no way of determining, beyond a shadow of a doubt, that these paintings had been done by Sheng — or anyone else, for that matter.

I needed to do more research. Were there other books or paintings that had been attributed to the Chinese artist? Would I be able to tell the difference between Sheng's work and that of James Audubon?

And if Sheng's work had been co-opted by the great Audubon, were there other painters who had suffered the same fate? And why did it matter? Hadn't they all been hired specifically to help Audubon complete his masterwork? There was no subterfuge. Was there?

And if there was, how would we find out? And what did it matter? I asked myself for the hundredth time.

Staring at the bluebird on the cover, I suddenly remembered Socrates McCall railing against Audubon in favor of his hero Alexander Wilson. I'd forgotten all about him. What if this book had been illustrated by

Wilson? And again I asked myself, what did it matter?

It mattered to me because I loved solving these kinds of wonderful bookish mysteries. There was always a chance that these vague threads of stories and details might lead to a bigger story with a grand solution.

Or maybe not. But I was having fun.

I chuckled as I packed up my satchel, locked up the house, and drove off to the Covington.

I went straight to Ian's office, and his charming and efficient assistant, Wylie, told me to go right in.

"I need your help," I said, as I crossed his large, luxurious, art-filled office.

Ian stood and bowed. "I'm here to serve."

I chuckled at his sarcasm. "I'd like to study the Audubon book up close. It won't take long. Can you close down the exhibit for a little while?"

He snorted. "You're such a diva. What's this all about?"

I recognized the irony of my request, given that I'd criticized Bai for thinking he could pull off the same thing. I reached into my satchel for *Songbirds in Trees* and showed it to him. "This is supposedly attributed to Audubon, but his name doesn't appear anywhere in the book. I have no idea if he painted these birds or not."

He studied the book cover from all angles. "This is sweet."

"This is the one Jared Mulrooney gave me the night he died."

"Oh, yeah." He opened up the book and stared at the first few drawings. "I never took a good look at it beyond seeing the damage he'd done. You did an amazing job. It looks pristine."

"Thanks. I live for your praise. But look at the paintings themselves."

He took a good look at several of them. "They do look different than Audubon's."

"I think so, too. It might just be the smaller canvas. Or a different type of paper that holds the color better."

He held the book up to the light. "It's not a different paper," he murmured.

"How can you tell?"

"It has the Havell watermark." He set the book down and looked at me. "Havell was the engraver of the artwork."

"I know. I was just reading about him." I grabbed the book and held it to the light, as Ian had done. I could barely make out the watermark. "I noticed the watermark but couldn't make out what it said."

"You'll notice it doesn't occur on every

page," Ian said. "And I'll tell you why."

"I'm all ears." I was always ready to learn more about books.

He grinned. "Audubon sold his *Birds of America* paintings by subscription. One hundred and seventy-five subscribers paid to receive his work in lots of five over the course of a decade. All of the engravings were made on the same double-elephant-sized paper. By the end, each subscriber would've collected over four hundred of these amazing paintings. And Havell, the engraver, was responsible for transferring the original prints to hand-colored copperplate engravings that were created in his London studio."

"So where do you think this little book fits into the story?"

"Here's my theory," Ian said. "The double-elephant folio paper had Havell's watermark on it to guarantee to their subscribers that they were receiving original limited-edition Audubon works."

"Right."

"But for this smaller book, I'm going to speculate that the paper was cut down and given to the artists to create whatever they wanted. And when the book pages were sewn together, the watermark wasn't always visible on every page, but here and there in a few random spots throughout the book."

I smiled at him. "That's fascinating."

"If it's true. Who knows? But I like it."

"I do, too." I sat back in my chair. "You're a pretty smart guy."

"And devastatingly handsome as well," he said, grinning. "Look, neither of us is an expert in art provenance. As far as I know, these paintings could've been done by Audubon or anyone else. Unless we can track down an expert, it's just a guess."

"There's the rub."

"Sorry, kiddo." He picked up the book again. "It's possible that this is a collection of paintings — or aquatints, really, since they're engraved from the paintings — that Havell thought was worth turning into a book. Who can say?"

"But this book was published in Scotland. Havell was in London."

"But he had to have had control over the project because it's his paper and his watermark and his copperplate engravings. And as an illustrious engraver, he probably had contacts in Edinburgh. And yet truly we know nothing more than we knew an hour ago."

"So I'm essentially back where I started."

"You know about the watermark now. So maybe we can find something else that will indicate who the artist is."

"I wonder if there's anything in your art book collection that would help."

"Our art department is huge, but I'm not sure you'll find examples of an obscure Chinese artist from the early Victorian era."

Dejected, I put my elbow on his desk and cradled my chin in my hand. "I would love to be able to give this book to Crane as a definitive collection of his ancestor's works. But it's not mine to give."

"You know, we have someone in residence, temporarily, who's working on Chinese artists from that era."

"You do?"

"His name is Sheng Bai."

I folded my arms on the desk and buried my head. "Oh God."

"What's wrong?"

"That's the guy I was telling you about. The brother of Derek's friend, the one who's looking to cause some turmoil around here."

He let out a dramatic sigh. "Are you sure? He seems like a nice guy. And his girlfriend's a beauty."

"You've met her?"

"I've seen them together a few times."

"So what does she look like?"

"Gorgeous," Ian said. "Asian. Supermodel type."

"Must be nice to be Bai," I murmured. It didn't sound to me as though Bai had much to be jealous of Crane about, despite what Derek had said.

"They make a very attractive couple."

"Yeah, Bai's pretty cute. But his brother, Crane, is even better-looking."

"Really?" Ian grinned. "In that case, I'd love to meet him."

I had to laugh. "Sorry, sweetie, but he doesn't play for your team."

"A boy can dream."

"Now that I think about it, you might've seen him here on opening night. I would've introduced you if you'd been free for a minute."

"Okay, wow, I just remembered something. I'll assume Crane is Chinese, right?"

"Yes."

"In that case, I think I did see him that night. But there's something else."

"What?"

Looking perplexed, Ian rubbed his forehead. "I was so frazzled at the opening, I completely forgot to mention this to you. But Bai asked about you and Derek that night."

"Bai? Okay, that's weird."

"Yeah. We were talking, and he pointed to you two and asked who you were. He thought you might be friends with his brother."

"We *are* friends. We were with Crane that night. Didn't you see him?"

"Like I said, I was frazzled."

"You're never frazzled."

He frowned more deeply. "I know. But you're right. I saw a good-looking Chinese man with you."

"Which means Bai saw us, too."

"Yes."

So Bai had seen us all at the event, but Crane hadn't seen him. Had Bai been avoiding his brother that night? Had he already begun his "Audubon Shame" plot to cause trouble for Ian and the Covington?

A big shuddering shiver rolled down my spine and caused the hair on my arms to stand on end. If Bai was there that night, was he looking for this copy of *Songbirds in Trees*? Had he met Jared Mulrooney?

Had he *killed* Jared?

I shook my head, wondering when I'd become so overly dramatic. Bai might have been a pain in the butt to his brother and even to Derek, but that didn't make him a murderer. How would he even have known about this obscure little book, and what possible connection could it have to his ancestor? There was no attribution, either way. I was getting ahead of myself.

"Speaking of Bai," I said, "I need to tell you something." I related everything I'd heard about the "Audubon Shame" scheme to Ian. As I predicted, Ian accepted the news with interest but not much trepidation. He repeated his belief that both good and bad publicity worked in his favor.

I was no closer to answering the questions surrounding *Songbirds in Trees* than I had been before, but it was fun talking to Ian about it. As always, he had a million vague facts and possibilities to ponder. But I still didn't know if we would ever be able to attribute the book to Sheng.

Nevertheless, to my delight, Ian allowed the Audubon exhibit to be closed down to give me a chance to look at the opening pages of the big double-elephant-folio book. One of the curators pulled the book from the large glass case and took it into the back room, where a wide utility table was set up for that very purpose. Placing the book unopened on the table, he handed me a pair of flimsy white cotton gloves.

"Please wear these."

"Sure." I pulled the gloves on and opened the book. I had to stand up to do so because the pages were too big to turn while sitting down.

It was a rare honor to examine the Audubon masterpiece up close. Each page was more illuminating than the previous one. "You guys have the best job in the world," I said, smiling at the curator.

"It doesn't get much better than this," he said, nodding.

I stared at the next page, of a large wild turkey traipsing over leaves and twigs. His feathers were vibrant and I could see almost every color represented in his wings.

"What's this?" I asked. "Is this the artist's signature?"

The curator moved closer and squinted at the page. "Yes, that one is signed."

"Can you read it?"

After another moment of study, he said, "I assume it is Audubon's signature."

"Yes, I would assume that, too." I pulled out my portable magnifying glass. "It looks a little like John Hancock's on the Declaration of Independence, doesn't it?"

He took another look through the glass. "You're right."

I turned the page using both hands. "Oh, but look at this one. This cuckoo painting has no signature."

He shrugged. "It might've been a different day or he might've been in a hurry. And the painting itself is not done in the same style, either, is it? The turkey is painted in its habitat, and all that wonderful detail fills the entire page. This picture of the cuckoo, on the other hand, is more of a study. There's no real context. It's a bird on a branch, and it's beautiful, but there is no background to ground it in reality. So perhaps Mr. Audubon didn't want to sign it for that reason." He gave a self-deprecating shrug. "If that makes any sense."

"It does." I gave him a big smile. "Thank you."

I turned a few more pages and studied the signatures wherever I could find them, along with some other details I realized might be important. After twenty minutes, I took off my gloves and stood. "I really appreciate your time. Thank you."

I'd seen what I had to see.

CHAPTER FOURTEEN

I spent another hour in front of a computer in a tiny carrel in the Covington's basement research lab. I had been racking my brain, trying to figure out what to call my searches. I looked up "artists who paint birds" and studied a list of names from the early to mid-Victorian era. None of the artists listed appeared to paint in the same style I'd seen in the smaller book. I had the book sitting on the desk next to the computer and I glanced at it often.

"Songbirds in Trees," I murmured. "Spill your secrets." I wasn't even quite sure why I was bothering with this, but my curiosity was definitely tweaked.

"Songbirds in Trees." I stared at the title. "Trees." I stared at the computer screen and typed "Victorian artists who paint trees." At the last minute I added "Chinese."

And up popped the name Sheng Li.

I stared dumbfounded at the screen.

"Trees." I had to breathe in and out a few times because seeing his name was like taking a blow to my solar plexus. "You painted trees. Not birds. I mean, of course you painted birds, too, but your specialty was trees."

There were images of Sheng's work on the Web site I clicked onto, although the online photos of cherry blossom branches and juniper sprigs didn't do the actual paintings justice. On the same Web site, I found all sorts of legends and philosophies and fanciful writings about trees. There was a list of virtues represented by different trees. Bamboo, for instance, was a symbol of old age and modesty. The five petals of the plum tree blossom represented the five gods of good luck.

"Who knew there were five?" I muttered. Reading further, I found out that if a bamboo shoot was shown with a plum tree branch, it represented husband and wife. A pine tree symbolized longevity, steadfastness, and self-discipline. But the peach tree blossom was the most symbolic of all. It, too, represented longevity, but it was also used to keep demons at bay and its petals were helpful in casting spells on men.

There were many more examples of trees and symbols, but those were the most fascinating. And now that I was studying images of Chinese artists, something occurred to me. I pulled my magnifying glass from my portable tool set in my satchel, and after opening the *Songbirds* book, I tried to make out the tiny doodle I had been seeing on many of the pages. It was an inconspicuous squiggle, usually tagged onto the end of a branch or hidden at the edge of a bird's foot. Was it a Chinese symbol? Was it Sheng's signature? Or was it just a random scribble? The fact that it showed up on every page made me certain it had to have some meaning.

I shut down the computer and sat for a long moment, thinking about what I'd read and seen. All of it, combined with what Crane had told us about his ancestor's journey, his association with Audubon and his travels through Scotland, made me think that Sheng was almost definitely the painter of the beautiful artwork in *Songbirds in Trees.* Maybe I would never verify it beyond a shadow of a doubt, but I would bet money that it was true.

I was bummed that I couldn't go back and take another look at the big Audubon book. What if I could find more of those discreet Chinese symbols in some of the bigger paintings? It might not come to anything, but it would be totally cool if I found some. On the other hand, given the artist's humble ways, I doubted that he would be so vain as to sign the work he did on Audubon's behalf.

I packed up my tools and left the basement workroom. It wasn't until I stepped outside and saw that the sun had set that I realized how many hours I'd spent at the Covington. I'd always been prone to losing track of time when I stepped inside those doors and walked through those quiet halls. Whether I found myself upstairs in one of the cozy book carrels, studying the finer points of conservation, or downstairs in one of the dozen or so basement bookbinding studios, repairing a rare book or a medieval manuscript, I always felt like a happy little mole blinking its way to the surface when I left for the day.

I couldn't wait to get home and tell Derek what I'd found. I had called him once but had to leave a message. I was hoping he would get in touch with Crane and I could tell them together. Preferably over a nice glass of wine.

As I drove across town, I thought about the copy of *Songbirds in Trees* tucked safely away in my satchel, and wondered again about the copyright date that was years after

Audubon's death. Was it a clue, too? Was I grasping at straws again? It wasn't unusual for a book to be published posthumously by someone's disciples or his family, but still, it was another puzzle piece. Would it fit into the whole picture or would it turn out to mean nothing?

Even if my research fizzled to nothing, I couldn't wait to tell Derek about my discoveries. So, where was he? I had left him a message and I'd sent him a text. I'd asked Corinne to have him call me as soon as he was available. Maybe he was in the process of leaving town again. I hoped not.

My cell phone rang and I pressed the button on my Bluetooth to activate the call. "Hello?"

"Oh, Brooklyn, dear. I'm so glad I caught you."

"Hi, Corinne. Did you hear from Derek?"

"Not exactly. I heard from his friend Mr. Crane, who let me know that they are out at a business dinner and asked me to pass the message along to you."

"Oh." My lower lip popped out involuntarily. Pouting wasn't pretty, but sometimes it was justified. Momentarily. I sucked it in and tried to behave like a grown-up. "Thank you, Corinne. I appreciate the call."

"You're welcome, dear."

I was bummed that Crane had called instead of Derek, but I figured he must've been busy and didn't dwell on it. Except now I wouldn't be able to talk to either Derek or Crane for hours. My frustration tempted me to drive to Tasty Burger and drown my sorrows in a double cheeseburger, french fries, and a chocolate milk shake, but that would've been childish. Or would it? I faced a real dilemma while waiting for the light to change at the corner of Van Ness and Eddy, but I was more than halfway home now. I could always phone in a pizza order if I wanted to. So I continued on my way, knowing I would survive alone for a few hours, thanks to pizza. But I owed myself a burger. Really soon.

I pulled into my parking lot and was momentarily thrilled to see Derek's Bentley parked in his space next to mine. My excitement was short-lived when I figured out that Derek had probably come home and then Crane had picked him up. So it was settled: I would eat pizza and be perfectly happy. Plus a glass of wine. I wasn't about to forget the wine.

Instead of going upstairs, I walked out of the building and straight down the block to Pictro, our favorite local pizza place. While I waited, I thought more about *Songbirds in Trees.* Where had the book come from? A small bookshop in Scotland, yes, but how had it wound up there? And what odd twist of fate had brought Jared Mulrooney into that shop to start this strange, mysterious ball rolling?

And with regard to the book, what was I to make of those little wisps of signatures — if that was what they were? When I got home, I would use my high-powered microscope to study them even more closely and maybe find some answers.

"Pizza's ready, Brooklyn," Pete said, ten minutes later. "Chicken wings and salad are in this bag."

"Thanks, Pete." I grabbed the bag with the salad and wings and the pizza box and walked home. My mind was bouncing all over the place and now I was thinking about Bai and his girlfriend. What was up with them? Why were they giving Crane so much grief? Since I was crazy about my family, it was hard to understand how siblings could be so much at odds. I felt bad and wished there was something I could do to help Derek's friend.

A half block away from my building, I noticed a man standing out front waiting for someone. I didn't think anything of it, since our street was lined with apartments and shops and restaurants, and it was early evening. There were always people walking around, going from here to there. I was perfectly safe if maybe a little jittery after all the traumatic events of the past few weeks. I pulled my key from my bag as I got closer.

"Thought you were so smart, didn't you?"

I blinked, not expecting the guy to talk to me. It was hard to see his face with the night darkening, but I realized who it was. Bryce Flint. The cheating spouse who had tried to get away with larceny.

Oh boy. Nerves jangled and I gave a quick look around. Normally, our street was a bustling hive of activity. Naturally, when I needed the crowds, there was no one nearby. But I didn't want to let the man see how nervous he made me. It wasn't as if he would attack me on a city street. Would he?

"You should go home, Mr. Flint. You got caught and that's too bad, but you don't want to be here threatening me."

"Oh really? You think you know what I want? You don't know jack." He was furious, his face florid, his eyes wild. "Thanks to you, I was fined and had to spend a night in jail."

"What for?"

"Contempt of court."

I nodded, unsurprised. "You're lucky. You committed fraud, Mr. Flint. You'd be spending a lot more than one day if you were convicted. Think of it as a warning."

"I hate women who think they're so damn smart."

"And I hate cheaters who waste my time. I spent hours working on that book and it was all for nothing."

Right now I didn't care about the book. It occurred to me that Flint had either been staking out my place or actually been following me. Either way, he was a total creep and I couldn't believe he was going to all this trouble over one single book.

But then I had to remind myself, people had killed for one single book.

Flint adjusted his stance and I realized he was getting ready to attack me. My first thought was that if he made me drop my pizza, I was going to be very angry. I tried to remember some of the defense moves Alex had taught me. Last week's lesson had been on breathing and how it helped to center me in my environment, so I tried to remember to breathe.

Flint took a step toward me and I hastily set the pizza and salad bag down on the sidewalk.

"You don't want to do this," I said again,

racking my brain to remember one or two self-defense moves. Darn, it had been too many days and I had to admit I was afraid. My mind couldn't stop spinning, all wrapped up in this clown's threats. "You just walk away now and we'll forget it ever happened."

"You need to learn a lesson," he muttered.

"Which lesson would that be? That you tried to cheat your wife? You're the one who broke the law. You're the one who needs to learn a lesson."

"You women are all the same."

Nerves were gone now and irritation was winning the day. I didn't have time to deal with a liar and a cheat who was furious that he'd been caught. "If you mean we're all too smart to be cheated by you, then yes. We are."

He growled and rushed toward me. His stocky upper body carried him forward and I remembered Alex and her partners telling me to use the man's body weight against him. So I did, ducking out of the way at the last possible second. Flint went right into the wall. Stupid man.

Now he was really fired up. "You're dead," he grumbled, and tried to grab me again.

I used my elbows to counter his attack. Then I yanked his left arm and it surprised him so much he didn't fight back. I had a feeling he'd been drinking, because he was clearly stronger than I was but he wasn't reacting quickly enough. I pulled his arm as hard as I could and bent it back. His scream of outrage was immensely satisfying.

I yelled, too. Even though he was no real threat in his intoxicated state, I was afraid to try to deal with the man completely on my own. "Help! Somebody help me!"

"Hey!" Halfway down the block a guy started shouting and running toward us. "Leave her alone. Get out of here!"

Flint finally got wise and took off — as soon as I let him go.

The good guy stopped and watched my assailant racing around the corner. Then he looked at me. "Are you all right?"

"Yeah," I said, mentally surveying myself. Amazingly, Flint hadn't laid a hand on me, so I was okay. And I was looking forward to the moment when I could call both his wife's attorney and the police to report him. I wanted him in jail. And I couldn't wait to tell Alex how awesome her lessons had been and how great they'd just worked for me.

"I'm good," I said, feeling pumped up. "I really appreciate you coming along. That guy was not in the mood to listen to reason."

"Someone you know?" he asked.

"Vaguely."

"You need to call the cops."

"Believe me, I'm going to," I said. "Thanks again. Really."

The guy waited while I grabbed my pizza and salad bag and let myself into the building. Then he waved and jogged off.

I should've been scared to death, but I was frankly psyched up. I had refused to show fear and I'd actually remembered some of the lessons Alex had given me. Thankfully, Flint was a big oaf and his own lack of coordination had worked against him, but still, I had fought back and managed to make him squeal. Not much, but enough to cause a scene and attract the attention of my Good Samaritan neighbor.

"So yay, me," I said to myself, alone in the freight elevator. I felt powerful and happy to be home. I let myself into the house — and was shocked to see Crane standing in the living room.

"Crane, hi! I'm so glad to see you. But what're you doing here?" I glanced around and called, "Derek? I'm home."

Crane stumbled across the room and I started to laugh, thinking he was teasing, but then I stopped. He looked ill. "Crane? Are you all right? Where's Derek?"

Crane folded up and collapsed onto the

floor in front of me. "Crane! Oh my God!" I dropped the takeout and looked around. "Derek? Derek!"

I knelt down next to Crane, grabbed him by his jacket lapels, and tried to shake him. He groaned but didn't come to.

"Crane, wake up! Where's Derek? What happened?" I scrambled to my feet and ran back to the phone in the foyer between the living room and my workshop. I pressed the two-number speed dial that connected me to Inspector Lee. I heard her voice say, "Hello," and I yelled, "Help!" But she kept talking and I realized it was her voice mail.

"Put the phone down."

"Crane? What are you talking about?" I looked around but didn't see him. I didn't see anyone. "Hello? Inspector?"

"I said, put the phone down."

Bai stepped out from the dark shadows cast by the bookshelves along the wall. His eyes were focused on me as he pulled a very old, very sharp, curved knife from his coat pocket and pointed it at me. "Give me the book."

I dropped the phone and it clattered to the floor. My throat was dry and my mouth was open, but no words were coming out.

"Nothing to say?" he asked.

"What book?" I found my voice. "What're

you doing here? What's wrong with Crane?"

"My brother ran into a little trouble." Bai giggled, and the sound disturbed me almost as much as the knife did. Was he on drugs? I couldn't figure him out, but that had been true from the first time we met.

"We need to call an ambulance," I said.

"No."

"He's your brother," I cried.

"He's nothing to me now." Bai didn't even glance at Crane, collapsed and groaning on the floor.

You're nothing, I thought furiously, but didn't say it. The man was obviously psychotic. And he was holding a really scary-looking knife. One that had probably been used to kill two people. And where the heck was Derek?

As if I'd conjured him, Derek shouted from somewhere near the kitchen, "Brooklyn! Run! Get Alex!"

"Derek? Derek!" I started for the kitchen.

"Hold it," Bai said, waving the knife close enough to my face that I cringed. "Stay right where you are."

I held up both hands in surrender — for now. At least I knew Derek was alive. "I don't know what you're trying to prove, Bai, but you need to call an ambulance. Take whatever you want from my house, but we need to get help for your brother."

He scowled. "I told you I don't care about him."

Bai was blocking my view, so I leaned to the side to get a look at Crane. "Did you drug him?"

"You could say that."

"But why?" I was starting to panic. If he'd done that to his own brother, what had he done to Derek? "Why are you here? What do you want?"

"I'm here to get the book."

I frowned. "Which one?"

"Don't play dumb," Bai snarled, and slapped me across the face.

I screamed and pushed him. I couldn't help it.

Angry now, he grabbed my arm and flung me toward the bookshelf wall at the opposite end of the living room from where I imagined Derek had to be. I managed to keep from falling, but not by much. Had Derek been drugged, too? Had he been tricked by Bai? Impossible. Something else had to have happened here. Was Crane involved? Had he been helping his brother and then Bai had turned on him? Blood was thicker than water, after all.

And even as I thought the worst of Crane, I knew it couldn't be true. He would never betray Derek. The two men were closer than brothers. Bai was the odd man out here, and it had infuriated him for years. So what had really happened here?

The thought occurred to me that if Flint hadn't tried to attack me outside, I would've been up here ten minutes sooner. I might've been able to help Derek. And that was one more strike against that stupid scumbag.

"Give me the book." Bai said it quietly, which was almost more disturbing than his shouts.

"If you're talking about the book of birds, I don't have it."

"You're lying."

"I'm not." That much was true, technically. I'd left it in the car when I went to get pizza and I forgot to go back for it. The car was locked up, so the book was safe for now, unless Bai took my keys. "I left it at the Covington Library."

"Liar."

"It's true. I was showing it to Ian McCullough and he asked if he could keep it overnight." I almost groaned. Had my lies just put Ian in danger? No, simply because if Bai had hurt Derek, I would make sure he didn't walk out of here alive.

I watched as Bai glanced around, looking uncertain as to what he should do next.

Who was in charge here?

"Does she have the book?" a woman demanded from somewhere in the other room.

I frowned at this new voice. "Who is that? What's going on?" I raised my voice. "Who are you?"

"Shut up," Bai said, scowling at me.

"Does she have it?" the woman repeated, louder.

"She says she left it at the Covington," Bai said loudly in response.

"She's lying."

"No, I'm not," I shouted, fed up and sick to death of idiotic intruders and worried that Derek might be in real danger. I felt my teeth grinding down as I looked at Bai. "Who is that?"

"It's a friend."

"A friend?" I said sarcastically. It had to be his girlfriend. I wondered if she was the one Alex saw running away from here the night we were almost broken into. A female. Tall and thin. Was she Goose's killer? And what did she have to do with Jared Mulrooney? Had they tried to get the book from him first? Was that the connection?

I wanted to smack myself. Of course it was the connection. I was an idiot. Gazing at Bai, I said, "So you killed Jared Mulrooney because he wouldn't give you the book."

Shrugging off my accusation, he clutched the knife tighter. "He was a loose end."

A loose end? I wanted to scream. Who was he trying to kid? He himself had left loose ends streaming from one part of the world to another. His entire life had consisted of loose ends.

"He was a human being," was all I could say.

Bai rolled his eyes and I knew I would have to do something drastic or I would wind up the next victim. Was Crane still alive? And where was Derek? He hadn't spoken again. Was he unable to?

"Jared Mulrooney thought he was protecting the book from us. He refused to hand it over, so he had to die."

"No, he didn't," I muttered. "And who is *us*?"

"Give him the book, Brooklyn," Crane whispered from where he still lay curled up on the floor. "He won't leave without it."

"I'll give you the book," I said. "I just have to get it from the Covington tomorrow. Please. You can follow me there and you can have it. I don't want it. I was going to return it to the Bird-watchers Society as soon as I repaired it."

…l frowned. "Why did you have to repair

"Because Jared spilled wine all over it and asked me to fix it."

"Wine?" the woman cried. "That stupid jerk could've destroyed everything!"

Bai blinked. So there was something he and the woman didn't know. Could I use that against them?

"Did you fix the book?" she demanded to know.

I'd just about had it with the disembodied voice. Was she the one guarding Derek?

"Let me see Derek and I'll give you the book."

"Just give me the book." Bai waved his hand dismissively toward Derek. "He won't be any help to you."

My entire body trembled. Chills ran from my spine outward to every extremity and I knew what it meant to say my blood ran cold. "If you hurt him, I'll kill you myself."

My threat seemed to provoke him and he waved the knife menacingly. "Brave words for someone who's powerless."

It was true, but only for the moment. There was no way this smarmy little jerk would win. He kept a tight hold on my arm and continued brandishing the knife with his other hand. He had pushed me into the archway between my office and the living room, so I couldn't see the dining room where I had a feeling Derek might be. I needed to get to him. Save him, somehow. I had to do something. I would have to distract Bai. But how?

"Derek!" I screamed suddenly. Bai flinched and I took the opportunity to punch him in the stomach with my free hand and pull my arm away. I dashed across the living room floor, almost sliding into Derek sitting at the dining room table. He had his head resting on the table. My heart dropped.

"What's wrong with him?" I screamed. "Derek, wake up!"

The woman standing on the other side of the table had a gun pointed at me. She was tall, thin, Asian, and very beautiful. She reminded me of the risk analyst at Derek's office. What was her name? Lark. The one who had run her fingers along his lapel. This woman was striking as well and clearly deadly.

"Who are you?" I asked, all the while trying to get close enough to Derek to see if he was still breathing.

"That's my girlfriend," Bai said, sounding like a ridiculous love-struck teenager. "Her name is Kea."

I glanced at Bai and knew immediately that Kea was the brains and the power behind this duo. Her eyes were beautiful, but empty. She had probably killed Goose. I couldn't see Bai doing it, although he was surely twisted. I hadn't seen that side of him before and I wondered if I should have. "Why do you want this book so badly?"

"None of your business," Bai said.

"You've broken into my house, you've killed two men, you've attacked me and my fiancé and your own brother in my house, and it's none of my business?"

"I didn't kill him," he groused.

"Shut her up, Bai," the woman said. But now instead of sounding harsh and dictatorial, she sounded nervous.

"You shut up," I snapped, well beyond thinking cautiously. Back to Bai. "If you didn't kill him, who did?"

"Bai, shut her up," the woman repeated urgently.

I glared at her, then back at Bai. "She killed him, didn't she? She probably killed Jared, too. I can't see you doing it."

"Bai!" she shouted.

"I'm trying to shut her up," he shouted back, then scowled at me. "Shut up."

"You won't shut me up. You're in *my* house now." I yelled, subtly pressing up against Derek's arm. I needed to make contact. I could tell he was still alive, but very weak. "And what did you do to Derek?"

I heard my workshop door open and someone walked into the apartment. It was obviously a woman by the sound her high heels made clacking against the hardwood floor. What now? How many people were in on this, anyway? The newcomer walked through the foyer and into the living room. Bai and his girlfriend flashed each other a warning look.

"Kea, aren't you two finished yet? Do I have to do everything?"

Bai was seething, obviously insulted, but he said nothing.

"No, Mommy," Kea said. "Not yet."

Mommy?

I turned around — and almost stopped breathing at the sight of Marva Pesca, the new president of the National Bird-watchers Society. What in the world? I stared back at Kea. "She's your mother?"

"Yes," she said. "And she's not going to like your stalling one bit."

"Who's stalling?" I asked. "I told you I don't have it."

"Did you get the book or not?" Marva asked her daughter.

"She says she left it at the Covington,"

Bai explained.

Marva glared at me. "You're lying."

I almost rolled my eyes but resisted. These people needed to get their act together and take it on the road. "Why would I lie? At this point I would give you anything just to get you all out of my house. So no, I'm not lying."

"We can get it tomorrow," Bai said.

Marva pinched up her face. "Oh, so we'll just leave all these lovely people here and come by tomorrow. Is that what you're suggesting?" Marva pinned her daughter with a look. "Did you have to get involved with another moron?"

"Oh, Mommy. Just go wait in the car."

"No. I'm taking charge." She pulled a gun from her purse and pointed it at me as she said, "You kids stand over there."

I felt Derek give me the slightest nudge, and it was the best moment ever in the whole world. I wanted to burst into tears, but this wasn't the time.

"Okay, okay," I said, "I've got the book in my car. It's repaired. Let me go down and get it."

"Now, was that so hard?" she asked, giving Bai and Kea a look that only a mother could give. They both glanced away.

"Wait," Marva barked, and Bai and Kea

416

froze. "Why did it need repairs?"

"Jared Mulrooney splashed wine on it," Bai explained.

Marva made a sound of disgust. "That slob. I'm glad I killed him."

Oo-kay, I thought, my stomach flipping. So Marva had killed Jared and her daughter had killed Goose. Glad to know it was all in the family. Each of them was capable of cold-blooded murder. That settled it. "I'll get my keys."

"No, you won't," Marva said. She jerked her head at Bai. "You get them. Where's her purse?"

"It's in my office," I said, ready to give them anything they wanted, if they would only just leave us alone. But there probably wasn't much chance of that.

Bai went to find my purse and came back holding up my car keys and jiggling them as though he'd accomplished something brilliant. "I'll be right back."

With a spring in his step, Bai jogged over to our front door. But just as he twisted the doorknob, the door swung open, and my mother and father walked in.

"Special delivery," Dad called. "Hey, who's this?"

"Hi, sweetie," Mom said. "Oh, you have company."

"Mom, Dad! Run down the hall and get Alex. Call the police!"

Kea was so distracted by the tumult that she dropped her arm, and the gun was no longer pointing at me.

Dad went running out, but Mom took one look at Derek and gasped. "What happened to him?"

Marva's heels clattered across the floor and I suddenly felt the gun against my back. "Who the hell is this dimwit?"

I bristled and knew I'd reached the end of my rope. There was no way I was going to let her hurt my parents or anyone else.

"That's *my* mommy," I said with a growl, and elbowed her. Catching her by surprise, I whipped around and smacked the gun out of her hand. Then I pounced on her. We both fell to the floor with me on top, luckily. I punched her with my left fist, breaking her nose.

The woman screamed and blood went flying. I rolled off and was thrilled to see Derek, despite his weakness, reach up and slap the gun out of Kea's hand.

Now we just had to worry about Bai. He had been momentarily stunned, but now he raised his arm and flourished the knife in his hand. He started toward Derek and I screamed, "No!"

At that very second, Gabriel and Alex stormed into our place. Gabriel was on Bai in a heartbeat, and the knife was kicked across the room. Dad walked over, picked up the weapon with two fingers, and set it on top of the bookshelf, where none of our visitors could reach it.

Alex easily overpowered Kea with one swift kick to the woman's knee, causing her to buckle. She lifted Kea up with one hand and shoved her into a chair. Then she grabbed the gun that had skittered across the floor. Turning it on Kea, she said, "You're going to want to stay put."

My hand was beginning to throb from punching Marva's big, hard head. But I didn't mind the pain. In fact, I savored it. She deserved a bloody broken nose and a lot more besides.

"Cops and ambulance are on their way," Alex said.

"Thank you." Pointing to the man lying on the floor, I said, "Can you please check to make sure Crane is still alive?"

"Sure, honey. You take care of Derek."

"I will. Mom, can you make some coffee? They gave Derek and Crane some kind of drug."

I rushed over to Derek. He was still groggy and could barely hold his head up. I held him for a moment, then cried, "Mom! Hurry!"

"Coffee's coming up," she said, and pushed me out of the way. She gave Derek a few light slaps and whispered something in his ear. He mumbled a few words.

Mom reached into her purse and pulled out a packet of herbs and odd chunks of something. Pills? Crystals? "I need that coffee!" she shouted.

"It's coming," I said, wondering at what point we'd traded places.

She began to chant while sprinkling some kind of sparkly crystal substance and crushed herbs over Derek.

"Oh my God," I muttered. I set the coffee mug on the table and patted Derek's shoulders. "Drink this, love. Come on, you can do it."

Mom and I both urged him to swallow a full cup of strong coffee. A few minutes after that, Derek began to revive.

Mom dashed over and gave Crane the same treatment of strong coffee, crystals, and crushed herbs. Alex grabbed one of the small pillows from the sofa and slipped it under his head. Finally, he blinked and glanced around. Alex was still kneeling over him.

"Hi there," she said.

"Hello," he whispered. "Are you an angel?"

Alex nodded at me. "He'll be okay."

She stroked his cheek softly and then stood. Crane looked ready to protest her leaving his side, but he was still too weak.

"Darling," Derek whispered.

Thrilled that he was able to speak, I pulled a chair close to his and wrapped my arm around his shoulder. "What is it, love?"

"I'm . . . sorry. I brought a . . . killer into our home. Crane . . . tried to warn me."

I wanted to cry. For the first time in my life, I looked into his eyes and saw his confidence completely shaken. And that scared me more than anything that had come before.

"I love you . . . more than . . . life," he murmured.

"And I love you even more."

"But . . . evil . . . our home. Wrong."

I knew what he was trying to say and I quickly spoke up. "It wasn't you who brought them here. Look around. This was all about that stupid bird book. And that's on me. I was the reason these creeps came into our home. So don't you dare go thinking —"

"Darling, please. I need to finish saying this."

I huffed out a sigh. "Go ahead."

"If you want to call off the wedding, I'll understand."

"What?" I blinked in surprise but quickly recovered. "Sorry, pal. Nice try, but you're stuck with me."

"But —"

"No." The good news was that my arguing seemed to give him strength and he sat up and looked at me straight on.

I leaned forward. "May I remind you that *I* once brought a killer into our home?" I could see the moment realization dawned. He knew what I was talking about. "You didn't banish me from your life, Derek, so I'm willing to return the favor. I'm marrying you and we're going to be the two happiest people in the world."

He reached out and wrapped his arms around me and I buried my head in his embrace. A good thing, because I felt a few tears escape.

"So we're even," he muttered finally.

I laughed. "Yes. We're even."

Crane was finally able to lift his head and scan the room. He found his brother, still being held down by Gabriel. "Why? Why did you do this?"

"I was trying to save our family name."

The look Bai shot Crane was pure contempt. "Someone had to do it."

"Instead you have tainted it," Crane said. "And these women who helped you are nothing but common criminals."

"You think you know everything, but you don't. That book belongs in our family, and Kea was just as devoted to finding it as I was. She loves me."

I was pretty sure she was incapable of loving anyone but herself, but it wasn't my place to say so.

Crane snorted weakly. "She wanted the book for her mother, not for you. They were only in it for the money they could make selling it."

"That's not true." He appealed to Kea. "Tell him."

Kea rolled her eyes but said nothing.

Marva wasn't inclined to be as quiet as her daughter. "He's been talking about that damn book ever since he showed up at the society. He said he had traced it from a Scottish bookshop to our meeting place. I quickly realized the book had to be more valuable than we first thought."

"So you decided to steal it," I said.

"Aren't you brilliant?" she said, baring her teeth at me. "But then the book disappeared. I confronted Jared and he said it was being audited. I pumped him for more information and he became suspicious. He told me he would report me to the police if the book went missing."

"Did Jared tell you he found it in a bookshop?"

"Yeah. While he was on vacation in Scotland. What are the chances?" Marva rolled her eyes, something she did with alarming frequency. Just like her daughter. "He found it within days of Bai tracking the book down to the bookshop. Bai's a good little tracker. I'll give him that. It's just too bad his timing sucks. The book was gone, but he finally tracked it to Jared and the National Birdwatchers Society. Once he told me about how valuable the book was, I told Kea to get close to him. Didn't realize I'd have to deal with Dumb and Dumber."

Kea slumped in her chair, apparently fed up with her mother's criticism of her and her boyfriend.

Derek reached for more coffee and I glared at Bai. "What did you drug them with?"

"It's a mild derivative of curare," Bai said smugly. "It causes the system to slow down. I thought it would give us enough time to get the book and get out."

I wanted to slap that smirk off his face,

424

but I was just grateful he didn't have the killer instinct like the two women. But that brought up another question. "How did you get them to take it?"

"It's on the knife," he said brightly. "The blade was coated with a liquid form of the poison. So while Kea had the gun trained on them, I sliced both of their arms."

I knew the horror showed on my face, knew I would be perfectly happy to grab that stupid knife and slice all three of them, so I turned away.

"That knife," Crane said slowly, "has been in our family for a thousand years. You have betrayed our ancestors and your family by using it this way."

"Oh, cram it, big brother," Bai muttered.

Crane shook his head and I could see the pain he felt saying the words. "I will rejoice to see you behind bars permanently."

I couldn't agree more but said nothing. Bai looked as though he wanted to lash out, but Gabriel tightened his grip on him.

Something else occurred to me and I glanced at Marva. "Was Micah Featherstone working with you?"

None of the three reacted to the name.

"Who's that?" Marva asked.

"Just some random book thief," I muttered, thinking about Billy's sociopathic buyer of *Poor Richard's Almanack.* "I figured you all stuck together."

"That book was important to our family," Bai said, trying again to justify his actions. "Our ancestor was robbed of his work and his dignity. Audubon stole both from him and used Sheng's talent for his own benefit."

"You're wrong," Crane insisted. "Sheng was honored to work with Audubon and be a part of the great painter's most ambitious project."

"That's not true."

"It is true," Crane countered. "I told you to read Sheng's journals, but you never would. You thought you already knew everything, but you were wrong. Sheng was aware that he was a great painter, but to have that skill acknowledged by the master of ornithological art was one of the crowning glories of his life. We both know Audubon would never have hired Sheng if he didn't agree that our ancestor was as highly talented as himself."

"You just want to keep Sheng in the shadows," Bai protested. "He should've been famous. He should've been known as an even greater painter than Audubon."

"Perhaps so. But perhaps you're conflating your own dismal career with our esteemed ancestor's," Crane said softly. "You should've been famous. You should've been known as the greatest painter in China. Instead you'll spend the rest of your life in an American prison."

Bai was silent after that. I wanted to weep for Crane. He had tried his whole life to make his brother happy, but it was ultimately a useless exercise. I wanted to give him a hug, but I would wait until Bai was taken away.

"So your family never had a copy of *Songbirds in Trees*?" I asked.

Crane had to take a few slow breaths before he could speak. "The book was thought to have been lost in a poker game and then it was won back. But it was lost again by the next generation." He smiled. "Another version of the story has it that the book never left Scotland. As with so many things, there are family legends attached to the book. Some of us weren't certain it ever actually existed."

But it did exist, I thought. I glanced at Alex. "The police should be here any second. I'll be right back."

By the time I returned, Inspector Lee and her partner had arrived and two uniformed cops were handcuffing the three thieving killers. Crane sat at the dining table, quietly commiserating with Derek. I walked over and joined them.

"This is for you," I said, sliding a wrapped package across to him. I didn't care if I could ever prove that Sheng had actually painted those *Songbirds in Trees,* and I didn't care that the book wasn't actually mine to give. Jared might have paid a few dollars for it in a Scottish bookshop, but after watching the deadly Marva Pesca in action, I swore there was no way I was going to hand the beautifully restored volume over to the Bird-watchers Society. It rightfully belonged to Crane and his family.

Crane glanced from me to Derek, then unwrapped the package. *Songbirds in Trees* looked perfect in his hands.

It took him a long moment, but he finally gazed at me and his lips curved slightly. "Thank you, Brooklyn. I will never forget your bravery and friendship."

I reached out and covered his hand with mine. "I'll never forget yours, either."

In between the reading of rights and the arrests of Marva, Kea, and Bai, I had a chance to catch Inspector Lee in a quiet corner of the room.

"Any word on Micah Featherstone?" I asked.

She scowled. "It's like he disappeared in the wind. We haven't found any trace of him, and he never returned to the bookshop to get his book."

I shook my head in disbelief. "But he gave them five thousand dollars."

"Yeah, about that. He must have known it was a setup because the bills he gave them were counterfeit."

"What? Wow." I'd never seen a counterfeit bill before. As far as I knew, anyway. I rubbed my arms to ward off the sudden chill I felt at the news of Featherstone's disappearance. "I just hope I never run into him again."

"Yeah, me, too."

I had another question I was almost afraid to ask, but I plunged ahead anyway. "So how did your mother like the book?"

She grinned. "She loved it. You did a fantastic job, Brooklyn."

I barely resisted clapping my hands with glee. "I'm so glad," I said, and couldn't help adding, "And she liked the modern art crayon work?"

Lee chuckled. "Yeah, she did."

"Oh, good. I'm really happy you decided to leave it as it was."

"Yeah, I guess I owe you one," she said.

"No, you don't," I said, frowning. "You

already paid me."

"True, but I still owe you one because you were right."

"Was I?" Not that I was fishing, but how often had Janice Lee told me I was right about something? I had to hear the details.

"Yeah," Lee said, smiling fondly at an image in her mind. "Because when she opened that beautiful box and found the book, I had the infinitely pleasurable experience of seeing my indomitable mother dissolve into sloppy sentimental tears for the first time in years. And that, my friend, was worth everything."

After the police had dragged the three stooges away, Mom, Dad, Gabriel, and Alex sat with me in the living room and listened to Derek and Crane fill in the blanks.

"I had just arrived here when Bai pulled up," Crane said. "He was conciliatory, humble. He told me he needed to talk and wondered if he could come with me upstairs. When I agreed and Derek buzzed me into the building, Kea ran up and joined us."

Derek continued where Crane left off. "As soon as they walked in, Kea pulled the gun on me. I felt like a bloody fool."

I had my arms wrapped around Derek like

430

a neurotic koala bear and I wasn't about to let go for a while. I glanced over at my parents. "Now that we've heard their story, I'm wondering about you guys. Not that I wasn't thrilled to see you, but what are you doing here?"

"We came to drop off a present for Derek," Mom said. "We wanted to surprise you, but it looks like we were the ones who were surprised."

"We'll always be grateful that you chose that moment to visit," Derek said, still sounding a little sluggish. But his eyes were able to focus and his skin had returned to its healthy natural color, no longer that pallid sheen I'd found so frightening. "I personally owe you my life," he said, "and I can't imagine what you brought me, but it wasn't necessary."

"Except for the part where they showed up and saved our lives," I said, smiling at Derek.

Derek grinned. "Yes, except for that part. I'm not sure I'll ever be able to thank you enough."

"Seeing as how we weren't able to walk in and foil Goose's killer," Dad said, "this is sort of a nice full-circle thing."

"Very well said, Jim." Mom stood up and handed Derek a large gift bag. "I hope you use this in good health."

"Unlike the last guy," Dad muttered.

Perplexed, I gave him a look, then got distracted watching Derek pull out the wads of pretty tissue paper to get to the treat at the bottom of the bag.

"What's in there?" I asked.

Derek lifted the rich, thick navy material out of the bag and beamed at my parents. "A new bathrobe."